Extreme Difference

David Reynolds-Moreton

sci-fi-cafe.com

Extreme Difference
David Reynolds-Moreton

ISBN 978-1-910779-28-6 (Paperback)
ISBN 978-1-908387-46-2 (ePUB)
ASIN B005PB0RRA (Kindle)

sci-fi-cafe.com

One:
Of Myth and Legend

AT FIRST THERE was a nothingness. He was aware of being aware, but that was all. Then came the blackness. It was so deep and intense that it seemed to suck the very life out of him, and a surge of panic ensued. He felt he was fading away, tenuously expanding outwards to fill the entire universe until he would be scattered out so thinly that there would be nothing left of him.

The sensation stopped. Was he now nothing? There was still a deep blackness, but the awful pull had gone.

One by one, tiny pinpoints of light appeared, scattered about in the blackness like star dust.

Stars. That was it! Stars! But where was he? They seemed to be all around him, so he must be suspended in something.

But there was nothing attached to him and he felt nothing beneath, in fact he had no sensation at all, he just was. He tried to turn, but nothing happened, there were just the stars and him, a something suspended in space, and for all he knew, suspended in time as well.

Desperately he tried to remember what he was before this strange state he now found himself in, but there was no recall, no memory seemed to exist before the blackness. There was just an emptiness, a non-existence, a nothingness.

A sudden wrench of his very being took him by surprise, it seemed as if space itself had been twisted and then turned inside out, and him along with it. He would have been sick if he had had anything to be sick with.

The feeling slowly faded, and he became aware of his body. He could feel his fingers, and wriggled them to make sure they were real. He pinched his arm, he could feel that, so he must have a body. Turning his head to see what lay beneath him, he was in for another shock.

The blackness beneath had no stars, although they were all around him like a huge dome of tiny lights, but there was nothing below. Was he suspended over a hole in the heavens? What would happen if he fell? And then he did.

The black hole hungrily rushed up to meet him, and he hit the ground with a sickening thud which drove the breath out of his already aching body in a whistling gasp.

For a moment he lay there, stunned, and then spat out the mouthful of ice cold metallic tasting sand he had inadvertently acquired upon hitting the hard cold ground.

Whatever he was lying on was sucking the heat out of his body at a terrifying rate, so he tried to push himself up using his arms. He flopped down again, the pain in his fingers intensifying to an excruciating level as his hands sank into the freezing sand with the effort.

The crunch crunch of approaching footsteps caused him to look up. A tall figure stood before him, only discernible because it blocked out the light from the glittering star field.

'Let me help you up.' The dark shape bent down and a grip of steel encircled his arm, yanking him to his feet in one easy motion, steadying his weak and swaying body.

'Quick, we must be away from here, the sand life will be active soon, and that would spell the end of us both.'

The dark shadowy shape took a firm grip on his elbow, and urgently propelled him forward at an ever increasing pace until they were almost running, only slowing down when the stars were blanked out by the towering black mass of something ahead of them.

'We should be all right now. What's your name?' the dark shape asked, between panting breaths.

'I don't know.' he finally gasped out, the words punctured by throaty whistles as his heaving lungs worked overtime.

'I don't know anything. I can't remember who I am supposed to be, where I've been, or how I got here. I just remember hitting that bloody sand at a high rate of knots, and getting a mouthful of the foul tasting stuff for my trouble.'

'Ah, good. You speak our tongue. That'll save much time getting you oriented into our system. Not many speak like us these days, and that makes things very difficult sometimes. I had hoped you would be a female, but a male is just as welcome, really.'

They had reached the dark opening in the ominous rock wall which seemed to reach up to impossible heights until it merged with the midnight black of the heavens, its extremities delineated by the bright sprinkle of dust like stars.

'My name is Nan. We'll soon have a name for you, and then you'll feel better. A sense of identity always does that for a person.' the dark shape said clearly, having got its breath back.

'But Nan is a girl's name. You don't sound like a girl to me,' he said, 'unless you've had a very strange operation.'

'Nan is my given name, given to me by the group when I arrived. I find it quite acceptable, and I can assure you I am a man, in every sense of the word.' His voice had hardened, with a sharp edge to it, a warning that this was not someone to upset unnecessarily, if at all.

'Sorry, I didn't mean any offence.' he replied, realizing he was on dangerous ground in a strange land, and would need all the help he could get. 'It's just that I am so confused, I don't know what's happened to me, or why.'

'Don't worry,' the voice softened a little, 'we'll soon get you settled down and explain a few things, and then you'll feel better. It's always a shock for new arrivals, but as they say, time and knowledge is a great healer.'

The steel grip on his arm lessened, and although he could feel himself swaying a little, he remained ambulant as the steadying hand of Nan was slowly withdrawn.

'Do you think you can walk unaided now?' asked the dark shape, 'the dawn is coming up, and there's a lot to do.'

A faint glowing light on the high horizon now clearly differentiated the sky from the blackness of the surrounding land, giving the impression of being at the bottom of a giant bowl, its dark jagged edges ripping into the soft glow of the approaching day.

'Please follow me, you'll need food and drink after what you've been through, and then we'll try to explain what has happened.' The dark shape strode into the even darker opening in the rock face and disappeared. Before he could move to follow, a pale yellowish splash of light lit up the opening, the tall figure of Nan silhouetted in its gentle glow.

'Come on, we can't waste time, the dawn is nearly here.' and with that the tall dark figure marched off into the tunnel, darkly muttering something under his breath.

As he followed Nan into the narrow passageway, he drew level with the light source on the wall. A thin pipe with a control knob near its base had a small flickering flame dancing on its upturned end, and as he passed it by, he hugged the opposite wall in case the draft from his body should extinguish its feeble life.

The tunnel took a sudden turn to the left, and he found himself in a large cave with several guttering flame lights dotted around the walls. These cast lurid shadows from a bedraggled group of stern and haggard looking people, who seemed none too pleased at his arrival.

Nan stepped forward, and taking him by the arm, pulled him firmly into the middle of the group.

'This is our new arrival,' he began authoritatively, turning and smiling at the wretched figure who had followed him into the cave complex, 'so let's give him a nice welcome.'

A feeble chorus of 'hello's' expressing little enthusiasm from the ragged group of hermits left him wondering just what he had got himself into, not that there had been a great deal of choice in the matter on his part.

'Hello,' he answered back, trying to inject some zeal into his reply, 'I'm sorry, I can't remember my name, or anything very much, but I am grateful to be here.' He later wondered why he had added that last bit to his response, and put it down to inborn politeness.

'Before we give you a name, I'll introduce you to our merry little band, we are glad to have you into our midst.'

Nan stepped forward and raised his arm towards a cloak clad figures who looked the most likely to be female.

'This is Bell, she looks after our growing bins and is generally in charge of all food production and collection.'

Bell did her best to smile, but two missing front teeth added little to her effort. Realizing this, she gave up, and let her mouth take up its normal droopy look.

Nan turned to one side and pointed to the next apparition in grey brown sackcloth, almost a twin of the first.

'Here we have Mop, she does all the cooking, helps to gather food, and generally keeps the place tidy.'

Mop had a full set of teeth, albeit a little stained, and a pleasant smile. Long black matted hair framed a pale pock marked face. Any other semblance to the female of the species was hard to find, as a solid thickset jaw jutted out in an almost threatening manner, and the eyes were cold and hard. She did at least make the effort, and extended a stained and grubby hand for him to touch in greeting.

In the dim light their hands touched briefly, leaving behind a sour and rancid smell which lingered in his nostrils for some time to come. He felt his stomach turn over, and was glad it was empty.

'Karry is so called because of her immense strength, for a female that is.' He thought Nan withdrew a little from the amazon like figure, her eyes glaring hard and cold.

'If we get into a scrape, she is the one to have by your side.' Nan offered in a placatory tone, and the eyes softened a little.

'Ben here, is our weapons man. He maintains the gas guns, and just about everything else you will see in our little haven. All bits of metal and other material you might come across should be passed to him, and he will make something useful from it.' The short stubby man took a step forward and grabbed his hand in a vice-like grip. He could feel the bones grinding together as the grip increased, the pain shooting up his arm. He tried not to wince, but his eyes watered a little.

The weapons man, having made his point, whatever it was, relaxed his grip and stepped back, an ill concealed grin on his dark and greasy face.

Nan, sensing that their new acquisition was feeling increasingly ill at ease, hurried the rest of the introductions through with indecent haste, briefly mentioning the name of each individual and the functions assigned to them, but it remained a hazy blur to him, as had everything since his awakening on the cold dark sands a few nightmarish moments ago.

'We must get the growing bins out,' Nan said in the same breath as the last introduction ended, 'the sun will be up any minute now.'

Everyone was galvanized into action, as if their very lives depended upon some indefinable and immediate response.

With Nan leading the way, the sombre little group of troglodytes hurried out of the cave-like room and along the tunnel, turning off into another cavern, where a row of trough-like boxes sprouted an assortment of plants. Some had bright red berries dangling from thin spindly branches, while others bore larger plump rounded yellow fruits, the like of which he could not recall having seen before.

One by one, the troughs were carefully lifted and carried out of the cavern, one person at each end, taking great pains not to jostle the contents of the boxes and even more careful not to bump into those preceding and following. The sombre little procession trundled along the main tunnel until it opened out into the vast expanse of sand which formed the centre of their world.

The troughs were laid out in rows on stone ledges, close up to the towering rock walls of the extinct volcano, and away from the sparkling lake of sand which seemed to stretch out almost to the horizon.

Those who had placed their troughs in their appointed positions, then hurried back to bring out the rest of the plant containers, until the ledges around the tunnel opening looked like a neatly laid out small market garden.

Nan stood back, running his critical eye over the neat rows of troughs, indicating with a casual wave of his hand a slight adjustment here, an extra tilt there, until all were positioned exactly as he wanted them, according to some unspoken ritual which he alone seemed to understand.

There was little doubt that Nan was in overall control. Whether by election, skill, or age, he could not tell, but he was surprised, as Nan seemed to be a quiet gentle man, not the sort of person one would expect to hold a position of authority, especially in the prevailing circumstances.

The rising sun poured forth its hard brazen light, glistening off the high peaks on the massive volcano's rim and turning the ice cold stone into flaming fingers of red and yellow.

Already the air had a slight touch of warmth about it as the reflected light from the shiny rocks above danced about on the barren sands, giving the momentary illusion of a large lake of shimmering water.

'We'd best get back inside.' said Nan softly, as though if he spoke any louder he would break the spell of the warmth to come, or awaken some unimaginable monster from its slumbers. 'Kel, I think it's your turn to guard, please be extra vigilant today.'

With that he turned, and herding his newly found recruit before him, went back into the tunnel followed unenthusiastically by the others, except for two who lingered outside for a few precious moments to savour the ever brightening and warming light.

'We must give you a name.' Nan began when the rest of the group had joined him. 'Do you have a preference? Or would you like us to suggest a suitable name which you would like to be known as?'

'I don't know if I even had a name. I can't remember anything much, except the biting cold of that bloody sand. I'm still spitting out bits of it now.'

Even thought his mouth was dry, he managed to eject a small globule of spittle to emphasize his point. It glistened and sparkled as it spun downwards in the flickering light of the gas lamps, to be quickly absorbed by the bone dry floor of the cave, leaving no trace of it ever having been there.

The utter silence which followed his little display made him wonder if he had inadvertently broken some important taboo, or even insulted the motley gathering.

The stillness was broken by Nan, insisting that a name be given to their visitor, explaining that without it he would not feel a real person, and would be of little use to the group.

'Do we have any suggestions?' Nan asked again, looking from one to another of the sullen assembly, but all just glared back at him, except Ben, who grinned.

'I get the feeling that no one wants me here, so why don't you just let me go. I'll manage somehow. Perhaps there are others I can join.'

'No!' Nan was adamant. 'We found you, and with us you will stay. The other groups are mostly a barbaric lot, and if they don't like you, you could well finish up being eaten, or something worse. Come on, someone must have an idea.'

The silence dragged on painfully, with a few muttered comments and grunts from the ragged gathering, but nothing constructive or helpful was offered.

'Alright. How about Sandy? That seems fitting, I landed in the bloody stuff, it went up my nose, in my mouth, and given enough time it probably would have found its way up the other end. I'll settle for that.'

Nan looked around to see if there was any reaction to the suggestion, but apart from a few half hearted nods, the silence ensued as before.

'That's settled then. You will hence forth be known as Sandy. Now we can welcome you into our midst properly.'

Nan waved the others into some semblance of a line, and standing at its head alongside Sandy, beckoned the others forward one by one.

'I'm Mop, welcome to our family, Sandy.' She clutched his proffered hand in the customary manner, the now familiar rancid smell lingering on long after the others had done likewise, reluctantly going through their ritualised greeting.

When the official inauguration into the 'family' reached its somewhat pathetic conclusion, Sandy asked Nan to explain what the place was all about, and why he was here.

The others filed out of the cavern, no doubt going about their allotted business, or just getting out of the way of any other rituals Nan might suddenly feel inclined to implement.

Several crude benches were scattered about the cavern, mostly up against the walls, but apart from two, which were obviously made from some kind of metal, the material used for the others remained unidentifiable.

'Please sit down Sandy, and I'll do my best to answer any questions you have, although you may be disappointed in my lack of knowledge of this place.' Nan had now assumed a much more relaxed attitude towards him, and almost seemed like any other normal human being, except he had difficulty in trying to recall anyone in particular.

'What the hell is this place?' asked Sandy, the words stumbling over themselves in his eagerness to get them out.

'It is where we live, and have done so for a very long time, long before I came here. Stories are handed down from the elders to those who take their place upon the elder's death. I am an elder, and I try to keep the stories as true as possible when retelling them, but it is thought that some have embellished the history of this place to suit their own ends.'

'That doesn't surprise me one bit, but what *is* this place?' Sandy asked impatiently. 'Where is it, and what does it consist of?'

'It was created for us by some higher power, and we are created to populate it. Some people claim to be able to recall things from a past existence, but I think that's heresy, and there's no proof that we have existed before the creation. I think it's just imagination on their part, and not healthy.'

'First I'll tell you what we know about the physical world, and then about the different types of people who live here.'

Sandy opened his mouth to speak, but Nan raised his hand to silence any interruption of his narration.

'Imagine a large shallow bowl, where the smooth rim has been cut into a series of ragged points, and then plaster the inside with a two or three centimetre layer of mud or some such material, taking it right up to the top of the points. Now half fill the bowl with fine sand, and where the sand meets the mud layer, make some small holes to represent caves.

'That is basically what our world looks like, except that it is very much bigger, in fact it is nearly sixty kilometres across, as far as we can tell. The sun is very fierce, and during the day the sand gets so hot that if you were to walk on it, you would burn your feet very badly.

'At night the temperature drops to below freezing, and even a quick venture out onto the sands would result in severe frostbite. This leaves a short time in the early morning and evening when we can safely venture out into this inhospitable world, and we have to be careful about that.

The growing bins are taken out in the early morning as soon as the frost has disappeared, and brought back in before the sun climbs over the mountain rim to bathe the sands in direct sunlight. The same thing happens again in the evening, once the sun has dropped below the high rim of the mountains, the bins are brought out again to utilize the softer reflected light from the shiny peaks, and returned to the caves just before the cold cycle begins.

We have to do this to enable us to produce enough food to live on. There are other sources of food, as you will see, but green plants along with their fruits and berries, are essential for our well being.'

'The caves and tunnels are part natural, and part man made. Over many generations, extensions have been made to some of the caves to house our artefacts and growing bins, and connecting tunnels have been laboriously hacked from the rock to make access a little easier. Some of the tunnels go very deep into the body of the mountain, and so it is believed, those who enter them never return.

'The sand itself is not so innocent as it might at first appear. There are creatures who live in it, and are not adverse to sampling human flesh if they can get their teeth into it. I have never seen them, but I did know someone who was taken by them. All that was left was a small blood stain on the sand to mark where the incident had happened, and no one has seen any trace of him since.

'The only time you can safely walk on the sand is when it is frozen, or very hot from the sun, and then you must protect your feet with wrappings. We assume the creatures can't tolerate the extremes of temperature, and go down to a lower level.' Here Nan paused to see if Sandy was absorbing what was said, which gave him the chance to ask, 'What's on the other side of these mountains, as you call them? And why do you stay here if it's so inhospitable?'

'As far as we know, there's no way through the mountains. We can't climb over the top, it's too high, and the rock gets more shiny and slippery the higher you climb. In the past, there have been several attempts to see what's on the other side, but no one has ever found out.

'There may be nothing on the other side anyway, so we would be no better off even if we could get there. It would seem that here is where we are meant to be, so there's little point in trying to go anywhere else, not that there's anywhere else to go, as far as we can tell.'

'Oh, come on, you can't have a sand bowl ringed with a mountain chain, and nothing on the other side of it,' Sandy interjected quickly, 'there's got to be some land, or something on the other side. Anyway, where did you get the idea that you're meant to be here, who said so?'

'It has always been so. We arrive on the sands, and are taken into whichever group gets to us first.' Nan's face hardened, and he continued in a defensive tone. 'None of us has a memory of being anywhere before, so we must be created here, by some superior force or being. We are the servants of that greater force, here for a purpose, it is intended we remain here to do whatever the greater force wants'

'What a load of crap,' Sandy exploded, 'you've been here too long, and you're beginning to believe your own myths.

'Just think about it, you arrive here with a usable language which you all understand, you grow food, make things, you know how to organize yourselves into working groups, and you really think some benign being created you and filled your heads with all this information and abilities just to watch you running around like a lot of scruffy bloody hermits living in caves? You've got to be joking, or seriously off your heads.'

Nan's face darkened thunderously, and drawing himself up to his full height, he pointed a long shaking finger at Sandy.

'You've been here a few hours, and you have the gall to make fun of us and the purpose we've been created for. How dare you!' He spat out angrily, his mouth continued to flap open and shut silently, having run out of words to say.

'All right,' Sandy replied, 'think about this, where did you get the concept of 'a few hours' from? I don't see any clocks here, so that idea must have come from somewhere else.'

Slowly Nan's anger subsided, and he looked confused for a moment, opening his mouth several times to speak, but closing it again as he rethought what he wanted to say.

'Come on,' said Sandy, 'what do you know of time? How long is an hour, or for that matter, a day? How many hours in a day?'

'Twent.....twentyeight,' stuttered Nan, 'but how do I know that? I don't know what a clock is, do you?'

'Yes, of course,' began Sandy, and then found he was unable to recall it. A look of confusion spread over his face.

'I'm sure I did know, but for the moment it eludes me.'

The two men stood staring at each other for some moments, neither wanting to be the first to speak in case they were unable to find the right words, and later have to explain their meanings.

Nan slumped down on his bench, all the spark had gone out of him, and he was a mere shadow of the man he had been only a few moments earlier. He raised his hands twice, and then dropped them back into his lap in resignation, this stranger had shattered his cosy concept of life by asking a couple of questions, what would he do if the stranger tore down the whole structure of their existence with a few more questions? He felt it was quite possible.

'I'm sorry to have shaken you out of what you have taken for granted for so long, but you can surely see, just because you have accepted it, it doesn't make it a fact, and only by looking at actual facts can we make accurate judgements. Anyway, how do you think you got here?'

'The same way you did, from the Great Light, that's how we all get here.' Nan brightened up a little, he was back on familiar ground, talking about things he felt were real to him, things he could identify with.

'The Great Light comes down to the sands just before dawn, creates us, and drops us onto the sand. Sometimes, pieces of old broken machinery are left behind, also packets of seeds, cord, cloth, all manner of things are left for us to make things with. They are gifts from the Great Light. Those are facts, they actually happen, ask anyone here.' Nan was looking his old self again, assertive, confident, and in control.

'OK, how do you know about 'broken machinery'? How do you know it's broken in the first place? How do you know what to do with seeds? Who told you what to do with these things?' Sandy knew he was being unkind to press the point home so hard, but he wanted answers which made sense, and he was determined to get them at all costs.

The confused look came over Nan's face again as he desperately tried to recall the meaning of the items Sandy had mentioned, but there was nothing to recall, just an emptiness, and it made him feel dizzy to look at it.

'Now do you see what I mean?' Having got the thin end of the wedge of doubt neatly in place, Sandy was intent in hammering it firmly home.

Nan began to sway on his bench, and Sandy leapt forward to steady him, holding him in place until the spasm passed.

'I'm sorry to do this to you, but you must realize that you have all been fooled, for God knows how long. It's about time the truth was pulled out of this pitiful charade.'

Tears ran down Nan's grime streaked face, and his shoulders heaved as he tried to suppress the turbulent emotions which tore at his very being. Why had this stranger come to upset their world? Everything was just fine yesterday, the plants were growing well, their water bowls were full, there had been no raids for many a day, and now this.

The very fabric of their existence was being torn apart.

'How do you know these things?' asked a sobbing Nan, doing his best to control the turmoil which was racing through his mind, threatening to tear apart the fabric of all he knew and understood.

'By the same means you know about 'machinery', and other things you do here. I just know. I know the words, and I know what some of them mean. There's no way I could have learnt them here, so they must come from my past somehow. I can't explain it, but I know it to be true, and so will you if you'll only let go of this claptrap you hold onto.'

The two men sat huddled on the same bench, one comforting the other, both trying to make sense of the seemingly unfathomable situation they found themselves in.

Nan eventually pulled himself together, and had assumed some semblance of dignity by the time one of the others came into the cavern, stating it was time to get the growing bins inside, as the sun was just breaking the top of the peaks.

They all hurried outside into the harsh light of a brilliant white sun, shielding their eyes until they had acclimatized to the powerful glare, and working in pairs, brought the growing bins back into the relative cool of the bin cavern.

'Please don't say anything about what we discussed earlier,' said a somewhat demure Nan to Sandy, as they trouped back into the main cave, 'it's hard enough trying to keep this lot working as a team as it is, God knows what will happen if they start thinking for themselves.'

'Don't worry on that score,' Sandy replied, 'we have a lot more to sort out before we can let them in on it, I'm not really a destructive fool, I just don't like being taken for a ride by some unknown force, that's why I'm trying to pick this sorry mess apart, and make some sense of it.'

Nan nodded in tacit agreement.

When the entire group had assembled in the cavern, Nan stood on a raised section of floor to address them, physically reinforcing his authority over them by his elevated position.

'It is noticeable that some of you seem reluctant to accept our newest arrival into our midst with the degree of welcome usually afforded a stranger. This is most unfortunate, as he has much to offer us, and we would be the losers if he should decide to leave us and join another group.'

'Such as what?' someone asked, all heads turning this way and that to see who had dared to be so outspoken, but the originator of the tart remark remained a mystery.

Bell did her best to give Sandy another welcoming smile, but the two missing front teeth along with the other misshapen and discoloured ones, did little to reassure him that he wanted to be welcomed into such a dishevelled and grime streaked rabble.

'I can understand your hesitation in accepting me into your cosy little group,' Sandy began, 'but I can offer you something you don't have. First, I shall need to settle in and find my place among you, and then we can begin to bring about some changes for the betterment of you all.'

If he expected a rousing blast of applause, or even a mild cheer, he was going to be disappointed. Apart from scowls from a couple of men, his speech of reassurance did little to change the stolid sullen attitude which seemed the norm for the group. Sandy realized that if he was going to make any headway in the popularity stakes, he would have to work on them individually, and very carefully.

Nan, who had the wind taken out of his sails by Sandy's outburst, realized there was nothing constructive he could add to what had gone before, and quickly stepping down said, 'Let us get to work, there's much to do.'

The scruffy little group of cave dwellers melted away as quickly as they had assembled, leaving behind the sour odour of greasy hair and unwashed bodies, their shuffling footsteps gradually fading away in the distance as they went about their allotted tasks, leaving Nan and Sandy alone.

'I would assume that water is in short supply,' Sandy began, to break the awkward silence, 'and I doubt anyone's washed their hair since they arrived, let alone cut it. Why do they let themselves get into such a filthy state?' he asked, and then realized he had inadvertently included Nan in his disparaging remarks.

'As you say, water is in short supply, we only have what we can collect from the dew which trickles down from the rocks outside, and there is never enough of that.' Nan was obviously hurt by the remark. 'Drinking water is our first priority, and we recycle what we can to add to that used for the growing bins. I noticed the aroma when I first arrived, but I soon got used to it as time went by. Do you really find it so offensive?' he asked, hoping Sandy would not make too much of it.

'Well, let's put it this way, if one of the females were the most gorgeous creature alive, I would think twice before taking her to bed!' Sandy replied, trying to make light of the issue, and failing completely.

'Seriously though, is there no other way of obtaining water? Do any of the tunnels go downwards, and if so, have you looked for it there? If it trickles down on the outside of the rocks, there's a good chance some of it may collect within the rock formation.' Sandy concluded.

'That would take us into regions we aren't meant to go into.' Nan replied, looking worried that this newcomer might break well established taboos and endanger them all.

'There you go again, *who* said you couldn't go into certain tunnels? I'll bet it started because someone a long time ago got careless, and didn't return. That's no reason to put certain tunnels out of bounds, that's just stupid superstition.'

'Would you be willing to go into the forbidden zones then?' asked Nan, hoping to see terror at the prospect.

'Certainly, if we take care, and don't go falling down any holes, I see no reason why we shouldn't go where we please, I'll bet there's lots of things we could find out which would enhance our lives, if only you'd all forget the superstitious crap you've build up around the place.'

Nan assumed the hurt look again, mixed with a little fear.

They talked on for some time, finally being interrupted by Mop bearing two bowls of something which gave off copious wisps of water vapour and an indescribable smell.

'Here we are,' she beamed pleasantly, 'you'll both feel better with this inside you.' She had sensed that Nan was not quite up to his usual bright state.

They took the proffered bowls and crude metal spoons, Nan tucking in hungrily before Mop had left the cavern.

'Come on, eat up,' Nan said between mouthfuls, 'it tastes better than it looks and is very nutritious, you'll get used to the smell after a while.'

Sandy dipped his spoon into the gruel-like mess, hooking out a piece of something he could not identify, and was grateful for the lack of recognition. Nan was right, it tasted quite palatable if he held his breath while chewing and then quickly swallowed, the liquid remains in the bottom of the bowl was something else, and Sandy put it aside.

Nan quickly scooped up the bowl, and asked hesitatingly,

'Are you sure you don't want it?' and drank it down in a couple of gulps before Sandy could reply.

'You have fire then?' Sandy asked, a little surprised at the hot goo they had been served up with.

'No, why do you think that?' asked Nan, a puzzled look on his face.

'Because of the hot...,' he had to force himself to say 'food.'

'Oh, that's heated by the hot gas vent in one of the caves.' Nan replied, relieved another assault on their beliefs had been avoided, for the time being.

'I'd like to see that,' Sandy said, suddenly finding something of real interest to investigate, 'can we go now?'

'I suppose so, although it's Mop's domain really, and we should ask her first.'

Nan led the way down a series of tunnels, one of which eventually opening out into a cavern lit by three gas lights, and equipped with a rough table littered with pots of various sizes, two shelves, somehow fixed to the wall, but he could see no obvious means of attachment, and a copious amount of Mop's body odour.

A large bundle of rags in one corner suddenly moved and unwound itself, revealing the dreaded Mop. She had been stooped over a pile of wrinkled brown and black things, sorting them out into two piles.

'I was just getting something tasty together for the evening meal,' she offered, giving Sandy a welcoming smile.

'What are those?' he asked, dreading the answer.

'Mushrooms, of course. We grow them in one of the caves near here, would you like to see them?' she replied, pleased that someone had at least acknowledged her presence and possibly her culinary skills. Sandy went over to the pile and looked closer at the wrinkled and shrivelled objects, wondering if these were the extra chewy bits he had had so much difficulty in swallowing.

'These aren't mushrooms,' Sandy exclaimed, 'mushrooms are rounded white things, on a stalk. But they are of the fungi family. How do you know they aren't poisonous?'

'No one's died yet!' exclaimed Mop, sounding hurt.

'I didn't mean to be disrespectful,' he hastily added, 'but some fungi are deadly poisonous, I was just wondering how you knew these were edible.'

Nan, fearing an argument was about to ensue, and upset the delicate balance of his charges, interrupted the conversation.

'Sandy would like to look at the hot gas vent you use for your excellent cooking, that's if you don't mind.'

'I don't mind,' Mop replied, still a bit huffy, 'it's over here.

As they drew near a recess in the cave wall, a faint hissing noise could be heard. Picking up a piece of dirty rag, Mop took hold of a stone plug and withdrew it from a hole at the back of the recess. The hiss was now more of a deep whistle, and Mop stood back to let Sandy look into the exposed hole.

The roundish hole went in about half a metre, and then expanded out to form a small cavern of its own. A small slit in the floor of the cavity emitted a stream of high pressure gas, only visible because of the shimmer it imparted to the surrounding air.

'It's very hot.' Mop warned. 'You'll burn yourself if you touch it.' she added as an afterthought.

'Have you got a long piece of metal I could use for a moment?' Sandy asked, reaching one hand out behind him in anticipation.

Mop rummaged about for a moment in one corner of the cavern, returning with a metre long strip of metal which she gently placed in his outstretched hand.

'Be careful,' she said, sounding concerned, 'it's very hot in there, you could easily burn yourself.'

Taking the proffered strip of metal, Sandy pushed it into the opening, being careful to let only part of the hot gas stream impinge on its end. Withdrawing it a few moments later, he ran his finger along the beads of condensate which had been deposited on the metal strip, and touched it to his tongue.

'That's water!' he exclaimed, 'you've a water supply here you didn't know about. That's not hot gas coming out of the vent, it's steam. If we can cool it sufficiently, it will condense into water droplets.'

'How did you know it was water vapour?' asked Nan, puzzled by Sandy's ability to be so certain of his discovery.

'It's not water vapour,' Sandy replied, 'it's steam. Water vapour is like a mist, you can see it, and it's not usually very hot. Steam is very much hotter, and is invisible. What made you think it was gas?'

'My predecessor said it was gas, so I took his word for it,' a somewhat contrite Nan answered back, 'it's hardly my place to query his knowledge of things, he was a very clever man.' he added defensively.

'Obviously,' Sandy commented, 'but it's only when you query things which are taken for granted, that you find out the truth.' He paused for a moment, deep in thought, wondering if it was wise to disclose his idea for water production, and what effect it might have on the rest of the group.

'We could certainly do with more water,' said Nan, breaking the uneasy silence, 'but how can we get it without getting burnt by the hot gas?'

'If we had some metal pipes, we could let some of the steam go through them, and water would collect on the cold surface and run out into a container, but the difficulty would be keeping the pipes cold.'

'The main difficulty is the pipes, we don't have any.' Nan sounded disappointed at the thought of the extra water supply suddenly disappearing.

Sandy looked into the hot cavity again to see where the steam was going, as it didn't come into the main cavern.

'There's a hole in the roof of the cavity, like a chimney, and by now it's so hot the steam can no longer condense in it. If we could divert some of the steam into another cavern, it would condense onto the walls, and we could collect the water, allowing the cavern to cool down again every so often.'

'There's a cave next door,' Mop suggested, 'but we don't use it, as it is so cold. We keep it blocked off with a cover, or we'd all freeze to death.'

Sandy looked at Nan, and he nodded.

The next door cave had a small opening covered with a dark brown piece of cloth, stuck to the rim of the hole with what looked like pitch. Whatever it was, some of it transferred to Sandy's hands as he tried to pull the cloth away from the opening, and Mop giggled at his failing attempts to remove the offending compound.

She was right, the air in the cave was certainly chilly compared to the tunnel they were standing in, and when Sandy squeezed through the hole he found out why.

'There's a strong draft blowing from a hole in that corner, and it seems to go out of a hole in the top of the cave. Don't know why it should be so cold though.'

'How will we get the hot gas in there?' asked Nan, still a little hesitant about the project, 'it's solid rock between the two caves.'

'Perhaps we can knock a hole through,' said Sandy, 'and then make up a piece of pipe to connect up the steam supply,' he paused before adding, 'I think it should work.'

They put the fabric cover back over the entrance to the cold cave, Sandy getting some more of the black sticky stuff on his hands, much to Mop's amusement.

'I'll put your idea to the rest of the group when we have our evening meal.' said Nan. 'I'm sure they'll be pleased to have an extra supply of water.'

'Wouldn't count on that,' Sandy replied, as the men made their way back to the main cavern, 'it'll mean they might have to wash, and I can't see that going down very well.'

Sandy wanted to know just how hot it was outside during the day, so they went to the entrance of the cave complex, the radiating heat from the baking sands reaching them when they were still three metres from the opening.

'My God, it's lethal out there.' was all he could think of saying. 'But why is it so hot, surely it can't be just the sun?'

'I fear it is, but it does have one benefit, no one else can go out either, so that only leaves a short time in the early morning and late afternoon for raids, so we don't have to keep watch all day. At night, it's too cold, the sand freezes and you wouldn't last more than a few minutes.'

'If it's that cold, how come you and I didn't get frozen to death when you came to get me?'

'Ah, that's because it was near dawn time, and the temperature goes up a little then. The Great Light only comes to leave people at dawn, otherwise they would be frozen by the time we got to them.' Nan was on home ground again, talking about things he knew well, and his self confidence returned.

The rest of the time before the evening meal was taken up showing Sandy some more of the cave complex, the store rooms for their pitiful little collection of raw materials, and a crude weaving loom used for their garment manufacture.

When the others had all trooped in for their evening sustenance, and the greasy bowls had been passed around and the contents consumed, Nan mentioned the possibility of the new water supply.

Sadly, little enthusiasm was shown for this major breakthrough in their survival potential, two of the men mumbling something about going against the natural order of things, and the old elder wouldn't have allowed it. When asked by Nan to be a little more explicit about their beliefs, they backed down, scowling at Sandy whom they considered to be the instigator of the blasphemy.

Ben was asked about the possible supply of metal to make a connecting pipe to go between the two caves. He thought there might be some, but if there was not enough, a quick raid on their neighbours would probably solve the problem.

'You mean, if you don't have something you need, you just go and take it from other groups?' asked a somewhat shaken Sandy.

'They would do the same to us.' Ben replied defensively, and the others chorused their agreement. While the others argued the finer points of thieving, Sandy questioned Nan a little deeper on the supply of materials from the Great Light, and when it might be expected.

'There's no set time,' he replied, 'it just comes whenever the Greater Powers decide to give us something.'

'And that's only their rubbish.' Sandy added. 'Lets face it, they've never given you anything in working order, have they?'

'No, that's true, but it's a test for us to make something useful from what they have graciously given us.'

'Face facts,' said Sandy, 'they're only giving us their junk, and they're probably glad to get rid of it.'

'Anyway, I'm not happy about raiding other groups for materials, can't we have a look at Ben's supplies, there might well be enough bits and pieces to make the tube.'

'I don't think it's up to you to decide if we raid the others,' said Nan, feeling his authority was slipping again, 'it's been going on for as long as I can remember, and it's part of our life.'

'That doesn't make it right. Surely the more we raid them, the more they'll raid us, so who wins in the end? And what about casualties in the meantime? I would have thought your life here was tough enough, without adding unnecessary punch-ups with your neighbours to it.' Sandy was losing patience with the older man and his bizarre ritualistic beliefs.

Ben saved the day by coming over to them, and suggesting they visit his store to see if there was anything which would meet their needs, as he was not too sure what they wanted.

On the way, Sandy asked about the gas lights, and how they were fuelled, but Nan did not seem conversant with the operation, and suggested he ask Ben when they had sorted out the pipe requirements.

The materials store was a positive gold mine of bits and pieces, and Sandy earmarked those items he thought necessary for the water condenser.

Nan suggested they visit Mop's kitchen to get a better idea of what had to be done, and Sandy took a long metal bar and a lump of some hard material he found at the bottom of a pile of odd chunky shaped pieces of metal, to make the break through hole.

Luckily, Mop was off doing something else when they arrived, and Sandy got to work right away with Ben, taking it in turns to hold the metal rod, while the other hit it with the hard mystery lump. Just before they broke through the intervening wall of rock, they made a useful discovery.

Ben had insisted he do the major part of the hammering, and getting a bit tired, his aim faltered. The hammer lump only grazed the metal bar instead of hitting it squarely, and the subsequent shower of sparks caught them all by surprise.

Ben dropped the lump, Sandy dropped the bar, and Nan was already in the cave opening, ready to flee even further if the need arose.

When they realized that none of them had caught fire, and it seemed safe to pick up their tools again, Sandy suggested they try to duplicate the fireworks display.

Leaving the lump on the ground, as it seemed most likely that was where the stream of sparks were coming from, Sandy swung the bar, just grazing the lump of mystery material. This time they were ready for the sparks, and were not disappointed at the display.

'You have made fire,' exclaimed Nan, 'so now we won't have to trade for it when our lights go out.'

'Making a shower of sparks is one thing, getting it to set fire to something is another matter.' Sandy said gently, not wanting to down Nan's new found enthusiasm. 'I expect we'll find a way to do it though.'

The breakthrough to the next cave soon followed, and it was now just a matter of fabricating a length of pipe to transfer some of the steam into the chilly chamber to generate a new supply of water.

'The end which goes into Mop's cooking cavity will have to be made such that we can swing it out when she wants to cook,' Nan remarked, 'and we'll have to warn her not to touch the pipe, as it will be as hot as the steam it carries.'

Sandy noticed Nan had used the word 'steam', instead of hot gas as he usually did, and considered he had at last begun Nan's process of re-education.

Ben was quite happy to be left with the job of hammering the bits of sheet metal into a pipe, and making a jointed swivel end for the connection into Mop's cooker, while Nan and Sandy returned to the cold cave to remove any dust and rubble from its floor.

They were fortunate in that the floor level in the cave was a few centimetres below that of the outside passage, so if there were no leaks in the side walls, quite a lot of water would accumulate in the shallow well before it ran out into the tunnels.

Sandy was allocated a sleeping cave, in which he could also keep his possessions, not that he had any at the moment.

He retired for the night, exhausted, but his mind was still in a whirl after what had happened in one short day.

'Three more days at this pace, and I'll be a gibbering wreck.' were his last thoughts as he gratefully slipped into a deep sleep on the smelly bed of rags which passed for a bed, for the time being.

He was shaken awake next day by Ben, who was in a state of great excitement. It took him a few seconds to remember where he was, and Ben looked hurt by the lack of instant recognition.

'What's the time?' he asked, rubbing his sore eyes.

'Don't know what you mean,' Ben replied, 'I don't think we have any time here, at least not that I've heard of.'

'Oh God. Alright, what part of the day is it? How long have the others been up?'

'They've been up since dawn, it's now nearly midday. Nan said to let you sleep on, but I thought you would want to see the steam experiment set-up before we try it out.'

'Damn right I do.' Sandy replied, heaving himself out of the pile of disgusting rags he had cuddled all night.

'Lead the way, Ben, I'm a bit wobbly on me feet this morning.' Sandy staggered about like a drunk, after a night out he was unable to recall.

'Probably lack of food.' Ben said cheerfully.

'Oh, that's what you call it.' Sandy remembered the last greasy offering. 'I had something else in mind.'

Mop greeted them with her usual hopeful smile, mainly directed at Sandy, on whom it was totally wasted.

'We'd like to try out our water maker.' Ben said, doing his best to smile at the unlovely heap before him.

'Go ahead, Benny, I don't need the hot hole for a while, it's a cold midday meal today.'

The look on Ben's face at that cheery news said it all, and Sandy wondered what frightful concoction she had dreamt up to tickle their taste buds this time.

Mop disappeared down the tunnel, either disappointed that no one had taken advantage of her charms, or on some culinary errand for the evening meal. Sandy was in two minds as to which was the least formidable option.

Ben removed the stone plug from the steam cavity, and swung the jointed pipe into the hole. It was a perfect fit, and he went up several notches in Sandy's estimation.

'There's a deflector on the end, so most of the steam should be guided into the pipe.' he said cheerfully. 'Can't say I like the sound of it though.'

The pipe vibrated like a tin snake with a severe case of the shakes, accompanied by a shrill whistling noise as the steam was bent off its normal course up the vent hole, and into the transfer tube.

'Let's see what's happening in the cold cave.' said Ben, hurrying out of Mop's kitchen and into the tunnel.

'Yes, let's.' said Sandy, 'after you.'

'Who's going to open the cover and take a peak inside?' asked Ben, with a grin.

'I'll give you that honour,' said Sandy, 'I got messed up with that filthy black stuff last time, it took ages to get off.'

Ben grinned again, and took a small metal blade from somewhere about his person, and gently prised the fabric cover away from the rim of the hole.

The gas lamp in the tunnel shone directly into the hole, and there the light stopped. A thick white mist swirled energetically about in the cave, totally obscuring the opposite wall and any other details.

'Put the cover back for a short while, and then turn the steam off, after that we'll see how well it's condensing.' Sandy was well pleased with the experiment so far, but would the water be drinkable?

They went back into the kitchen, and Ben picked up something from the table and began to chew.

'It's better raw, I don't know why she bothers to cook it, it only makes it tougher and all the flavour is lost.'

Sandy didn't dare ask what he was chewing, his stomach was feeling a bit delicate as it was.

Mop came back in with a bowl full of plump glistening yellow berries just as they were about to leave to check the mist cave.

'We're just going to see if we have any water.' said Ben, vacating the room in a hurry. As Sandy went to follow him, Mop came alongside and coyly pressed half a dozen berries into his hand, giving him a long slow wink.

The cover was prised back, and most of the mist had cleared revealing several little puddles on the floor next to the wall of the cave, and multiple runlets of moisture trickling down the walls to join them.

'Well done Ben, it looks as if we have a new water supply, although the first few lots will have to be used for plant watering until all the dust has been washed off the walls. I'll just see what it tastes like.'

Sandy bent down and dipped a finger into one of the nearest puddles, and then put it to his tongue.

'Not too bad, a bit metallic and gritty, but that should clear after a while. Let's give the good news to Nan, although I'm surprised he's not here to see the trial. Oh, by the way, Mop gave me these just now,' and he showed Ben the berries clutched in his other hand, 'would you like some?'

Ben did his knowing little grin while taking half the berries.

'She's got her eye on you, I think she's a lot younger than she looks, so if you're not feeling energetic, watch out!'

They hurried past Mop's kitchen, giving her a brief wave as they went, and headed for the main assembly cavern.

It was empty when they arrived, so they both sat down to await the arrival of the others for the now late midday meal.

'Tell me about the gas guns,' Sandy began, 'Nan mentioned them yesterday, but didn't say very much about them.'

'Not much to tell really. It's just a metal tube with a bulbous container on the end. We fill it with a mixture of air and gas, push a round stone in the end of the tube and then seal it with a bung of material. If anyone threatens us, we just point it at them and flip the little lever at the end. It goes bang, and the stone flies out of the other end. If we're lucky, it hits them. It frightens the hell out of them anyway, and they usually run off, especially if we point it at them again.

'But it won't fire again, will it?' asked Sandy.

'No, but they don't know that!'

'How did you know how to make the gas guns in the first place?' Sandy asked. 'That's quite an advanced weapon.'

'I didn't make them, they were here when I arrived. I just maintain them, and fill them with gas every day.'

'How does the lever make them go off?'

'I don't know. I did try to look inside one once, but it wouldn't come apart. I suppose there must be something inside which lights the gas, but I don't know what it is. Perhaps it is something like the hammer lump we used, making a spark when you hit it.'

Sandy's next question was cut short by the shuffle of footsteps coming down the tunnel. The rest of the group trooped in, headed by Nan, who was looking very pleased with himself. Something must have gone right.

'Sorry I wasn't at the water experiment, how did it go?'

They told him, and for the first time the others seemed pleased as well, several offering 'well done' to both Ben and Sandy, which surprised him after their former treatment.

Mop appeared with several large bowls strung one above the other, and plonked them down on the table.

'It's a cold meal today, but there's a hot one for tonight,' she said cheerily, 'and it's rather special.'

The few feeble cheers were drowned out by the groans, but Sandy could not tell which meal was being referred to.

A mixture of fungi, green leaves, berries and a large bulbous looking fruit which had been sliced into many thin sections was on offer, and Sandy suddenly realized that if he wanted a mixture, he would have to fight his way to the front, as the berries and green leaves were disappearing fast.

Although the fungi looked hideous, it tasted the best of all, except for the berries, but he didn't manage to secure many of them in the general melee around the table.

Mop gave him a sly smile, and popped two berries into his hand as she passed him on her way out of the cavern.

The meal, such as it was, soon finished, and Kel, the general dogsbody who could turn his hand to anything, asked Sandy if he had any other bright ideas. Not quite sure what sort of answer was required to remain on friendly terms with everyone, he answered 'Not at the moment.' and thought he heard a sigh of relief from those nearby. Then again, it could have been the result of the green leaves, which they had all enthusiastically tucked into.

The afternoon was spent working the new water condenser, after Mop had finished cooking her special evening meal.

By late afternoon, they had recovered several containers of water, the last few being free from the fine gritty particles which had been in the first morning sample, and Bell gave her plants a good dousing for the first time in their lives.

While the others took it in turn to gaze in wonder at the mist filled cold cave, Sandy took Ben to one side and asked him about the gas lights.

'I think they were here before any of us arrived,' Ben informed him, 'and so was the gas generator.'

'Do you know how that works?' he asked, hopefully.

'Yes, it's quite simple really. There's two big tanks in one of the caves below us. We put all our waste, and I mean *all* our waste into the tank. All the scraps of Bell's plants which we can't eat, bits of rotten cloth, anything which will decompose is dumped in. It rots down producing gas which is piped along fine metal tubes to the gas jets. Each jet has a little knob which will give a full flame in one position, and a tiny 'keeper' flame in the other, that way we don't waste the gas when no one's around to need the light.

'When the contents are fully decomposed, we start the other tank, removing the remains from the first tank for Bell's plant bins, mixed with sand, the plants love it!'

'But wait a minute,' said Sandy, 'even if you put every tiny scrap of waste possible into the tank, it wouldn't produce enough gas to light two or three lights continuously, let alone the huge number you have here. There must be another source of gas to keep this lot going.'

'No, just the two tanks, when one is full, we switch over to the other one and empty the first, as I said.'

'Could I see this gas producing plant?' asked Sandy hesitantly, 'I mean, would anyone mind if I did?'

'Don't see why not.' Ben paused for a moment. 'I suppose you should see Nan first 'cos he's in control of everything, and then Jez, as he's in charge of the tanks.'

Interest was waning on the water producing cave, and most of the group had drifted away to go about their other tasks, so Sandy, never one to waste an opportunity, approached Nan, and asked about the gas producer.

'Why are you so interested?' Nan looked surprised at Sandy's request. 'It only makes gas for the lights, there's nothing special about that.'

'It's the amount of gas it produces, I don't see how it can make enough to supply all these lights.'

'Hadn't thought about that.' Nan looked pensive for a little while, and then the moment of doubt cleared, 'But it does, somehow. Take Jez with you, he can explain how it works in more detail than I can, he runs the thing.'

Finding Jez was another matter. No one had seen him or knew what his allotted task for the day was. Sandy, and Ben who insisted on being in on the investigation, were about to give up, when Jez came hurrying out of one of the maze of tunnels and caves which comprised their world.

'You bin looking for me?' he asked, his short guttural tones matching his solid stocky looking body.

'Good God,' Sandy thought, 'he looks more like an ape than a human being.' But when he tried to visualize what an ape looked like, he was unable to do so. He shook his head, as if to clear away some misty impediment in his mind.

'Yes please. I'm interested in how your gas plant works, I've not seen one before.' He saw no purpose in revealing the real reason for the visit, at this stage.

It was a long walk to the gas producing cavern, and on the way Sandy began to count the number of lamps with their guttering little flames. In his mind, there was no way this many lights could be fed by the gas plant which had been described to him. He was sure there must be another supply to the system, and he was determined to find it.

They went down a steep incline, which took them to a level well below that which they normally lived in, and Sandy noticed a sharp drop in temperature.

'Bit cold down here,' he offered in conversation. 'Can't say I'd like to work in this atmosphere for too long.'

'Don't notice it,' Jez grunted, as he padded down the tunnel, 'jus the same as above to me.'

They came to the gas producing chamber. It was big, and the plant looked lost in so much space. Two large metallic bins, nearly as tall as a man, stood side by side. A network of pipes ran from bin to bin, then into smaller bins, turned, twisted, and eventually ran up to the ceiling and into a box, where a pair of pipes exited to continue their wandering until they disappeared into a hole in the wall which divided the gas cavern from the next chamber.

'This bin's makin gas,' Jez said, pointing with a stubby finger at the nearest container, 'an that one's bein filled with muck, an'll be started up in a day or two, if we's git enough muck, that is.'

'How often do you change them over?' asked Sandy, trying to be casual in his manner.

'When they's full.' Came back the curt reply, Jez did not waste words, or anything else, for that matter.

The system for switching from one tank to the other was explained in great detail, and Jez warmed to the two inquisitors after a while, as no one usually came down here and showed any interest in him or his work.

'What do you think?' asked Ben on the way back up, leaving Jez to tend his effluent digester. Sandy turned.

'That plant couldn't possibly produce enough gas to light the chamber it's in, let along the passageways leading to it. As for the rest of the place, we'd all be groping about in the dark if it were left to those two tanks to produce the gas.'

'Bet Mop would enjoy that! Do you really think there is another supply coming in then?'

'Damn sure of it. I'll have a word with Nan, we'll have to get his permission for what I want to do, and that is take a closer look at where the pipes go through the wall.'

'You could have done that just now.' Ben commented.

'I mean, dig out the hole they go through, I think that's where the extra supply must come in. Anyway, what gives with Mop? Doesn't anyone want to, er, satisfy her?'

'Would you?' exclaimed Ben with a giggle. 'Poor 'ol Mop's got a heart of gold, but look at her! Can't say I'd like a close encounter with her, even if I was starving. I know we all look a bit of a mess, except you, who look as if you've just been created, but Mop is a right smelly heap.'

'That's another thing, why is everyone so unkempt? The only way you can tell the women from the men is that they don't have beards, and as for their hair, that can't have been washed or cut since they arrived here.'

'Lack of water mainly, I would think, plus the fact that it's a damn hard struggle just to survive here. Anyway, you get used to it after a while. You look so totally different, you could have come from another world with your short hair and smart clothes.'

'I'm beginning to think you might have got something there. I certainly don't feel part of this bunch, no offence meant. As for my clothes, I consider them to be rags, the remains of a uniform I used to wear. Good God, why did I say that?' Sandy exclaimed, 'the word uniform seemed the right thing to say, but I can't get a picture of it in my mind.'

'No good asking me,' Ben replied, 'I've long since given up any attempt to try and explain things. I just accept 'em for what they are, and try to make the best of it.'

'That's why you lot are in such a bloody awful mess, you don't *try* to make things any better. There're many things which could be done to improve your lot here.'

'Such as what?' Ben replied, sounding hurt.

'The water supply, for a start. Now you can all wash, you can drink as much as you like, and if everyone gets a hair cut, we can make a couple of hundred metres of rope.'

What do we need rope for?' asked Ben, completely missing the point. Sandy did not even bother to reply.

When the suggestion about the gas supply was put to Nan, he seemed surprised that anyone would want to do such a thing, until Sandy explained at great length that it would prove the point that things were not quite as they seemed, and therefore if they understood what was really going on, they may be able to better their lot.

Nan's permission was eventually given, with the proviso that Jez was 'otherwise occupied' at the time, the less people who knew what was afoot, the better, for now.

Mop had been right, the greasy stew she provided for the evening meal was almost palatable, and Sandy tucked in with a degree of relish which surprised him. He put it down to the fact that he was almost starving, rather than Mop's culinary abilities, which was perhaps a little unkind, as she had very limited resources to hand.

To say they all engaged in convivial conversation after the meal would be stretching the point to its limits, a series of muted monosyllabic grunts with their equally short replies dribbled on for a while, and then, one by one, they drifted off to their sleeping quarters, as there was little else to do.

Holding his breath, Sandy tucked himself into his pile of smelly rags and tried to get comfortable, cursing the day some fatherless person had dispatched him to this hell hole.

He felt sure that was what had happened. Nothing else made any sense, and as for the 'created' theory, he had rejected that out of hand almost immediately.

He was just drifting off into sleep, listening to the protesting gurgles from his tortured stomach, when a shuffling sound snapped him wide awake again. The cave light had been turned down to its lowest level, so all he could see was a shadowy hulk advancing towards him. His heart raced, and he wondered what best to do, leap up and attack, or feign dead to see what would happen next.

'It's only me,' the now soft dulcet tones of a predatory Mop announced silkily, 'I've brought you some more of those delicious berries you like so much.'

The hulk lowered itself down onto his pile of rags with a wheeze, pinning one arm firmly to the ground, and making it difficult for him to sit upright in the gloom, which he thought was the most effective defensive position he could take up under the circumstances.

'I'm only half awake, and full to the brim with your delicious stew,' he lied, trying to sound mumblely. 'I couldn't possibly eat any more just now.'

Mop's greasy fingers groped around his face trying to find his mouth, and having done so, forced the berries in.

Sandy gagged, but managed to hold the stew in its place for the time being, emitting a grunt as his head went back and banged against the cold stone wall in the process.

Mop, sensing that high jinks of a sensuous nature were not on the menu that night, reluctantly heaved her not inconsiderable mass back onto her feet, bruising his trapped arm as she put her full weight on it.

'See you in the morning, Sandy.' she purred, and shuffled away into the gloom.

The three supplicationary berries flew explosively out of his mouth to splatter themselves on the opposite wall as he let out the breath he had been holding for so long.

Luckily the stew remained where it was in his stomach, mainly because he was doubled over, and it could not find an easy means of escape.

The heady aroma of his amorous visitor lingered on for some time, and he wondered how he could institute compulsory washing in the future. Something would have to be done, even if it meant plugging his nostrils and breathing through his mouth.

Eventually sleep came, taking him out of one nightmare situation, and depositing him into another, complete with sounds and smells.

Sandy awoke next morning with a thick head, a foul temper, and the decision that after he had scrubbed himself clean, the bed linen would get a good boil, along with the rest of the troglodytes.

He made his way to the main cavern where a jovial Ben was patiently awaiting him.

'You look a bit shattered!' If nothing else, Ben was observant. 'Didn't you sleep well?' he asked solicitously.

'Don't ask,' a grumpy Sandy replied, 'life has become a bloody nightmare since I've been here, and I'm sure it wasn't always this way.'

'What do you mean, always? You were only created a short time ago. Life has always been like this, you'll get used to it soon enough. It's just a matter of accepting the routine we have here.'

'Wouldn't bet on that,' he replied grumpily, 'anyway, surely you don't believe you were 'created' out on the sands? Come on, think about it, where did you learn to speak, to remember the very words you use? That has to come from somewhere else. This 'creation' stuff is a load of s...' at that moment Nan came into the cavern.

'Ah, hoped to catch you two. This poking about in the gas generating cave, I'm not really happy about it. You might destroy the whole system, and then we would have no lights. Why do you really want to do it? Surely the fact that it works is enough, so what do you hope to prove?' Nan was visibly agitated, having spent half the night thinking about it, and fearful of the status quo being upset beyond his control.

'Oh it's nothing much really,' Sandy responded, trying to sound casual, and failing, 'I'm just curious how so small a plant can supply so much gas, and at a constant pressure.'

'Well it does, so why question it?' replied Nan, seeing the argument slipping out of his control, once again.

'Don't worry, we'll not harm it, just want to see how it works. We'll tell you what we find out, if anything, and then you'll know a little bit more about this place.'

Two:
Defence and Attack

REALIZING THAT SANDY would do his investigation of the gas plant one way or another, Nan reluctantly gave in to his persistent attitude, insisting that he did not fiddle with anything he did not understand, in a last vain attempt to assume some degree of authority.

'Jez is helping Bell plant up some new growing bins, so he'll be out of your way for a while. Don't take too long though,' Nan said as he left the cavern, 'he'll not like you messing about with his equipment.'

'I don't think Nan liked that,' Ben said a little timidly, as they left the despondent Nan, 'he didn't look very happy.'

Sandy gave him a withering look, and asked him to bring along the bar they had used the day before, and something to hit it with.

On the way down to the gas generating cavern, Sandy pointed out the sections of passageway which had been cut out, as opposed to being naturally worn by water, or whatever nature had used to form them.

'If you look quickly, you'd not notice the difference, so why would anyone go to the trouble of trying to make 'em look natural?' Sandy asked a perplexed Ben, who just shrugged his shoulders and grunted in reply.

'It seems to me,' he continued, 'that someone is trying to make us believe in something other than what is really going on, and that's what I want to find out.'

'But why?' asked a worried sounding Ben. 'You can't do anything about it, things are as they have always been, and if we alter them, we may not survive. There's only just enough food, water is strictly rationed,...' before he could continue his list of excuses not to interfere, Sandy interrupted him with,

'Not now it isn't, with the water cave.'

After a quick check around the darker corners of the cavern to make sure Jez was absent, Sandy went over to the two digester tanks in the middle of the cavern.

'The first thing I want to do is reduce, and then cut off the gas supply.'

'You can't do that!' exclaimed a startled Ben, 'you'll plunge us all into darkness and we'll never get out of this maze of tunnels.'

'Don't be so bloody silly, I'll reduce the flow first, and if the lamps don't dim down a little, then we'll know there must be another supply coming in somewhere.'

Ben was terrified at the prospect, but did not have the courage to physically restrain Sandy as he rummaged about in the tangle of pipes connecting the two big tanks and the subsidiary cylinders comprising the gas generating plant.

'It looks as if these two valves control the flow of gas from each tank, sending it eventually up to the main delivery pipes up there,' he said, indicating a pair of tubes which snaked along the ceiling of the cavern, to later disappear into the wall adjoining the next cave.

'I'll turn this one off a little,' he said to a trembling Ben, 'and see what happens.'

Nothing did, so he turned it off fully, and then the other valve was shut down. Still the little gas lamps on the wall of the cavern flickered, sending ghostly shadows dancing around the walls as the two of them moved about. Sandy looked for the extra supply inlet he was so sure existed.

'Well, so far the lamps haven't gone out, and the gas supply from the tanks is off. That proves my point, there is another supply feeding the lamps, so why do you think that is, eh?'

Ben had stopped shaking as he realized Sandy had been right all along, but what did it imply?

'OK Sandy, you've convinced me that the digesters are not supplying the gas, but does it really matter where the gas comes from? We seem to be getting it from somewhere and we've never run out, as far as I can remember.'

'But that *is* the point,' Sandy retorted impatiently, 'don't you see? If the digesters are not producing our gas, then they have been set up to fool us into thinking we are keeping the supply going ourselves, when in fact what we are doing is just a waste of time, and producing nothing, except perhaps some compost for the growing bins. Someone doesn't want us to realize that this whole place has been set up to house us, hence all this subterfuge. Anyway, I still want to know just where these pipes really go.'

'You'll need something to stand on if you are going to reach where they go into the wall.' said a chastened Ben.

They both hunted around in the gloom of the big cavern, Sandy finally falling over a box-like thing in a dark corner and uttering a rude expletive in the process.

'Must be what he sits on when he's not twiddling the gas controls.' Ben offered, feeling he should say something.

They dragged the heavy box over to the wall, Sandy climbed up and stood looking intently at the point where the pipes disappeared into the stonework.

'Pass up the metal rod, and standby with the lump to hit it with. A little poke about should reveal something.'

A small shower of stone chips fell on the unsuspecting Ben as Sandy chipped away at the point where the pipes disappeared into the wall.

'Looks like they have stuck the small pieces back with something.' Sandy mused as he jabbed away at the wall, finally getting the rod into a position where he thought he could do some real damage.

'OK, whack it one,' Sandy called out, 'but not too hard, I only want to chip away a little of the wall where the pipes go in to see exactly where they go.'

'They go into the next cave,' Ben replied, 'I thought you knew that.'

'I'm not so sure they do, at least, not directly.'

A few minutes later and they had removed enough of the friable stone to reveal where the pipes were actually going, a large lump slipping out of Sandy's hand and hitting Ben on the head. This brought forth a very strong expletive which surprised Sandy, and he hastily reinforced his earlier point,

'Bet you didn't learn that word here!'

'I've never used it before.' said a mildly embarrassed Ben, going a dull pink. 'I'm beginning to see what you mean.'

A few more chips, and the gas pipe mystery was solved.

'If you look up there, you'll see the pipes from the gas generator bend upwards, and disappear up into the rock. Another pair of pipes come down besides them, and then go into the next cave, carrying the real gas supply. That's where the gas supply is really coming from, not the generators down here.'

'Why would anyone want to do that?' asked a surprised Ben, after he had taken a look at the two sets of pipes, 'surely that's a bit deceitful, and why make us go to all the trouble of working the generators when there's no need?'

'This place is all about deceit, nothing is quite what it seems. That's why I want to solve some of these mysteries, and so get a better idea of what it's really all about. Come on, we'd better put back as much of this stone a possible, although it's so gloomy in this corner I doubt anyone will notice our handiwork.' Most of the stone was wedged back in place, and the exploration reasonably well concealed.

'What do we tell Nan?' asked Ben, when they had redistributed the remaining rubble on the floor of the cave into convenient dark corners, 'I don't suppose he'll like it.'

'It's about time Nan faced up to some of the odd things which happen here, instead of just accepting everything at face value and then building a mythical ritual around it.'

Sandy turned the gas supply from the generator back on, being careful to leave everything as it was before.

'Are you going to tell Jez what we've found?' asked Ben, eager to spread the news now that he had had his interest awakened in matters mystical.

'No, I think we'll keep that a little secret to ourselves, and Nan of course, the fewer people who know about this sort of thing the better, for the time being. I would like us to get into a position where we can really look after ourselves without the help of any outside force before we show our hand, as it were, 'cos who knows what will happen then.'

Ben promptly assumed his worried look, as the idea of major changes to their regime looked more than likely, if Sandy had his way.

They met up with Nan in the main cavern just before the midday meal.

'Well, what did you two find out?' asked a somewhat complacent Nan, not really expecting any disturbing news.

They told him what they had found, and Sandy's theory that the gas supply had been rigged a long time ago to fool everyone into thinking that it was they who were making the gas for the lights, when the system could not possibly make enough for their needs. Nan did not look a happy man.

'Why do you think 'they', if 'they' really exist, went to so much trouble to fool us? I don't see any point in it. I think you're jumping to conclusions.' said a rattled Nan.

Just then, the rest of the group began arriving for the midday meal, so any further discussion on the faked gas supply was suspended. Nan suggested that they continue later on after the evening meal, as they would be less likely to be disturbed then.

Mop excelled herself with the food offering, although she would not divulge what the chewy bits were, except they were something she had recently discovered. The juice they were suspended in was thick and glutinous, and tended to stick to the teeth. Sandy dreaded to think what it was she had used, and did not dare ask.

Most of the afternoon was spent rummaging about in Ben's store of bits and pieces, Sandy not saying exactly what it was he was looking for, merely getting an idea of what was available, should the need arise. Ben was sure it would.

The growing boxes were taken out when the sun dipped below the highest peaks, the bowl of the crater taking on a more gentle glow instead of the white hot blast of light which constituted the main part of the day.

The boxes had hardly been out for more than a few minutes when a loud bell sounded, and everyone rushed out to the main entrance.

Karry and Kel were pointing their gas guns at a small group of cloak clad bald headed people who had crept up to the growing bins, and were intent on helping themselves.

'Shoot the tallest one,' Nan said quietly, 'he's most likely their leader, and that should throw them into disarray.'

A loud bang shattered the otherwise stillness of the crater, and several more cloak clad figures suddenly sprang into view from their hiding place among the rocks at the base of the towering cliffs. Karry must have been lucky, or a good shot, for the tall target fell to the ground, clutching his leg.

The fallen one made much of his damaged leg, while two of his henchmen tried to get him up onto his feet again. One of the bolder members of the raiding party took several steps forward, waving a long silver coloured rod at the defenders, and this prompted Nan to give the order to fire again.

This shot hit the rod waver in the forehead, and he too fell to the ground, blood spurting out from the gash, and staining the sands a deep crimson as it soaked in.

Both gas gun carriers took a step forward and pointed their guns at the remaining group of attackers, as if to fire again.

Not realizing the guns were now inoperative, they took to their heels, dragging the last casualty rather carelessly by one leg, until they were well out of range.

The group reassembled, shaking their fists at the triumphant defenders and yelling unintelligibly before marching off defiantly, trying to rescue some degree of dignity from their failed attempt to acquire what was not theirs.

'Well done,' said Nan, 'that was good shooting and should teach them a lesson they won't forget in a hurry.'

Ben stepped forward to take the gas guns for reloading, and Sandy followed him down to his workshop, to see how it was done. One of the gas lamps had a piece of flexible tubing attached to the outlet of the lamp, and Ben thrust the tube into the end of the gun, after removing the bung. Unscrewing a small knob on the bulbous end of the weapon, he then turned on the gas and held a burning taper which he had lit from one of the lamps, over the hole.

Nothing happened for a moment, and then a small flame appeared at the hole, burning brightly. Ben then turned off the gas, removed the tube, and inserted a rod with a leather like plunger on the end, into the gun barrel, pushing it in as far as it would go, and then the little flame went out.

The rod was withdrawn from the barrel end of the gun, the little knob screwed back in and small wad of some fluffy material pushed down the barrel. This was followed by the round stone missile and another wad of material to hold it in place, and then the bung, still attached to its string, was firmly pushed home, to seal the end of the barrel.

When Ben had recharged the other gun, Sandy asked him to explain exactly what he had done, and why.

'It's really very simple. When the gun is fired, burnt air is left in the tube, so the bung is put back to keep it that way.

'Whoever fires the gun, removes the bung just before they fire. The bung stops the gas mixture from leaking out after it has been charged, and is attached to the gun by this piece of string, so that we don't lose it each time the gun is fired.

'When I get the gun back for recharging, I connect up the gas pipe and hold a light to the little hole where the knob was, so that when the incoming gas has driven all the burnt air out, the gas will light, and I know it's full of gas.

'Next, I push the rod with the little flange on it into the barrel, pushing some of the gas out the other end, and when I withdraw the rod, it sucks air back in to mix with the gas.

'This gives the perfect mixture for an explosion, so propelling the stone out when it's fired. The wadding is to hold the stone in place, and the bung is put back to seal the barrel,' and then Ben added as an after thought, 'I would have thought you could have worked it out for yourself.'

'Well, I had, sort of, but I wanted to make sure I had understood it properly.' Sandy replied, when in reality he was checking to see if Ben understood the principles involved, giving him a measure of the man's intelligence for future use. With the guns recharged, they both headed back to the entrance of the cave complex, to rearm the guards.

'Looks like we got back just in time,' said Sandy, handing over the gun he was carrying to what he thought was Kel, although the difference between Kel and Karry was hardly discernible despite the fact that she was a female, 'we have another visitor on the way.'

Kel shielded his eyes against the glare coming off the shiny peaks above and stared into the distance indicated by Sandy.

'You've got good eyes!' he exclaimed, 'damned if I would have spotted him so soon. I think it's one of the men from the group next to us, there're all right, we trade with 'em quite a bit, that's when they have anything to trade with.'

The distant figure quickly grew in size as it raced across the intervening sand, little spurts of silver dust like particles flying out behind him as he sped towards the waiting group.

Red faced and sweating profusely, the stranger blurted out the news between gasps of air to satisfy his bursting lungs.

'We bin raided, most of our stock of plants 'ave bin taken, an' three of our men be lying injured. One ran off into the sands, an' somethin got 'im, couldn't see what it was though, it gist grabbed 'is legs, an' he went under.'

'God, he smells worse than our lot,' Sandy quietly said to Ben, who had moved up wind of the odorous visitor. 'They must be *really* short of water.'

'Do we smell as bad to you, as that man does to me?' asked Ben, with an anxious look on his face.

'If you want me to be honest, yes, but I'm getting used to it, I suppose. We could all do with a good wash, if the truth be known, and as for a hair cut, you'll all have to get an estimate first.'

'What do you mean, an estimate? asked a perplexed Ben.

'It means...., Oh, forget it, just a little joke of mine.' Sandy replied, moving a little further up wind of their visitor.

'What do you want us to do about it?' asked Kel, warily.

'Git 'em back for us. We's short of food anyway, an' now we's hardly got any,' the visitor said miserably, 'we could help you, that would out number 'em.' he added as an afterthought.

'Where were your guards?' asked Karry, 'you should have seen them coming and beaten them off, or at least got your growing boxes back inside.'

'Don't know. We just heard a noise, an' when we went outside half the boxes was gone, an' three of our men was lying on the ground, injured.' He wobbled over to a rock and sat down, thoroughly dejected, the rest of the group moving over to one side to avoid the aroma which seemed to follow him like an invisible but pungent cloud.

'We don't even know who they are,' Kel said defensively, 'and even if we did, there's little chance we could get the boxes back without heavy casualties. Sounds like they're the same lot who paid us a visit earlier, but we saw them coming and fought them off with our gas guns.'

'We don't 'ave any gas guns, perhaps we could trade for some?' the wretched creature suggested, but with little hope in his voice.

'We only have two, and your lot probably couldn't look after them properly, anyway.' Kel wasn't going to deplete his armoury at any price.

'Could we trade for some growing boxes an' plants?' the odorous heap asked, this being the main purpose of his visit.

'What do you have to trade with?' asked Ben, thinking this would put an end to the request.

'Don't know. We's got lots of bits an' pieces you might find useful. Stuff the Great Light gave us.' he added brightly, as if this would increase the value of their stock.

'I very much doubt you'll have anything of value to us,' Kel said, 'anyway, we don't have any spare growing boxes at the moment, so I don't see how we can trade.'

Sandy felt sorry for the emissary from the raided group, he had slumped down on his rock, all hope gone from his dejected face, and a trickle of tears threatened to dislodge some of the ingrained dirt from his grimy cheeks.

Sandy casually moved closer to Kel and said very quietly,

'It might be worth a quick look to see what they've got, could be there's something we could make use of.'

Kel hesitated for a moment, deep in thought, and replied, 'OK, we'll have to get Nan's approval first, and if we do, we'll go over first thing in the morning. You might be right, I don't think even they know what they've got. They're such an inept bunch, I'm surprised they are still in existence.'

'He's got a funny way of talking, too,' Sandy said, nodding his head in the general direction of the pathetic bundle of rags, 'I can only just understand him.'

Kel grinned, 'You should hear the rest of 'em, they've got a different language to us, and he acts as translator for them. We've dealt a little with them in the past, and that's when I found out that when he arrived here, he didn't speak their language at all, so had to learn it. I suppose he's lost a little of his own in the process, or it's just a bit different to ours.'

Nan suddenly appeared on the scene, and Kel went over to explain what had happened. Agreement was reached on a possible trade the following day, and the odorous emissary was dispatched homewards, with copious warnings about the coming cold of evening, and the nasty things which lurked below the surface of the fast cooling sand. The others of the group had already begun to retrieve the growing bins, and soon the crater was devoid of all visible life.

On the way back to the main cavern, Sandy asked Nan about the black sticky stuff which held the fabric covering over the hole in the cave they now used to condense water.

He thought it came from a cave deep below the gas generating cavern, a long time ago, but no one had been there of late that he could recall.

'Why are you interested in it?' asked Nan, 'do you have a use for some sticky stuff?'

'It's a raw material, and there may be some other undiscovered use for it.' replied Sandy cautiously, not wishing to go into deep discussion of what he had in mind at the moment. Somehow the black goo around the hole reminded him of something, and he felt sure if he were to see it in its native state, he would be able to recall what it was.

By now, Ben had taken an interest in the proceedings, and as Nan moved away, disinterestedly, Ben moved in closer.

'What are you up to now?' he asked quietly, 'perhaps I can help. I know my way around these caves quite well, and I've been in some that no one else seems to know about, deep below us. There is a limit, below which you die. I've not been that far, but someone did a long time ago, and never came back, or so the story goes.'

'We'll sort that problem out if and when we come to it. Don't forget, there's much superstition attached to most stories in your history. Oh, and we'll have to find some way of making light if we are going outside the range of the gas lamps, so start thinking about that.' said Sandy, as they began assembling for the evening meal.

Mop looked very pleased with herself when she came in with her steaming cauldron, and liberally splashed several members of the party as she dished out the foul smelling brew. Luckily, it tasted better than it smelt, as usual.

With the meal over, the group slowly dispersed with the occasional ill concealed belch, leaving Ben, Sandy, and Nan still sitting at the table. Mop collected up the bowls and dumped them into the cauldron, wiped up the few remaining puddles of spilt stew, and giving Sandy a slight nudge as she passed by, swept out of the cavern with a look of triumph on her face.

'That was the best meal she has produced yet.' Nan said, picking a few vagrant particles from his beard and eating them. 'I only hope she can keep up this new standard for a while.' He sat back, leaning against the wall of the cavern, and looked expectantly at the other two.

'Can I ask a few more questions about this place?' asked Sandy hesitantly, knowing that Nan could easily be upset.

He nodded, his face taking on a furrowed and serious look.

'Tell me about the sands, and the creatures who live in them.' Sandy began, aware that Ben was showing interest.

'We've never seen them, only suffered from their attacks. They only come to the surface when it's not too cold or too hot, so we are free to walk on the sands between these times.

'Early morning and late evening, if your feet are well covered, are safe times, although that can't be guaranteed. Whatever they are, they're very quick, those caught by them just disappear into the sand, only having time to give a yell. Do you have something in mind?' he asked.

'Just thought they might be a source of meat, that's if we can catch 'em. If we could, they would be a good trading material, but we would have to keep the whole thing to ourselves, or we'll lose the trading value.'

Nan looked surprised at the idea, and then asked what 'meat' was, as it was not on Mop's menu as far as he knew, and he had forgotten the meaning of the word.

Sandy did his best to explain that it was a high protein food, although he wasn't quite sure what that meant, except that it was a desirable thing to have available, and then went on to elaborate on a possible and safe method of capture.

'If we bait a long rope with something edible on the end, and throw it out onto the sands as they are warming up, whatever is down there should grab it, and then we can haul in the rope a little, and leave the sun's heat to kill it.'

Nan didn't say anything for a while, but Ben was almost too keen to get on with the project. It was decided in the end to work out all the finer points of the capture, and then put it to the rest of the group to see how they felt about eating meat, and if they thought the risk was worth taking.

It was obvious that Nan wanted to change the subject, so Sandy took the offered chance, and brought up the Great Lights for discussion. It was then even more obvious that Nan would have preferred to have stuck with the creatures of the sands until all were ready for bed.

'Just what are these lights?' asked Sandy, feigning innocence, as he thought this might be most productive.

'They are the great providers, the creators of people like us. They visit us every now and again to bring new people, and materials for us to make use of. Without them, we would not exist, nor could we exist here, for there is nothing to sustain us without their help.' Nan adopted the look of someone who had just delivered the final statement on a subject, and considered that subject to be at an end. He had not reckoned with the tenacity of purpose which drove Sandy to find out what had happened to him.

'Why do you think they create us, and then dump us in this godforsaken place to struggle for a miserable existence which I wouldn't wish on my worst enemy?'

'It is their will,' said Nan, falteringly, 'they have a purpose which is unknown to us.'

'I bet they bloody have.' Sandy muttered under his breath.

'But what could that purpose be?' Ben interjected, sensing a battle of wills was about to commence, and was enjoying the mental sparring which underlay it.

'Do you consider them to be Gods, a higher type of being, an almighty power able to create whatever they want?' Sandy was now getting into his stride, and sensing the confusion Nan was going through trying to rationalize his beliefs and explain them, he remorselessly pressed ahead.

'If they could create anything they wished, why not create a pleasant world, with plenty of food and tolerable conditions, instead of this hell hole of heat and cold and its lack of the most basic comforts?'

'It is their wish.' Nan replied defiantly, looking more uncomfortable by the minute.

'You keep saying, 'It is their wish', as if that answered everything. It answers nothing. Everything has a reason or purpose behind it, and I think there is a purpose behind our situation here. It's nothing to do with a God or Gods creating us and a world for us to play in, while they look on for amusement. I think there is a more rational purpose behind it, and I mean to find out what it is, and turn it to our advantage.' Sandy sat back to see what affect his statement had on the otherwise unflappable Nan, and was disappointed to see him disintegrate into a mere shadow of his former self.

The man was clearly in mental turmoil, his old beliefs which had sustained him through many doubtful moments were now being systematically ripped apart, and no longer seemed to make sense when looked at rationally.

Why had this disturbing stranger come among them?

The silence dragged on, and eventually Nan gathered himself up for one last defence of his world, as he knew it.

'What you are saying amounts to sacrilege.' he began, drawing himself up to his full height as best he could while being seated. 'If what you're saying should ever get back to the Great Light, it would be the end of their gifts, and there would be no more people to replace those who die. Just think what that would mean to us, it would be the end of our world in a very short while. You are treading on dangerous ground, and I suggest you think twice before probing any deeper into things you don't understand.' He sat back, exhausted with the mental effort of overriding his suspicions of what might be true and trying to retain some degree of control over the situation.

Sandy patiently waited a few moments for things to calm down, before delivering the final blow to what he considered to be a totally false and useless quasi religious regime.

'Just think on this, you arrive here as fully grown adults, with no memory of your past, dumped into a harsh world where you have to continually fight for a miserable existence and no means of escape. People start life as children, and grow up into adults, but that memory has been denied you.

'If you had to be put somewhere to live out your miserable lives, it could be somewhere more hospitable than this harsh hell hole, unless there was a reason for choosing this place. So what could be that reason?' Sandy carried on before anyone could intervene and spoil his rapid train of thought.

'If I wanted to prevent anyone from digging back into an occluded memory, I would place 'em in an environment where their every waking moment was taken up trying to survive, that way they wouldn't have time to think about their past, let alone work out what had happened to them.'

'That makes sense to me,' Ben butted in, not wishing to be left out of the argument, 'and it certainly explains a few things I've been thinking about.' He turned to Sandy, willing him to continue.

'Do you really think the Great Light has some sort of hearing aid tuned in to our conversation, to see if we are being ungrateful for it's bountiful gifts, which I consider to be their discarded rubbish anyway, and, if so, are all the other groups being monitored at the same time? Come on Nan, just think about it, it can't possibly be true.'

Nan's eyes had gone out of focus, as Sandy's heretical suggestions clashed with his own beliefs, the internal struggle manifesting itself as a series of shudders rippling through his body. Somewhere, deep in Nan's partially occluded memories, connections were being made which had not existed for a very long time. Pictures of things he had not known in his present world were beginning to flash up, devaluing and displacing his present field of references.

'Do you think he's all right?' asked an anxious Ben, as Nan struggled to break out of the trance induced by the mind conflict. 'You don't think he's going to die, do you?'

'No,' Sandy replied confidently, 'he's just trying to adjust to a whole set of new ideas and reasons for being here. It must be like suddenly discovering you are someone else after thinking you are you, if you see what I mean.'

'I think so.' Ben sounded doubtful about the concept.

Sandy gently reached across to touch Nan's trembling arm.

'Are you OK? Sorry to have shaken you up like that, Nan, but someone had to do it. We can't go on living like this, it's disgusting to say the least of it, and not much fun into the bargain. The only way to improve things is to find out the truth, and then turn it to our advantage.'

With a final shudder, Nan wrenched himself back into present time, giving the other two a weak smile as he said, 'I'm sorry, I can't stop shaking. There must be something in what you say, because looking back it all seems a bit silly somehow. Can't explain it, it's just a feeling I have, a sort of numbness, difficulty in getting my thoughts together coherently. Please carry on with your questions, I'll do my best to answer them as truthfully as possible.'

'Are you sure you're up to it?' asked a concerned Sandy, thankful that the first hurdle in his quest for the truth had been cleared. Nan just nodded.

'What do you know of the Great Lights? How do you know when they will come?'

Nan slumped back against the wall, drew in a deep breath as if it would be his very last, and then relaxed out a little.

'I just know when they will be here. Can't explain it really, it's just a feeling I get. When I go outside, it's always just before dawn and the light is always there, like a big round sun, but there's no heat. By the time I walk across the sands, the new body has been dropped, and anything else they wish to give us. I bring the new person back to our home, as I did you, and they join the group. That's all there is to it.'

Sandy nodded sagely, looking for clues in every word uttered by the now contrite Nan, but finding nothing new on the subject.

'Have you ever seen anything above the light? For instance, when it is visiting another group?'

'I've only seen it twice when it was for the others, as I don't get the 'I should be outside' feeling then. All I ever see is the light, it's so bright it blinds one to anything else, and it's so big. There is no sound that I'm aware of, except a very faint whisper, like wind blowing through bare trees.'

'And what are trees?' asked Sandy innocently, hardly able to hide his smile.

'I don't know... yes I do, they're tall growing things, with leaves like our plants, only bigger, and if you have a lot of them together, it's call a wood! I didn't know that just now, but when I looked, I did!'

'Looks like Sandy was right when he said our memories have been hidden,' Ben chipped in quickly, 'I got a picture in my mind of a wood, and I've never had that before.'

Sandy sat back with that smile on his face you only get when you have been proven right against all adversity, and someone else has done it for you.

'What do you know of the other groups? How many are there, and are they all the same?'

'There are hundreds of groups around the mountain walls, I would think. I've only had dealings with two or three, as the distance between them is something of a barrier. We trade with the ones each side of us, and one other, but the others have nothing to do with us. The group on our left speak the same language as us, but the others on the right have a language of their own, but one of them translates for us, so we are able to trade. You'll be seeing them tomorrow. I've heard tell that most groups have their own language which others can't understand, but I've never met them.'

Nan was much more relaxed now, and seemed eager to talk to the other two. This was a relief to Ben, and encouraging to Sandy, a new question pouring out when the previous one had been answered. They talked long into the night, careful probing from Sandy producing the answers to fill the odd gaps in their history, until a detailed picture of their circumstances had been built, and the unbelievable truth was revealed at last.

The three of them eventually went to their separate sleeping quarters, tired but wiser of what had befallen them, and just a little angry at having been made to suffer so unnecessarily.

The night was very short, and it was a bleary eyed Sandy who was shaken awake next morning by a grinning Mop with a portion of 'bread', as she had been unable to find him the previous night. He was glad of the food, and was saved from the next course by the shuffling footsteps of Ben who appeared just in time. Mop left, giving Ben a filthy look in passing.

'My, she's got her eye on you all right.' Ben croaked, hoarse from so much unaccustomed talking. 'If she gets you into her cave, you'll never get out!'

'Perish the thought,' Sandy groaned, as an involuntary picture of the dreaded amorous Mop in full cry flashed before his eyes, 'I can only just stomach her stews.'

'We're due to pay our neighbours a visit this morning, and it's almost light enough.' Ben looked longingly at the bread, so Sandy broke it in half.

The shuffling of their footsteps was augmented by their noisy munching on the hard and dry gift from Mop, as they made their way to the outside world.

'You'll have to wrap your feet in these.' said Ben, handing Sandy two long dirty rags. 'It's to protect your feet from the frozen sands.'

The first hint of daylight broke above the towering crater walls with a soft pink glow, as the pair set off at a jog to arrange a swap of goods for a few growing bins, and their contents. Bell had already checked her stock, and found that she could spare four of them without jeopardizing their own food supplies.

They were greeted by the other group's translator, being careful to keep up wind of him and dreading the moment when they would have to enter the cave system and experience the closer proximity of the reeking creature.

'Weren't sure you'd turn up, 'cos we don't 'ave much to trade wiv,' he said, waving them into the entrance tunnel.

By keeping well ahead of their smelly escort and following the directions he kept calling out, they managed to avoid most of his noxious odours, until they came to the cave where the scavenged cast off's of the Great Light were stored.

'Don't show too much interest in anything you think would be useful, as it will weaken our bargaining power.' Sandy muttered to Ben, whose eyes had already lit up at the sight of so much metal.

'We can only spare three boxes and their plants.' Sandy offered, lightly treading on Ben's foot as he opened his mouth to correct the quotation.

The head of their clan had now joined the group, which brought them all into even closer proximity, and thereby intensified the aroma of long unwashed bodies.

'What's this?' asked Sandy, pointing to a very large bale of fine cloth lying in a corner of the cave, partly covered by thin sheets of metal which had been randomly thrown down.

'That's metal from the Great Light,' the translator said, 'that other stuff we got from a group who didn't wan' it.'

'What do you use that stuff for?' enquired Sandy, trying to sound as nonchalant as possible.

'We don't,' came the reply, 'tident no use to us, it's too soft 'an fine.' Sandy marked it down mentally as an almost free gift, if he played his cards right. They continued to rummage through the junk piles which had collected over the years, Sandy looking for metal tools and blades.

'We'll have to go soon,' Ben straightened his back with a loud click, 'the sun'll be up over the top of the rim, and then we'll have to stay here 'till evening.'

The threat of staying for a full day was enough for Sandy, and he began to gather together the items he thought would be of most use to them. The actual bargaining took longer than they had anticipated, as everything had to be translated via the man with the strange accent to the chief, and back again, also the chief proved to be a little more canny than they had expected.

In the end, they acquired a collection of flat pieces of metal, some wire of different thicknesses', various bits of plastic, and the huge roll of cloth was thrown in for good measure, as Sandy had predicted it would be.

The main sticking point in the transaction was a metal cylinder, with what looked like a pump attached to it.

In his eagerness to acquire it, he had been unable to disguise his interest in the piece of machinery, and so the 'price' went up. In the end, after much haggling, it was agreed that an extra growing bin would be exchanged for the cylinder and its attachments. Ben grinned to himself at Sandy's astuteness and foresight.

As the raided group would have to collect the growing bins from Nan's caves, and would have to go over there anyway, it was agreed that they would help transport Sandy's collection of materials as they went, and so the party set off, with the full sun just breaking the highest peaks.

As they rounded a small peninsula of rock which jutted out into the sands, a piece of sheet metal fell out of the over filled arms of one of the men. Before he could readjust his load and stoop down to retrieve it, it disappeared in a flurry of sand, as something below sensed a meal.

Everyone promptly leapt for solid rock, dropping several items in the rush for safety. They had barely turned around to see what had happened to it, when it came flying out with a flurry of sand to land at their feet.

It was a badly shaken little band of men, which after very carefully retrieving their goods, continued along the edge of the sands towards Nan's cave complex, reaching it just before the full blast of the naked sun hit the area.

Nan was none too pleased when he realized that the eight strangers, only one of whom spoke their language, would have to stay until the evening, as the sun was now bathing the crater with its full brilliance, and travel across it would mean certain death to anyone who tried.

Two other things were cause for concern, they would have to feed the strangers at midday, and the motley band were several grades up the rancid scale of smells, compared to the home team, and that didn't go down too well with anyone.

The four growing bins for the exchange were moved to a cave close to the opening, so that when the temperature had dropped sufficiently, they could send their malodorous visitors on their way as soon as possible.

When Mop heard she would have to provide extra food, she threw the expected tantrum, which was great entertainment for all, except the deliverer of the news.

The exchanged goods were taken down to Ben's store, Nan, more from habit than necessity, querying every item as to why it had been chosen, especially the metallic cylinder with the attached pump. Sandy tried to explain, without going into details, that he wanted it for a future experiment, hiding the fact that he was none too sure himself why he had chosen it, except it seemed a good idea at the time. He was a man who often relied on hunches in life.

'Why do you want that bale of cloth?' asked Ben, when they were out of earshot of the others, 'I thought the visitors said it was useless.'

'To them it might be,' Sandy replied, ' but I thought a new set of clothes for us would perk the place up a bit, and if we can include a hair cut and a wash down, we'll be the smartest lot in the crater.'

'Crater? What do you mean by that?' asked Ben, a puzzled look on his face. The word's familiar, but I can't define what it means.'

'A crater is the top of a volcano, a point on the earth's crust where molten rock is forced up and spills out, building up into a cone shape. The middle often remains hollow, like a bowl, and that's what we're in. Why it's filled with sand, I don't know, I've never come across that before, and it's the biggest crater I've ever seen, or heard of.'

Sandy put the idea of new clothes to Nan later that morning, and was surprised by his keenness to go ahead with the project. The idea of hair cutting and a good wash, while not rejected out of hand, failed to receive the degree of enthusiasm Sandy had hoped for, and he did not understand why.

The time for the midday meal arrived, and the whole group assembled in the main cavern to sample Mop's offering for the day, minus the visitors.

'Where are the others?' asked Nan, concerned that their hospitality might be open to question.

'Mop said she would give them some food in the cave with their growing bins, even she can't stand the smell.' someone volunteered, a muffled chorus of agreement rippled around the cavern, and then someone made a very unkind comment about Mop's general ambience, and Sandy heard the first really loud communal laugh since arriving.

The placid acceptance of the group's situation worried Sandy, and taking Nan to one side after their meal, asked him again why no one had ever tried to climb to the top of the peaks, and see what was on the other side.

'It was tried, once, long ago so I'm told, but the climbers never returned, I think they must have been caught by the night freeze up, unable to get back to the caves before nightfall. Why are you so interested in what's on the other side of the peaks?'

'I think there may be another world out there, something a little better than what we have here, and I think it's worth trying to find out.'

Sandy replied, firmly.

'I'd rather you didn't try, because I don't think you'll come back. Surely there's enough to interest you here, the new clothes for instance?' Nan had adopted his sad look to back up his feelings at the thought of loosing their new acquisition.

'Has anyone checked to see if there are any tunnels which lead upwards? We might be able to go up inside the rim and find an opening near the top which looks out on the other side, and then we would be protected from the cold and heat, and could take our time about it.'

'There are many tunnels we don't use, because you die if you go into them, especially the ones which lead downwards, or so I've heard, so don't try those.' Nan was now looking worried, and wondered how he could side-track the persistent Sandy.

'Perhaps Ben and I could have a little look around, just to see if there are any passages leading up. We won't go up, until we've cleared it with you. I don't see any harm in that.'

Nan knew when he was beaten, and gave in as graciously as possible, little knowing what the outcome of such an expedition would bring about.

Ben grinned broadly when Sandy told him of his intentions, and set off down the passage towards his store room.

'There's a small hole in one corner which has an up draft, I've noticed dust being sucked up into it when I disturb some of the materials down there. It might be a way up, but we'll have to enlarge the hole somewhat to get in.'

The store room was quite well lit compared to some of the other caves, and it only took a few moments to clear the corner fully to expose the hole.

'There you are, see the dust going up?' Tiny dust motes in the air drifted towards the hole, and then sped up to disappear into the darkness beyond the reach of the lamps.

Sandy put his arm in the hole, and could feel the steady cool flow of air agitating the hairs on the back of his hand.

'That air is going somewhere. If we could make some smoke down here, we could then go outside to see if it comes out higher up. If it doesn't, then that means it's coming out on the other side of the rim.'

'Or so high up we can't see it,' Ben added, 'but it's worth a try.'

A rummage through several caves produced a collection of very dirty and smelly rags, Sandy assuring Ben that no one would miss them. Using a bar of metal and the lump of stone they had previously used as a hammer, the hole was enlarged enough for Sandy to get his head and shoulders in. Ben passed him the rags, and he piled them up in a heap as far back into the cavity as he could reach.

'We'll tell Nan what we are about,' said Sandy, feeling pleased that they had made a start on the project, 'and then we can light the rags when the sun drops below the rim, it should be safe to go out then to see where the smoke comes out, if it does.'

'There's something we've not thought of,' said Ben respectfully, as they made their way back up to the main cavern, 'and that's how will we be able to see where we're going in this new tunnel?'

'I had thought of that,' replied Sandy, 'but so far haven't solved the problem. What we need is a burnable oil, but so far I haven't seen any oil-like substance here. Do you know of any?'

Ben, after querying what oil was, thought long and hard, but could not recall having seen anything like it. It was decided to ask Nan, and if that failed, they would approach the groups on either side of their complex.

'Although many things you mention are familiar words to me, I don't know what they mean,' said Ben, 'but you seem to know, like the oil, how do you explain that?'

'Can't really, I just seem to know. It might seem unbelievable to you, but I think we have been sent here for some reason, and our memories have been tampered with so that we can't find out about it.' Sandy paused for a moment, wondering if he should continue with his theory. Although Ben was more accepting of new ideas than Nan, there might be a limit past which he would lose Ben's co-operation.

'What you say makes sense, sort of, and certainly answers a few questions, but why would anyone want to do that to us?' Ben's interest was aroused.

'That's one thing I want to find out,' Sandy replied. 'I think the method of our arrival here might be something to do with it. Have you ever seen the so called Great Lights?'

'No, only Nan goes out to collect the new people, and anything left for us. He's very secretive about it, and never tells us when he's going. Do you think they're people like us, and not the Creator as Nan says?'

'Damn sure of it, but proving it will be another matter.'

At that moment, Mop appeared out of nowhere, accompanied by her own personal aroma, and grabbed Sandy's arm.

'What's this about new clothes for us?' she asked, giving him her best smile, 'I could help you make them.'

'Ah, there's a condition attached to that,' said Sandy quickly, 'to qualify for new clothes, that person has to have a haircut and a wash, otherwise the new clothes will wind up looking like the present ones, and that would just be a waste of time and effort.'

'Oh, will you be supervising that?' she replied cheekily, the smile getting even wider, and exposing several teeth badly in need of repair.

'I might have to, just to make sure it's done properly.' he said brightly, desperately hoping it would not come to that.

By the time they had found Nan and explained what they intended to do, the sun had lowered towards the top of the peaks, and the visitors began moving their growing boxes up to the entrance of the cave system.

A sudden commotion brought everyone running to find an indignant Karry standing with her arms folded across her chest, glaring into the cave where the boxes had been stored.

Apparently, one of the visitors, encouraged by his friend, had made a grab at Karry's ample bosom during the box shifting. Karry had responded to this affront on her person by grabbing them both, and banging their heads together.

They now lay in a crumpled heap against the cave wall, while the rest of the group were remonstrating at Karry from what they considered to be a safe distance.

It took Nan and the interpreter several minutes to calm the situation down to boiling point, and many more to restore some semblance of order among the visitors.

Eventually, an equable state of affairs was reached, the visiting party departing with what they thought to be the better side of the bargain, and a very huffy Karry explaining why she did what she did, to a disinterested Nan.

'Touchy bunch.' said Sandy, as they retreated into the comparative warmth of the tunnel system. 'What are the lot on the other side of us like?'

'Can't say I know much about 'em,' Ben replied. 'Nan's the only one who has any dealing with 'em, and he doesn't say much, but I'll try and find out.' he added enthusiastically, sensing another adventure in the offing.

They made their way down to Ben's store cave to light the rags they had pushed into the tunnel with the up draft, hoping not to see any smoke coming out on their side of the towering peaks.

Ben carefully lit a piece of rag from the gas lamp, and placed it at the bottom of the pile in the tunnel, fanning it with his hand until copious amounts of smoke were sucked up the chimney-like hole.

'Right, let's get outside and see what's happening.' Sandy called over his shoulder, as he left the cave and sped up the tunnel to the open crater. On the way, they nearly knocked a surprised Mop over as she was making her way down to them. They failed to notice the hurt look on her face as they raced by, causing the flickering gas lamps to dance even more vigorously in their passing draft.

The top of the peaks were bathed in fiery light from the fast sinking sun as the pair burst out into the open.

'God, it's cold already.' Sandy exclaimed, shivering. 'It should be safe enough to go out a short way, I suppose?'

Ben, a little out of breath, just nodded as they hesitantly walked onto the sands, looking for any sign of movement.

At only ten metres out from the edge of the chilling sands, they could feel the cold seeping through their footwear, another five metres and Ben began to complain vociferously.

'Hope this won't take long, my feet are aching already,' he moaned, 'and there's always a chance something will try and grab us from below.'

'Oh shut up, and look for the smoke.' Sandy exclaimed impatiently. 'If we can't see any, then it means it's coming out on the other side of the peaks, which will at least prove there is another side.'

They stood there for some time, gazing up at the peaks and stamping their feet to keep the circulation going, and not caring if it attracted the attention of the dwellers beneath.

As the sun finally dipped so low that only the very top of the highest peaks reflected its lurid red light, Sandy decided that they had been out long enough to have seen any smoke which was likely to exit within the crater's bowl, much to Ben's relief, and they returned to the cave system to inform Nan of their findings, such as they were.

The caverns seemed positively hot to the shivering pair as they sought out the elusive Nan, eventually tracking him down in Mop's kitchen, sitting in a corner, chewing. He immediately tried to swallow Mop's illicit gift, going red in the face from embarrassment at being caught, and trying to swallow and breathe at the same time.

'What have you two been up to?' he asked, when he got his breath back. 'Oh yes, the smoke test, what happened?'

'We didn't see any smoke, and we were out there quite a long time, therefore the smoke must have come out on the other side of the peaks,' Sandy announced triumphantly, 'so there must be something on the other side, and it might be better than this place.' he added firmly.

'I don't understand why you're so keen to find somewhere else, this place has supported us well for a long time now, and we have enough to eat.' Nan came back with, not happy that the status quo was about to be challenged yet again.

'Well, you do.' Ben added quickly, a sharp edge to his voice, and Nan went a deeper red at the instantaneous gibe.

Mop promptly produced a small handful of the berries she had given Nan, and equilibrium was restored as they all chewed on in silence for a few moments.

'I'm not criticizing this place,' said Sandy, after hurriedly swallowing the sweet tasting pulp, 'I just think there might be somewhere a bit better, and if we don't look, we'll never know.'

'I don't suppose I can stop you, just be careful, and don't take any unnecessary risks.' Nan seemed resigned to his slowly diminishing authority over the newcomer, and as Ben had seemingly aligned himself with Sandy, there was little he could do about the matter.

Sandy explained that he wanted to open the hole in Ben's store sufficiently for them to crawl in, and if they could make a light giving device, explore the new tunnel, looking for an exit on the other side of the surrounding peaks.

Nan suddenly seemed relieved as he realized that light was the key to the whole project, and the fixed gas lamps were the only source of light in their tiny kingdom.

Unfortunately, he had not reckoned with Sandy's determination or ingenuity, so his relief was somewhat short lived.

They chatted on for a while, and then Mop sent them off to the main cavern, as it was time for their evening meal.

As the meal was finishing, a bundle of rags staggered into the cavern and fell to the ground with a whimper, and then lay still. Everyone froze.

No one had ever visited them once night had fallen, as it was far too cold to be out and about. Nan was the first to make a move, going over to the heap of rags and gingerly giving it a poke with his foot. It remained motionless.

'Someone help me get some of these coverings off.' Sandy called out, as he began to unravel the bundled up figure lying on the floor of the cavern. 'Not much of a welcome for the poor sod. He must have been in real trouble to have ventured out in the dark.'

As the man's face was revealed, a large red bump stood out prominently on his forehead, with a trickle of blood seeping from a very bent nose.

'Looks like someone whacked him one,' Ben commented as he helped unwind the still unconscious creature, 'you don't get that much damage from a fall, surely.'

'Mop, see if you can rustle up some hot soup, or something, he's nearly frozen stiff.' Nan called out as the figure inside the bundle of wrappings took on a more human form.

She nodded, and hurried away, to return with a steaming bowl of gruel just as the last pieces of extra wrappings came off the spindle like figure of an elderly man, who was slowly gaining consciousness.

'It's the elder from the other group next to us!' Nan exclaimed. 'Prop him up and get some of that hot liquid into him, he must be chilled to the bone.'

Mop enthusiastically administered a ladle full of the hot gruel, most of which was returned at high velocity as the poor creature was trying to breathe at the same time.

Two more ladles of Mop's dubious concoction, which this time was swallowed as she had got the timing right, and the man came to life with a force which surprised them all.

'We've been attacked.' he croaked, slumping down again.

A sharp slap in the face from Nan, followed by another ladle of gruel, and he returned to the land of the living.

'What happened?' asked Nan, putting a comforting arm around the man's shoulders. 'You said you've been attacked.'

'They hi-hit us just after su-sundown,' the man stuttered. 'They came pouring into our ca-caves, striking everyone with long ro-rods. I think most of us are de-dead.'

'Who were they?' asked Nan, a frightened look momentarily crossing his face, 'have you seen them before?'

'No, they were dressed is sm-smooth shiny clothes, nothing like the sort of thing we all wear. I've never seen anything like it before.'

Another few portions of the hot gruel, and the man had recovered enough to sit up unaided, and his dazed look was replaced with one of fury.

'Why did they do that to us? We've never attacked anyone before, and we don't have much worth stealing, so why the murderous attack?'

'Don't know.' Nan was now looking concerned. 'I've never heard of that sort of thing before. We occasionally get the odd skirmish where a few things are stolen, but no one gets really hurt, and certainly not killed. You'd better rest up here for the night, and we'll take you back in the morning to see what can be done.' Nan sat back, bolt upright.

Karry and Bell got up as one to take the unfortunate man by the arms, and lead him out of the cavern. Mop sat down again, looking disappointed at being beaten in her effort to render assistance to the newcomer.

'We shall have to be extra vigilant in future.' Nan stated. 'At no time, except the dead of night or during the high heat of day, must the entrance be left unguarded, and we must come up with better weapons too, by the look of it.'

Nan turned to Sandy, both waiting for the other to speak.

'Can you think of anything more effective than pointed rods and the two gas guns, which is all we have to defend ourselves with?' Nan asked at last.

'Not off hand, but I'll give it some thought,' Sandy replied. 'I'm sure Ben and I can come up with something to deter invaders, after all, they might try to take Mop, and then where would we be?' His attempt at a jovial riposte to lighten the atmosphere fell flat, they were all too worried at this new turn of events which threatened their very existence.

One by one, the group shuffled off to their sleeping quarters, leaving Nan, Ben, and Sandy alone in the main cavern.

'I will make some enquiries tomorrow.' said Nan. 'We've got to identify this new threat, find out where they come from, and if they've done this before. Do you really think you can make us some new type of weapons?' he added, turning to Sandy.

'I'm sure we can.' he replied, being careful to include Ben with the use of the plural, 'I've had one or two ideas already,' he lied, hoping to restore a little confidence and thereby a good night's sleep for all.

Sandy awoke in the early hours of the morning, something had bumped up against him in his pile of rags.

'I'm frightened,' said Mop, with a well controlled tremble in her voice, 'if I could just snuggle up to you for the night, I'm sure I'll feel much better in the morning.'

'Oh no!' Sandy exclaimed, before he could stop himself.

'Why don't you like me?' asked a hurt sounding Mop.

'It's not that, it's just that I'm very tired, and you woke me from a deep sleep. I do like you, you're a very nice person, and very kind. I would have reacted the same way no matter who woke me up.' he hopefully lied.

Mop gave a deep sigh and snuggled up even closer, while Sandy, under the pretence of making room for her, repositioned himself such that he was now lying on those parts he thought the audacious Mop might make a grope for in a moment of affection.

Only breathing deeply enough to just sustain life, Sandy tried to get back to sleep, but this was difficult due to the almost continuous wriggling of Mop as she tried to get some response from her unwilling partner of the night.

In the end she gave up her amorous advances, and settled for just having someone to snuggle up to for the rest of the dark hours, a deep and contented snore announcing her withdrawal from active service.

Eventually, Sandy drifted into sleep of sorts, punctured by nightmares of a totally naked Mop nearly twice his size, trapping him in a cave with no exit in sight.

Dawn was a relief, when it came. Ben greeted the still entwined pair with an astonished look of disbelief and a poorly suppressed giggle, waving away with his hands the mumbled explanation Sandy tried to give justifying the compromising position he had been found in.

Luckily, Mop hurried away to her kitchen cave to produce something edible for the now awakening group, giving Sandy a little time to explain what had happened. He was far from convinced that Ben believed his side of the story, and just hoped that Ben did not approach Mop on the subject at some later date to hear her side of events.

During the first meal of the day, a worried Nan once more broached the subject of new armament, and Sandy had to think fast in order to cover up the fact that he had no fresh ideas in mind, nor did he expect to come up with any in the near future.

As the others drifted away to go about their duties, Ben came to the rescue concerning the weapons problem by asking Sandy what he intended to do with the cylinder and attached pump unit he had obtained in the swap for the growing boxes.

The idea suddenly came to him that a flame thrower could be made from the cylinder, if they could obtain a suitable combustible fluid, and then he remembered the apparently inexhaustible supply of gas for the lamps.

'I don't see why we couldn't fill the cylinder with gas, using the pump to obtain enough pressure to make a long reaching flame when it is released.'

'Sounds a good idea to me.' said Ben, brightening up at the prospect of doing something other than the normal routine.

'There is one problem though, how do we get all the air out of the cylinder before we put the gas in? If we don't, it could explode if the flame got back inside the cylinder.' Sandy could see the new weapon fading away as the dangers became obvious.

'What if we filled the cylinder with water first, and then let the gas push the water out? We've plenty of water now, and it could be used to water Bell's plants afterwards anyway.'

Ben looked pleased with himself at having come up with something useful towards the project.

'That's a damn good idea, Ben, well done.' Sandy heaved a sigh of relief as the possibility of a gas weapon was reinstated, and wondered why he had not thought of it.

'We could use the flexible piece of pipe you use to load the gas guns. Do you have any more of it?

'Yes, I think there's a little more somewhere, why do you want it?' asked a puzzled Ben, 'the piece I use is long enough to do the job.'

'We'll have to keep a living flame at the nozzle end of the contraption for when we turn the gas on, there won't be time to fiddle about getting a light from the nearest gas lamp if we get invaded.' Sandy could see the flame thrower design building up in his mind's eye, as they went in search of Nan to inform him of what they were about to do.

After explaining the basics, Nan gave his wholehearted approval to the project, and the pair hurried away to collect the necessary parts for the first trial of the new weapon.

The water cave was producing more water than they needed for their everyday life, and someone had already suggested that they use it for trading. Filling the cylinder with water was easy, using the pump and a length of flexible tube found in Ben's material store. Ben pumped away with great enthusiasm, until the water squirted out from the tube on the other end of the cylinder in a spray which soaked Sandy from head to foot.

'Right, now let's see if we can get the gas in as easily,' said a now dripping Sandy.

As the last of the water was expelled from the cylinder, the smell of gas began to drift up the tunnel, and that brought Nan and Karry running to see what had gone wrong.

Explaining that all was under control, Sandy began to pump more gas into the cylinder until he could no longer overcome the internal pressure within, and then shut off the valve and disconnected the supply pipe.

'OK, now we can try it out,' he said with a little more confidence than he really felt. 'Let's get it out into the open.'

Minutes later they had the cylinder at the entrance to the cave complex, and a length of flexible hose attached to the nearest gas lamp, the transferred flame bobbing about like a living thing in the gentle breeze from the hot sand crater.

'We'll have to put a permanent small ignition flame on the end of this thing.' Sandy said, as he heaved the contraption the last few metres out into the sun light, his eyes almost screwed shut from the glare. After making sure the pilot light on the end of the flexible tubing was still showing, which was difficult out in the crater, he was ready.

'OK, I'm going to fire it up now.' he called, a slight tremor in his voice. There was a faint squeak as he turned the metal control valve and a steady hiss grew in volume as the stored gas escaped into the open air. For one dreadful moment Sandy thought, as did the others, that the whole experiment had been a miserable failure, and then their fears were blown away by a mighty whoosh and a flash of searing fire as the gas cloud ignited at last.

All those who could see the fire ball and feel the back pressure of the exploding gas cloud were convinced beyond doubt that nothing much could have survived the roaring inferno the new defence weapon had produced, which was not the same thing as agreeing it should actually be used to defend their enclave.

Sandy feared there might be those who would not approve of the use of such a weapon upon other human beings, and the massive gout of fire the machine produced convinced him he may well have a struggle on his hands getting the dreadful device into actual operation against a foe.

After everyone had got over the shock of what the flame producer was capable of, it was dragged back into the tunnel.

It wasn't long before the first voice was raised in protest against the use of such a barbaric device upon other people, and those present promptly split into two groups, those who could see the necessity for such a thing, and those who could not see the danger of not using it.

Sandy could see the whole project being watered down, or even discarded, if he was unable to convince the others of the necessity to deploy the weapon in its most horrific form.

'Look, I don't like the idea of frying our neighbours any more than you do, but it's them or us. Look at what happened to the other poor sods, they killed them with no compunction, and unnecessarily, if stealing their goods was their only intent. I think they enjoyed doing it.' Sandy added.

'It's no good just frightening them off, they'll only come back, if only to steal our new weapon, and God knows what they'll do to us.' He looked around the group to see if they had changed their minds. Most reluctantly nodded their heads, but with little enthusiasm.

'If we injure them, they'll be back with a vengeance, if we only frighten them off, they'll certainly be back for the gas weapon, if only to use against other groups in the crater.'

Sandy looked around to see if any more had been swayed by his argument, and as there were no longer any vocal dissenters, decided to ram the point home. He had to get their undivided consent to use the weapon as he intended it to be used, for if anyone faltered during an attack, it could spell disaster for them all.

'We have two choices, either we carry on as we have in the past, and accept whatever fate befalls us, and bear in mind what happened to the others, or we use this new weapon at full potential, causing the maximum damage possible to those who would kill us. What do you say?'

'He's right,' Nan spoke up at last, 'we can't be half-hearted about this, I say we do as Sandy suggests.' He looked around the group for their approval, and was relieved to see everyone nodding their heads, with only Ben giving vocal agreement.

'Right, let's get it into position.' said Sandy, eager to set up the flame-thrower while all were in agreement. 'We'll hang up some material to disguise it, or they'll never come down the passage far enough for it to be fully effective.'

The cylinder was dragged down well into the entrance tunnel, and held in position with lumps of rock. Someone found some old rags which were hung across the passageway, with a small hole allowing the business end of the weapon to poke through.

'What we need is some means of keeping 'em in the passage when we fire up,' Ben said quietly to Sandy, 'or some of 'em might escape when they see what's happened to those in the lead.'

'Good thinking,' Sandy replied, 'I hadn't thought of that. Some form of net, or something we can drop down over the entrance should do the job. What have we got?'

'Don't think we've got anything, but I noticed during our trade with our neighbours that they had a big hank of thin rope, perhaps we could trade 'em something for it? And then we could make a net.'

With Nan's agreement, it was decided to venture forth next morning to set up a possible trade with their neighbours, water being the main commodity on offer as the group now had a surplus from the water cave.

During the evening meal, the subject of the fire weapon came up again, as some members of the group were still not happy with the envisaged effects the new defence device would have on anyone trying to raid them. After an even more graphic description of what might befall the group if they failed to wipe out the invaders, the dissenters reluctantly saw reason, and gave in to Sandy's demands for total destruction, should they be raided.

Three:
Light for All

THEY ALL SLEPT better that night secure in the knowledge that they could, if need be, repel all boarders. Nan decreed that only the more aggressive members of the group should man the new fire weapon, as he still doubted the ability of some to turn the weapon on fully if they should be invaded.

Next morning, after a quick meal, Sandy and Ben set off for their neighbours, staggering under the weight of the water container they hoped to exchange for the much needed rope.

The deal was struck, exchanging the water plus two more refills for the rope and four pieces of shiny metal Ben had spotted in a corner of their store. They had no use for the metal fragments and enquired what Ben wanted them for.

'Nothing in particular,' he lied, 'just thought they were pretty.'

On the way back with their bounty, Sandy patiently waited for Ben to offer an explanation for the shiny metal bits he had acquired, but as nothing was forthcoming, he asked.

'I thought we could mount them on the outside of the entrance so that we could stay inside in the warm, and still see anyone approaching.' he replied. Sandy smiled to himself, he had done well to choose Ben as his main aide.

They arrived back just as the sun broke over the crater rim, bathing all in its fierce hard light. Small drops of condensed moisture were already boiling off from their hiding places high up in the surrounding rocks, looking like thin white wraiths, twisting and turning as the blazing heat of the naked sun found them, and boiled them out of existence.

'The first thing we need to do is cut a channel in the roof just inside the entrance, so that we can roll up the net and keep it out of sight.' Sandy said, as they sought the cool interior of the cave system.

'Perhaps we can get some of the others to do that, while we make the net.' Ben suggested.

Soon, the sound of metal on stone echoed down through the tunnels as Sandy and Ben began to quietly construct the catch net. Although thin, the rope was a lot stronger than either of them had anticipated, and as the net neared completion, there was still plenty of the synthetic cord left over.

'Keep the rest of it hidden away in your store,' Sandy said to Ben, 'I think it might come in useful for something else I have in mind.' Ben nodded, knowing from past experience it was useless to enquire what it was, as Sandy would have told him if he wanted him to know at this point in time.

The stone cutters finished their groove at about the same time as the net was brought up for fitting. Ben, having found several short metal rods which they hoped to hammer into cracks in the tunnel roof to hold the net in place, suggested that two extra pieces of metal be driven into the floor of the tunnel to run the hold down cords through, thus preventing anyone escaping from under the entrapping net.

The two hold down cords were run back to a position next to the flame-thrower behind the rag curtain, the idea being that when all the marauding gang had entered and the gas jet lit, someone would release the net and pull the cords in, trapping all those who had been unfortunate enough to enter the tunnel.

'I think we should try out the system,' Sandy suggested, 'just in case there are any unforeseen difficulties we've not thought of.'

It took much persuading to get eight members of the group to pretend to be invaders, despite the repeated promise that the gas jet would not be lit, and the whole operation was perfectly safe.

With the unwilling volunteers interspersed between the flame-thrower with its concealing curtain of rags and the entrance to the cave complex, Sandy gave the order 'fire'.

Some were knocked to the ground as they met others going in the opposite direction at high speed, while most headed for the exit, only to wind up in a tangled heap as the net dropped just in front of those in the lead.

After much cursing and swearing as they untangled themselves, the exercise was pronounced a great success, and to some degree, the fear of an overwhelming attack from the raiders was diminished, but not totally dispelled.

A rota was worked out for manning the flame-thrower in two shifts, one in the early morning and another in the relative cool of evening, as these were considered to be the only times when an attack could be mounted, due to the extreme heat of day and freezing cold of night.

Nan came to survey the set up, but said little about it, Sandy reasoning the lack of enthusiasm for the project probably being due to the apparent and unintentional whittling away of his leadership as

Sandy instigated his various projects.

Some members of the group were actually looking forward to an attack, just to see the marauders given a dose of their own medicine, and these were incorporated into the guard roster as the most likely not to lose their nerve at the critical moment.

As they had now acquired the necessary roll of material to make new clothes, Sandy went down to the kitchen cave to approach Mop on the subject, thinking she was the most likely to make a good job of the project. After giving it some thought, he decided a tunic and trousers would be the most practical garments for all, and put the idea to her.

Mop, who was always willing to please Sandy at any opportunity, gave him her best smile and nodded enthusiastically.

'You'll need some help, perhaps one of the other women would like to lend a hand? Oh, and before the new clothes are worn, the person concerned must have a good wash and get their hair tidied up. We've plenty of water now, so there's no excuse not to.'

'How shall we know how to make the clothes fit?' asked Mop, thinking ahead quickly, 'everyone is a different size.'

'You can take measurements, and make any final adjustments while they're wearing them.' Sandy replied, quite unaware of what Mop had in mind.

Ben had made a crude pair of scissors from his supply of bits and pieces, and someone had found what passed for a needle, so, during the next few days, while the defences were manned, clothes were made, and after the first two or three outfits had been successfully fitted, everyone was keen to acquire a set for themselves. Sandy made sure that Nan was the first to receive the new uniform, and that immediately overcame any resistance to the change the others might have been harbouring.

Nan's transformation, complete with hair and beard trim, restored some of the confidence he had lost as leader of the group, and he now walked around at full height, asserting his authority wherever it was possible.

As Sandy's clothes were still in reasonable shape, he was the last to be fitted for the new uniform, a moment Mop had been waiting for.

'Come along young man,' she said with glee, 'you'll have to take some of your old clothes off, so that I can measure you for a good fit.'

'I don't think that's necessary,' Sandy protested, 'they fit quite tightly, not like the bundle of rags most of you have been wearing.'

'Surely you're not that shy,' she chided, slowly unbuttoning his tunic and savouring every delicious moment.

Stripped to his undergarments, which the others had long since discarded, he cut a striking figure, and Mop took her time over the measurements, checking each one several times until it became obvious what she was up to, and then she blushed a deep red.

'OK, Mop, you've had your fun. As I'm in charge of uniforms, I'll be around to measure you up for one.' Too late, he realized his quip would be taken the wrong way, and it was his turn to blush.

There had been no reports of attacks on any of the other groups in the crater, but Sandy still insisted that a keen watch be kept at all vulnerable times.

The shiny metal plates Ben had obtained were polished to a level of high brilliance which surprised even Sandy, and they were stuck on the outside edges of the entrance with some of the sticky black stuff from around the water cave entrance. With another pair just inside, a good view of the local area could be seen by those on watch by the flame-thrower.

When it was Mop's turn for a uniform, Sandy and Ben disappeared up the hole in the storeroom, enlarging it ready for the day when they could explore the shaft, but that relied on a suitable means of generating light.

At last, everyone had been decked out in the new uniform, been bathed, and had excessively long hair trimmed to a reasonable length. To everyone's surprise, except Sandy's, morale went up several notches at the change.

Shortly after the transformation of the group's appearance, several visitors from either side came to trade, no doubt intrigued by stories of the new look. One group wanted similar clothing, only to be told there was no more cloth, which was not strictly true.

As water was a scarce commodity to most groups, this enabled Ben, through the exchange system, to collect large amounts of material for his store, including the first proper tools which Sandy had seen since his arrival in the crater.

Word must have spread further afield than they had first realized, and no doubt had been embellished in the process.

They were now getting visits from groups who were on the very fringes of accessibility, there being only a finite time for safe travel across the deadly sands, and Ben's store cave over spilled into the next one.

When the attack came, it took everyone by surprise. It was still dark as far as using the mirrors was concerned, only the faintest glow in the sky heralded the coming dawn.

Karry was in charge of the watch along with two others of like mind, when a scuffling sound brought them wide awake from a dozing like state.

She checked the tiny flame on the end of the flame tube through a small hole in the rag curtain, and then nudged the other two, motioning them to silence as she strained her eyes into the gloom further up the tunnel.

The exit out onto the sands showed up as a slightly lighter patch against the surrounding darkness, and flickering darker shapes cut across it as the raiders assembled in the tunnel entrance.

When no more ghostly shadows moved across the tunnel opening, Karry reached for the gas control valve with one hand, and raised the other to signal when to drop the net.

Karry waited until she was sure the raiders were advancing towards the curtain, and then gave the signal to drop the net across the entrance.

In the stillness of near dawn, the net made a surprising amount of noise as it rattled down across the entrance, and several grunts signalled that the raiders had been alerted to the fact that something they had not anticipated was happening.

Karry's two helpers, each on the end of a hold down rope, braced themselves for the expected pull, in case the raiders tried to escape out of the tunnel.

She turned the gas control valve, a loud continuous hissing announced that high pressure gas was streaming out of the cylinder and into the tunnel. A surge of panic went through the guardians of the complex, as there was no expected burst of flame, and then it happened.

With a whoosh which was close to an explosion, the gas lit, and a sheet of flame raced up the tunnel engulfing the raiders, who now stood out like so many black shapes in the sea of advancing fire.

If it had not been for the rag curtain, the guardians would have been severely burnt by the back blast, as the heated air tried to escape in both directions. As it was, they were only slightly singed, and the two rope holders managed to retain their grip on the hold down ropes.

The ensuing screams of the raiders would haunt the members of the complex for some time to come, as they tried in vain to escape the furnace heat which pursued them up the passage, igniting their clothing and adding to the tunnel of consuming fire.

As the gas pressure dropped off, the roaring column of flame dwindled down, and then went out.

As darkness rushed in, it was somewhat alleviated by the flickering flames which still danced around some of the fallen raiders. The intense heat had broken down their body fat, liquefying it, and the remnants of their clothing, acting like wicks, continued to burn with red and orange smoky flames, adding to the horrific scene which greeted the rest of the complex members as they rushed up the tunnel to see what had happened.

Swirling clouds of acrid black oily smoke eddied up and down the passage, causing most to vomit copiously as the stench of burnt flesh assailed their nostrils.

Sandy pushed his way to the front of the crowd, singling out a smutty faced Karry who looked just as bewildered as those who had only recently arrived on the scene. He put an arm around her shoulder, realizing she was still in shock at the appalling mess which had once been the raiders.

'Well done, Karry,' he began, 'you've saved our lives, that's for sure.' The normally tough Karry put her arms around him, clinging tightly, and then broke into uncontrollable sobs. The pent up tension of the last few minutes released itself in a flood of tears, cutting two clean lines down her smoke darkened face. Gradually, her sobs subsided.

'God, I hope I never have to do that again.' she got out jerkily at last.

'I don't think any of us will, once word gets around of our new capabilities,' he replied, gently rubbing her hunched shoulders, 'unfortunately, it had to be done, otherwise we'd all be dead by now, you did well, very well.'

Once the initial shock was over, Nan took charge, ordering the still smoking remains to be dragged out onto the sands as the dawn light added even more detail of the horrific carnage which had taken place.

By the time the charred bodies had been removed to the edge of the crater sands, it was nearly full light, and time for the morning meal. None felt like eating, nor did Mop offer anything to the smut stained few who had done most of the work. Those made of less sterner stuff were nowhere to be seen, having retreated to their caves to get over the shock of what had happened in their own individual ways.

It was while Sandy and Ben were standing just outside the entrance to the cave complex, mainly to get some clean air, that they saw their first denizen of the sands.

Surprisingly, there was now only one body left, a few metres from the rock walls of the crater.

A rippling of the sand, some ten metres out, gave the first clue that something under the now warming sands was on the move. They both stepped back instinctively, ready to dive into the entrance should anything get too close.

Whatever it was, it reached the limit where the sand thinned out to meet the underlying rock, and the ripples stopped. A long thin grey tentacle broke the surface, and groped around for the remaining body. Having found its target, the rope-like appendage of the creature wrapped itself around one of the limbs and retreated back into the sand.

Either the body was too heavy for the creature below, or it was unable to anchor itself sufficiently in the yielding sand, for a large mound rose up, some three metres from the half submerged body of the burnt raider.

The tentacle seemed to relax its grip for a moment, and then gave a jerk, ripping the arm off the body, and both disappeared beneath the surface in a flurry of sand particles.

While the pair of onlookers stood there, transfixed, another commotion further out in the sand filled crater drew their startled attention.

Whatever it was, it was considerably larger than the first creature, and by the eruptions of sand, was probably trying to wrench the severed arm away from its initial captor. A few more spurts of sand, and the first creature escaped with its bounty, leaving the larger one to make a bid for a meal on the half submerged corpse.

All was still for a moment, and then a tentacle as thick as a man's waist slowly emerged, swinging to and fro, using the sensors on its tip to locate the remains of the burnt body.

'My God, how big's the creature itself then?' asked Ben, his mouth hanging open after asking the question.

'Too big for catching with what I had in mind,' Sandy replied, 'so I'll have to change my plans a bit.'

'You really mean to catch one?' asked an incredulous Ben, visualizing the struggle a creature of this size would put up.

'Yes, if I can work out how to. It would provide us with a good supply of meat, and we could trade the surplus for whatever else we might want, once we get the others used to the idea of eating meat.'

The tentacle had now located the remains, and hovered around it, trying to make sense of the unaccustomed smell of burnt flesh. Having decided its find was probably edible, the thin whip end wriggled under the remains of the body and out the other side, curling around the corpse, and then it was gone in a flurry of sand.

Seconds later, and no one would have known what had happened. It all appeared as normal as any morning in the crater, apart from a few remnants of charred clothing, and one of those was slowly sliding beneath the sands as something smaller and less discerning, took a fancy to it.

'I can see why everyone is so very careful about travelling on the sand.' Sandy said, to break the uneasy silence.

'Do you really think it's worth the risk trying to catch one of those things?' asked Ben, as they returned to the caves, 'we've no idea how big or strong they are.'

'I'm banking on the fact that they are in sand, and therefore can't get much of a grip, so if we can get a purchase on one of those whip like arms, it should only be a matter of hauling it out far enough for the heat of day to kill it, and then we can butcher it up in the evening.'

'I think we should talk this over with Nan.' said a still somewhat doubtful Ben.

'I already have.' Sandy replied firmly.

The stench of burnt bodies still hung around the entrance of the complex, and would do so for some time to come, but surprisingly little of it seemed to have penetrated further into the cave system, and Sandy wondered why.

Later that day, he did some tests with smouldering rags, watching the flow of smoke, and concluded that there was a faint air current coming from deep down within the complex, and resolved to find its source one day, as the only place it could originate from was the other side of the rim.

The trauma of the morning had eased a little by the time of the evening meal, and most had fortunately recovered their appetites for Mop's surprisingly good culinary efforts.

It consisted of the most tasty stew she had yet produced, accompanied by round bread-like buns made from crushed grain she had obtained during a trade swap with one of their neighbours. She later admitted it took several attempts to get the mixture right, the first few samples produced being more suitable for use as missiles against possible marauders.

Gradually, the tone of the group rose, even a few jokes were made, and everyone retired in good spirits, largely helped by Mop's sumptuous meal.

Sandy was just on the point of drifting off to sleep, having run through the events of the day to see if anything could have been done better, when the soft shuffle of footsteps brought him wide awake again.

'Can I talk with you for a moment?' Mop's soft tones dispelled the initial flush of fear he felt at the unexpected sound, and he murmured his assent as he relaxed.

Since having had a good wash, a hair cut, and a new suit of clothing, Mop appeared to be more like what he thought a woman should look like.

Despite her inclination to carry a little extra weight, probably due to frequent tasting of her culinary concoctions, she had a warm and friendly attitude, which he found quite pleasant and comforting in an obtuse way.

As she snuggled up beside him beneath the newly washed rags which passed for blankets, he was strangely grateful for her comely presence, and turned to face her. Never one to miss a chance, Mop slid both arms around him, and drew even closer, burying her head in the recess of his shoulder.

'I always feel so much safer when I'm near you,' she cooed, wriggling a leg between his, 'you always seem to know the right thing to do.'

Whether Sandy took the hint or nature took over, it matters little, suffice it to say, a good time was had by all, and it was a contented Mop who snuggled down for the best night's sleep she had had for a very long time.

The early morning meal was a little late, much to Nan's annoyance, and he showed it by his brusque attitude towards all who spoke to him. This brought the general conversation to a staggering halt, and the later part of the meal was taken in silence, except for the grinding of teeth on Mop's half cooked breakfast.

At Sandy's suggestion, after the somewhat sombre morning meal had concluded with hardly a word spoken, the pair made their way down to Ben's storeroom.

'Wonder what's up with the crotchety old sod.' Sandy commented, as they tramped down the tunnel.

'Nan likes everything done in order and on time, I expect Mop's late meal upset him a bit. I wonder why she was so late getting up this morning?' Ben added with a grin, giving Sandy an unappreciated dig in the ribs.

They looked into the water condensing cave on the way, and found the water level had almost reached the little ridge which prevented it from over spilling into the tunnel.

'I'll get Mop to remove some for her needs, and the rest we can store for exchange. Must say, I never thought it would be so productive.'

As Sandy turned back to go to Mop's kitchen, he raised a finger towards Ben, who had just opened his mouth to make yet another quip about Mop.

Upon his return, Sandy handed Ben a small dark stick,

'Chew on that for a bit, I think you'll like it.'

'What is it?' asked a suspicious Ben, mindful that Sandy might try to get his own back for the earlier jokes he had made about Mop.

'Don't really know. It's something she got from one of the new plants, looks like the stalk, and she left it in the steam oven to see what would happen to it. It tasted good to her, so she gave me some to try.'

Ben gave the end of the dark stick a tentative suck, his face brightened, and he began to chew along with his friend.

Some time later, after the chewing stick had given up all its flavour, and quietly watching Sandy rummaging about among the stores, he could contain himself no longer.

'What exactly are you looking for?' asked an impatient Ben, eager to get on with something constructive.

'Shan't know 'till I see it. I'm not being difficult, I'm looking for something to suggest a means of catching one of those things in the sand.' He paused for a moment, and then pulled out a roll of metallic netting from under a pile of metal sheets.

'Now this might do the job, notice the weave. If we made a cylinder of this stuff, and you put your arm in the open end and then I pulled on the other end, it would tighten, and you couldn't get your arm out.'

'Don't see how,' replied a baffled Ben, 'what would make it tighten?' Sandy patiently explained the principle behind the self locking effect of a spiral wound tube of threads.

'Let's try it, Cut out a small piece like this.' Sandy drew a pattern on the dusty floor, 'while I try to find something to run the holding ropes through.'

When it was time to break off for the midday meal, they had made a small cylinder of the mesh, stitching the two edges together with a strand of wire, tried it much to Sandy's satisfaction and Ben's amazement, made a larger one, and located two metal rods with an eye on one end of each.

Nan seemed his old self again as they all assembled around the table to eat, and Sandy told him what they had been doing, and the proposed capture of the sand creature.

At first, Nan would have none of it, but Sandy explained in detail how they would entice the creature to put a tentacle into the cylinder, tighten their grip on it, and then haul it part way out of the sand, letting the heat of the blazing sun complete the job. In the end, Nan gave in, realizing that for every good reason he could think of for not attempting the capture, Sandy had a more than adequate answer.

The afternoon was spent categorizing and restacking the traded goods they had acquired into neat piles, so that if something was required, it could be found without having to go through the whole cave in a random search.

Sandy insisted that the drop-net at the cave's entrance be repaired, the burnt sections being cut out, and new cord spliced in. The reason for this, he quietly emphasized, was in case the creature, not able to get back into the sanctuary of the sands, decided that the cave system might be a good place to retreat into from the heat of the sun.

With the net down, and the hold down ropes lashed in place, he hoped it would be sufficient to protect them from possible invasion.

When the sun had dipped below the crater rim, they set off with their equipment, and located two suitable positions for the rope anchor points, each some ten metres either side of the entrance.

The metal rods were hammered into convenient cracks in the rock, and a cord was run through each 'eye' and brought back to the entrance. The other end of both cords were then attached to the catching cylinder of collapsible mesh, and everything was ready for the morrow, when they would try to capture a creature of the sands.

Nan came out to survey the trap, nodding his approval as each item was explained, although he was still not happy with the overall concept, and the idea of eating the creature caused him to screw up his face in disgust.

Karry and Kel were co-opted into the capture team, and Sandy outlined the method he intended to use. With two of them on each rope, they would take it in turns to pull the creature from side to side, so loosening its grip on the sand and hopefully leave it stranded, to die in the heat of the sun.

Word had got out about the capture scheme, and the normally quiet evening meal was frequently punctuated by questions about the venture, the others on the team allowing Sandy to supply the answers on the principle that if anything went wrong, then he would be the one to take all the blame.

As each question containing a possible problem was deftly handled by an eloquent Sandy, who had gone over the scheme many times in his head, Mop's admiration for him became obvious to all, and this generated several ribald comments from those who were less favoured by the now desirable Mop.

Ben and Sandy returned to the stores after the meal, to sharpen the knives they would use to carve up their capture.

They thought that if they were quick, they could have it reduced to strips before the sun broke over the crater rim, leaving it out in the heat of day to dry out, thus preserving the meat for future use.

It was quite late when Sandy returned to his sleeping cave, and he was relieved to find it devoid of his new admirer. No sooner had he wriggled himself into a comfortable position and closed his eyes, when the now familiar flop flop of Mop's worn out footwear announced her imminent arrival. With a sigh of resignation he rolled over, making room for the copious Mop, who would soon acquire more than her fair share of the coverings, forcing Sandy to snuggle into her just to keep warm.

He could see at least one possible advantage of the arrangement, apart from the obvious one. If food ever became scarce, he would be well looked after by his admirer.

So he looked upon the situation as an insurance policy against the possible future, not that he could recall exactly what an insurance policy was in any great detail.

Next morning found the team up early, Mop having told them she would arrange an early meal so that they would have maximum time out on the sands before the sun got too hot.

With extra wrappings on their feet to protect them from the ice cold sands, they checked out the trap again, making sure the ropes would run smoothly through the 'eyes' when the moment of capture came.

Sandy took the trapping cylinder of mesh out onto the sands, despite a shouted warning from Ben about lurking predators, and then made sure the ropes ran back in straight lines to their terminal points.

'All we have to do now is bait it, and wait.' said Sandy, disappearing into the cave entrance, and reappearing a little later with a bundle of rags in his arms.

'What are you using for bait,' asked a puzzled Ben, and then wished he hadn't. Sandy unwound the rags to expose the charred remains of an arm, which had already begun to decay with the expected nauseous aroma.

'Oh God. That's disgusting,' Ben cried out, quickly moving up wind of the offending remains, and looking shocked.

'Oh shut up, you wimp,' Karry retorted crossly, 'you didn't have to handle it, anyway, can you think of a better thing to use as bait?'

Sandy walked out onto the sands as if the creatures below were just a myth, and thrust the rotting arm into the end of the cylindrical mesh trap, pulling the whole contraption taught against the holding ropes.

'Shouldn't be too long now,' he called out, as he walked back nonchalantly to the waiting and anxious group, 'the surface of the sand is beginning to soften a little.' Mop and a few others were watching from the complex entrance.

Mop handed around a large pot of some hot brew, flavoured, she said, with a herb obtained on one of their trading expeditions. The steaming mint tasting liquid helped to combat the still chilly morning air, as they waited patiently for the first signs of movement under the now thawing sands.

Ben instructed the onlookers to retreat well into the complex entrance once activity on the sands began, as they might have to beat a hasty retreat and drop the catch net if the creature displayed any inclination to shelter from the broiling heat of the sun in the inviting cool of their caves.

Time dragged, as it always does when waiting for something to happen, and then it happened.

Some thirty metres out, the sand rippled as something moved beneath its surface. A little wave of sand travelled towards them, slowing down and eventually melting away as it neared the underlying rock of the crater rim.

Everyone held their breath as stillness returned again to the quiet sands. Nothing moved, except their heaving chests and pounding hearts.

Gently, a thin grey brown tentacle broke the surface, rising up for two metres and slowly swayed to and fro, trying to pick up the direction from which the delectable smell of food emanated.

A large hump grew in the sand, as the creature below moved ever closer to the surface, drawn on by the smell of charred and rotting flesh. At last the tentacle homed in on the mesh cylinder, probing its outer edge as it sensed something strange and new, but urged on by the stench of rotting meat from the other end.

Gradually, the exploring tip of the creature's food gathering equipment crept down the cylinder, and then found the reward for its long and persistent hunt.

Having located its prey, the tip of the probing tentacle wound itself closely around the remains of the arm, tightening its grip and bunching up to fill the enclosing cage of metallic mesh, as the sensors on its tip were overwhelmed by the enticing smell.

At the first signs of retraction, Sandy and Ben heaved on their rope, elongating the mesh cylinder, and increasing its grip on the creature's pseudopodia. It froze for a moment, and then Karry and Kel put all their not inconsiderable weight on their rope, and a metre or so of the creature was dragged from the concealing sand.

The two teams alternated their pulling, and slowly more of the hidden creature became exposed as it lost its grip on the yielding sand. Two more tentacles now joined the entrapped one, waving about, desperately trying to find something solid to grip.

Both teams went sprawling as the tension came off the ropes when the main body of the sand dweller broke surface, the whole creature thrashing about, sending clouds of fine sand high into the now warming air.

Regaining their feet, they pulled the creature towards them, only stopping when it was well clear of the deeper sands, and then they ran back to the complex entrance, taking the ends of the ropes with them to be tied off, so preventing the creature from returning from whence it had come.

'Quick, drop the net,' Sandy yelled, as a tentacle began to stretch in their direction, 'tie those bloody ropes off quickly, we don't want it in here.'

They had successfully made their capture, but would now have to wait for the blazing sun to do its part in terminating the creature before they could see just what it was they had dragged up from the sandy depths of the crater.

The brilliant blue white light from the naked sun blasted down on the crater floor as the thermonuclear generator cleared the high rim for another day of torturous heat, evaporating any tiny drops of moisture which had collected in the cracks and crannies of the surrounding rocks.

Various members of the complex took it in turns to peer through the safety of the catch net to see the last death throws of the creature from the sands, its writhing and twisting struggle to return to the cool of the lower sands becoming weaker and weaker as the sun rose higher in the clear blue sky above the crater.

Ben gave the knives they would use to butcher the creature, a final honing. They would have to work fast when the sun dipped below the rim, as other sand creatures would be attracted to their dead relative, and would probably have no compunctions about eating a sibling.

Sandy's idea was to cut the tentacles into strips, as he assumed they would be mainly composed of muscle meat, and drape them over the highest rocks they could reach. The night time drop in temperature would in effect freeze dry them to some extent, and the sun on the following day would complete the job, dehydrating them to hard leather-like strips which could be easily stored and traded.

As yet, no one had seen the main body of the creature clearly, as it had drawn its tentacles back to cover itself in one last desperate attempt to preserve life. They would have to wait until the cool of evening to see the full horror of what they had captured.

By midday, the creature had ceased to struggle, and Sandy was surprised it had hung onto life for so long, being quite convinced nothing could only survive for a few minutes in the full glare of the sun.

Nan gave instructions for the driest cave to be found for meat storage, and some simple shelving to be constructed from the now not inconsiderable supply of materials they had acquired through trading. To maintain his position as leader of the group, he needed to issue orders, and by so doing on this occasion, had by default given his blessing to the meat project.

The midday meal was eagerly awaited, and the excitement level of the group rose almost to fever pitch as the afternoon dragged on. A shout from the entrance finally announced the imminent disappearance of the sun behind the crater rim, and everyone rushed up to the entrance, but few would venture any further until they knew for sure the creature was well and truly dead.

Sandy fearlessly strode out onto the sands, followed by Ben and the others who had been given knives and instructions on how to carve up the tentacles, which by this time had entwined themselves into what looked like a knot around the main body.

It took four of them to unwind and straighten out the first of the three appendages, thereby fully exposing the body for the first time. It was a huge ovaloid bulbous mass, covered in what looked like veins, the three appendages coming out of one end, and between them, a wicked looking beak, quite capable of biting off a human arm or leg.

The heat of the sun had done its work, the skin in some places having split open, revealing the powerful muscular structure beneath.

Once the tentacles had been laid out in a line, the amputation began, with little blood appearing, as most of it had congealed under the heat of the sun. The skin was stripped in one piece, as Sandy had a use for such a tough material.

Many knives flashed in the failing light which spilled over the crest of the high rim, and soon a steady stream of meat strips were being laid out to dry on the highest rocks they could reach.

The core of each tentacle seemed to be made up of gristle like interlocking rings, and these too were put out to dry, although they had no specific use for them at the moment.

It was when they cut into the main body, that they had a surprise. Just below the outer skin, which had been protected from the sun by the encircling appendages, was a thick layer of a white and yellow streaked fat like substance, nearly half a metre in depth, protecting the internal organs.

Sandy gave orders for the fat layer to be salvaged, and stored in whatever containers could be found. His thoughts were already racing ahead, the fat could provide the light he needed to explore the cave system, where the gas lamps failed to go.

As the light finally failed, and the chill of evening dropped like a cold blanket on those still on the crater floor, there was very little of the sand creature left. The internal organs, in their tough skin bag, were dragged out onto deeper sand, and left for the other creatures of the crater to scavenge when the sand warmed up again.

The butchery crew, sweaty, blood stained, and very tired, returned to the relative comfort of the caves to get cleaned up, and have a well earned meal.

Sandy had never heard so much general chatter at meal time, and realized that the members of the group had come up tone to a remarkable degree, probably caused by their having something useful to do, and a common purpose.

Everyone slept well that night, especially Mop, tucked up with her hero, as tired as he was.

After a very quickly consumed breakfast next morning, Sandy and

Ben went out when it was warm enough underfoot, to inspect the meat strips.

Everything was just as they had left it the night before, proving if nothing else, there were no night marauders.

As the reflected sunlight from the high rim began to warm the crater, the first sign of movement under the sand became apparent. Something had sensed a meal, and was on its way to retrieve it.

'Let's stay and see what it's like.' Ben suggested, and Sandy agreed, as there was little else to do now except wait for the meat to dry, and then he remembered the fat.

'OK, but we must make a start on our lamps if we're to explore the tunnel in your store cave.'

They did not need to wait very long. A large humped shape in the sand drew nearer, the fine sand flowing almost like water as it pushed its way towards the remains of the creature they had butchered the day before.

This time there were no tentacles, just a dark brown rounded lump, with no apparent distinguishing features, until the slit like mouth opened and swallowed the still frozen remains they had left on the sand.

With a roar which must have been heard half across the crater, the brown hump spat out the entrails bag, together with a considerable quantity of sand which it must have swallowed at the same time.

Both watchers were taken by surprise, and instinctively jumped back several paces, although the sand was too shallow for the creature to have reached them.

Ben began to brush off some of the sand which had landed on him, when they noticed the smell, and both were promptly violently sick on the spot.

Having divested themselves of their early morning meal, their attention was drawn back to the creature in the sands.

The brown hump had nearly disappeared from view, wriggling itself back beneath the sand, but a scaly arm suddenly flashed out, equipped with a set of claws which made them shudder, sinking them into the still frozen entrails bag and dragging it beneath the surface.

'So we have a mixture of unpleasantries down there,' commented Sandy, both hands clutching his still aching stomach. 'This place is full of surprises.' Ben felt too unwell to reply, and merely nodded.

They returned to the complex, getting strange looks from those they hurriedly passed, and went to the new washing cave to get cleaned up, and find a change of clothing.

'Where did that awful smell come from?' asked Ben, as he scrubbed himself clean.

'I suspect it was from the saliva that thing spat out along with the unwanted sand.' Sandy replied. 'It probably contains enzymes and bacteria to help digest whatever it catches. If the smell is anything to go by, it could strip paint.'

Mop, hearing the misfortune which had befallen the pair, waltzed into the wash room, quite unashamed, and dumped a handful of herbs into the water.

'These should make you two smell a little better,' she said, reaching forward to stir the water, and then thinking better of it, 'must away, I've got some cooking to do.' She left, grinning from ear to ear, and with a bounce in her step.

'What was that all about?' asked a puzzled Ben.

'Search me.' Sandy replied, knowing full well Mop's intentions, which had then been thwarted by Ben's presence.

It took the pair quite some time to eradicate the nauseous odour the creature had bestowed upon them.

'What do you intend to do with the fat we saved from the creature?' asked Ben, as they went along to Mop's kitchen to replace their breakfast.

'I hope to render it down to an oil, then we shall have fuel for lamps we can move around with. I left one container out in the sun to cook, after cutting up the fat, so by this evening we should have a little oil, if we're lucky.'

Mop had anticipated their visit, and thoughtfully prepared two plates of vegetables flavoured with her new herbs, beaming happily as they wolfed them down.

The pair went down to Ben's storerooms to look for materials to make the lamps Sandy was so insistent about, and while doing so, Ben asked him about the Great Lights.

'What do you really think they are?' he asked innocently.

'I think they come from some sort of vehicle which brings people like us to this godforsaken place, for whatever reason. I can't accept Nan's theory that we are created by them, that's a load of crap. God knows why he believes it.'

'But why would anyone want to send us to a place like this? We can only just survive here, why not send us somewhere where the living is easier?' Ben asked.

'That I don't know, but look at some of the facts.' Sandy was getting into his stride on a subject which intrigued him.

'We arrive here with no memory of our past, and we must have one, you don't just appear as an adult out of nowhere. I think our memories have been tampered with, so that we can remember some things, like language, and the names of things, but can't always understand what they are.

'Take meat for instance. I know I used to eat it, but can't recall where it came from, or what to do with it, until I saw the sand creature, and then it all came flooding back. If we work at it, I think our memories can be recovered.'

'I think you're right on that point, I've noticed that I know more now than I did before you came here. Perhaps we help each other by talking about things, and trying to make sense of them. I wonder why Nan hasn't noticed this also?' Ben looked thoughtful for a moment, not sure if he had explained exactly what he meant.

'He may well have, but hasn't said anything. Don't forget, Nan's the leader of your group, and can't reveal anything which would undermine his authority.'

'You said 'your group', don't you feel part of us?' Ben sounded and looked hurt.

'Well of course I'm part of the group, that was just a slip of the tongue. I'm the newest arrival here, so I'm bound to think of myself as being an outsider, and see things from an outsider's point of view. That's why I'm able to see the stupidity of Nan's unquestioned belief in the Great Lights as the creator of all. It's total clap trap, think about it.'

'I never felt really happy about it,' responded Ben, 'it's just what everyone else accepted, and it seemed reasonable at the time. But why do you think they dumped us here? There must be a reason.'

'Sure there is, but I can only guess at it right now. I suspect it's because we've done something somewhere, the recipients didn't like. They felt uneasy about terminating our lives, and did the next best thing, plonked us down here.

'Look at it from their point of view, if you place someone in a situation which makes life difficult, they'll spend most of their time trying to survive, not thinking about where they came from, or how to get back. In this hole, you spend *all* your time trying to survive, no wonder you stagger along from day to day, just accepting whatever is offered, there's little time or incentive to think, or bring about improvements.'

'See what you mean, it does make sense when you think about it,' mused Ben, not too sure if it did.

'Anyway, I don't intend to spend the rest of my life cooped up here, I think there's something else on the other side of the crater, and I'm going to find it.' Sandy added. 'I'll need some help, and I'm banking on you and a few others to join me. If Nan wants to stay here and mumble on about the Great Lights, that's up to him, but I'm certainly not.'

At that point, Ben found a small metal container with a screw lid, and thoughtfully turned it over in his hands.

'This could make the basis of the lamp you're on about,'   he said, offering it to Sandy, 'all we need to do is fit a tube on the top to hold a wick, and some means of turning it up or down to adjust the flame.'

'How did you know that, about the tube and the wick?' asked Sandy, with a grin.

'Don't know, I just did,' Ben replied, looking puzzled.

'Just goes to prove my point, we all know a lot more than we think we do, it just needs a little push here, a reminder there, and it comes flooding back.' Sandy had that self satisfied look on his face which had so annoyed Nan on earlier occasions.

'We'll need to protect the flame from being blown out by any drafts in the tunnels, and a piece of that reflective material you found would concentrate the light in a forward direction. All we need now is the oil, and I feel sure I can make that from the fat we saved.'

At the midday meal, they told Nan about the lamp, but he only listened politely, showing very little real interest in the project. Sandy's patience with the old leader reduced still further, and he resolved to waste no further time explaining his ideas to the unreceptive Nan, leader or not.

'Take no notice of him,' Ben said quietly, 'he'll come around when he sees what we're up to.'

The afternoon was spent setting up the last of the racks for storing the dried meat, helping Bell fill her new growing bins with compost from the digester, and then planting out the new seedlings in them.

They were now able to produce more food than they really needed, and some plants which were suitable for drying were exposed to the sun for the last part of the afternoon.

Unfortunately, those who took them out had to be completely covered in clothing from head to foot, and wear strange looking headgear with a semi-opaque eye piece to cut down the blaze of light in the crater.

This had only become possible of late, as the semi-opaque material had been obtained on a recent exchange with one of the other groups.

Sandy and Ben were waiting by the entrance for the sun to dip below the crater rim, so that they could see how the meat drying experiment had gone, when Nan came up to them. 'I understand that you have given orders that we must not disclose to other groups how we obtained the meat strips, and processed them.'

'That's correct.' Sandy replied, without looking at him.

'By what right do you do this, may I ask?'

'Makes sense,' Sandy replied tersely. 'If they know how we do it, then we lose the advantage of trading the meat.'

'Would you not agree, that I, as your leader, should give the orders around here? You have only just arrived, so to speak.'

'Then why didn't you give them? You've had plenty of time to work out the economics of the situation, but as yet, you've shown no interest in the operation.'

Sandy was still smarting from Nan's dismissal of his ideas at the midday break, and would give him no quarter now.

'I don't see the need for all this trading anyway, we were doing all right before.' Nan decided to try another tack.

'Oh yes? How would you have handled the attack from that load of barbarians who wiped out one of our neighbouring groups, without the flame-thrower? They would have massacred the lot of you. You now have an ample water supply, instead of the pathetic dribble gathered before from condensation on the crater rocks.

'We now have decent clothing, we are clean, and look more like human beings instead of the filthy smelly bunch of rock hermits of only a short while ago. Food has improved, and we can now eat our fill instead of grovelling for every dropped crumb. Most of these things have been brought about through using materials we either had in the stores which nobody bothered to utilize, or through trading for things we needed.' Sandy paused for breath, filling his lungs.

'Just how long do you think you would hold your post as so called leader if you returned the group to the former conditions you all enjoyed? I'd say ten minutes, and I'm being generous.'

Nan looked stunned at the onslaught, going a deep red beneath his normally healthy brown tan.

'The Great Light didn't create us to become super beings, we are placed here to do the Great Light's will, and make use of the gifts it so generously gives us from time to time, not to make strange devices with them. Anyway, I could have talked the raiders out of harming us, so there was no need to have used the flame-thrower so devastatingly.'

It was now Sandy's turn to look astonished, and all eyes turned to him to see what his response would be.

Most of the group had now assembled in the tunnel to help with the collection of the dried meat strips, not expecting to be witness to the apparent power struggle which was now going on between Nan and the newcomer.

Karry and Bell, followed by Kel, pushed their way to the front of the crowd, ready to take sides if it came to the crunch.

In the tense silence which followed Nan's last statement, grins were beginning to appear on the faces of those who held little credence for Nan's theory of the Great Lights, his almost hysterical outpourings finally convincing them of which side they would choose to follow if it came to a choice.

'I have nothing against you,' Sandy began, carefully controlling his voice to a steady even pitch, 'and as a person, I like you. But you know nothing, and understand even less. Look at the ridiculous statement you've just made, no one here believes such clap trap any more, that's if they ever did. I do not consider you fit to be leader of this, or any group. You are incapable of judging a situation on the facts present; preferring to abdicate responsibility to some higher force, which only exists in your warped imagination.

'I am willing to accept you as group leader, issuing your orders as you wish, just so long as they do not clash or hamper those things I intend to do to improve our lot here. I do not want to call a vote to elect a new leader, but I will if I have to in order to secure the group's survival. I think there are enough here who would back me in that.'

A surprisingly loud chorus of affirmations echoed through the tunnel, and Nan seemed to crumple under the rising volume of 'yers'.

'I think we should get the meat in,' Ben announced, looking at Sandy, 'we can sort out this leader thing later on this evening, after we've eaten.'

'Thank God for some common sense at last.' Karry said, and they all trooped out onto the still warm sands and began climbing the rocks to retrieve the dried meat strips.

A shout of surprise brought Sandy running to one group who were passing the strips down from a high ledge.

'What's the problem?' he asked, having some difficulty in clambering up the smooth rock face.

'Look at this, something's taken some of the strips.'

A neat row of some twenty meat strips lay along the ledge, with a gap in the middle which would have accommodated at least three.

'I don't like the look of this,' said Sandy, 'there's a slight stain on the rock where the strips have been, so it looks as thought we've had a visitor who can stand a lot of daytime heat.' He called down to Ben, 'Pass the word to the other gatherers, see if there are any more missing strips.'

Ben hurried off to do as he was bid, while Sandy looked for clues on the rock surface to see if he could determine who or what had raided their stocks.

By the time the light began to fade, and the chill of evening warned of the freeze to come, the last of the meat strips had been gathered up, and hurried down to the storeroom.

Sandy's container of fat lumps had been reduced to a thick oil, with the fat matrix tissue still floating in it like a half seen ghost, and the added bonus of an unpleasant smell.

Mop announced that the evening meal would be a little late due to the extra work she had done, but no one minded, as the exercise had been a great success, and all were amazed at the quantity of meat strips which now lay neatly stacked up for the future. Ben mentioned he was looking forward to trading some of the strips to top up his stores, not that there was much room left, even in the second chamber.

This prompted a few witty remarks from those who had seen his collection of what the 'Great Lights' considered to be their unwanted rubbish.

By the time everyone had cleaned up, and began to assemble in the main chamber for the evening meal, the atmospheric tension had begun to build up again.

One of the group, whom Sandy hadn't bothered to get to know by name, quietly came up to him and respectfully asked, 'Why don't you make an outright bid for total leadership, you're bound to get it. We're all fed up with Nan and his weird theories.'

'I'm not really fussed whether I'm leader or not,' Sandy replied, 'I just get on with what I want to do. I don't think Nan will try to stop me, and if he does, I'll just ignore him, politely of course. Generally, he doesn't do too bad a job as leader.' The other man looked disappointed.

'I think his wheels have got a bit loose. Just before you came, he tried to get some of us to go out, well wrapped up of course, and pray to the Greater Light. I told him what he could do with his prayer mat, and he hasn't spoken directly to me since. I think we need a change, and you're it.'

'OK, OK, we'll talk about it later. Look, Mop's bringing the food in.' Fortunately for Sandy, the attraction of food, after a hard days work, had greater pulling power than politics, and the matter was dropped for the time being.

As Mop moved around the crude table, dishing out her brew, exclamations of delight and the rattle of spoons in their bowls followed her ample body, as it went from person to person.

'Hey, this is great Mop, what did you put in it?' was eventually asked by an over curious someone, although most would rather not have known it later transpired.

'Can't you guess?' she asked brightly. 'I put some of those meat strips in, that's one reason I'm late, good isn't it?'

The silence which followed was only broken by the clatter of spoons being returned to their bowls, but before long, they were all chomping away again, she was right, it was very good.

No more was said about the leadership battle, and Sandy was thankful for that. When the meal was finished, and perhaps with indecent haste, Sandy and his faithful companion disappeared down to the storeroom, which in effect was now becoming a workshop.

'The oil has separated out quite well,' Sandy said, as he hooked the remains of the fibrous tissue from the container.

'Now we need to see if it will burn.'

Ben had already been working on a simple lamp, and it was only a matter of adding oil to the base container and adjusting the wick, to see if it would give them the light they so badly needed.

'I think we'll have to run this oil through some charcoal, to get rid of the smell, it's awful.' Sandy commented, as he poured the thick odorous liquid into the lamp.

'How did you know that would remove the smell? ... sorry, I needn't have asked.' Ben added quickly.

The lamp was taken over to the guttering gas flame on the wall, the oiled wick sputtered, and then burnt brightly, adding a considerable amount of light to the gloomy room.

'Hey, that's great,' exclaimed Ben, with childlike enthusiasm, 'would two wicks give twice as much light?'

'Should do, why not try it? If you can find something in your store which is reflective and flexible, we can make a lamp where the beam can be concentrated to reach into the distance, or be used for general light.'

They both worked on late into the night, experimenting with their lamps, and learning as they went along. When Sandy eventually went to his cave, Mop was already tucked up in the blankets, and he had quite a struggle to wrench some free to cover himself, without disturbing her. He was in no fit state for hi-jinks at this time of the morning.

Dawn came all too quickly, and Mop had already gone to her kitchen to prepare the morning meal when Sandy awoke.

He was the only one in the communal wash cave, the others having long since vacated it for the main cavern, and food.

When he arrived, the general mutter of conversation stopped dead, and all heads turned to face him.

The same man who had approached him the day before, now stood up, and clearing his throat nervously, he began,

'We have had a good discussion of the matter raised yesterday with you, and the feeling is unanimous that you be elected our new leader. We like the things you have brought about, and feel that you have a much firmer grip on reality that poor old Nan, so how about it?' He sat down hurriedly, as Nan was the only one not present, and might come in at any moment.

'That's up to you all. I'm not putting myself up for the job. I said more than I should have yesterday, and I have no wish to hurt Nan any further. I think if you leave things as they are for a while, they'll sort themselves out, and a leader will emerge naturally. That way, we don't cause any more upset.'

The others reluctantly nodded, accepting Sandy's ruling as if he had been their new leader, and the matter was forgotten when the food came in. 'What are you making down in the storeroom?' asked one man, between mouthfuls. 'I'd like to be in on it, if you need any more help.'

'You've no idea what we're up to, it might be boring or dangerous. You should never volunteer for anything unless you know what you're getting into.' Sandy didn't want half the group traipsing down to the workshop, cluttering the place up and asking stupid questions.

'I'm fed up with sitting on my arse half the day, trying to find something useful to do, so I'll take a chance on that,' the man replied forcefully. 'I noticed you had put some fat out, which turned to oil, and Ben has been bashing away with some tinplate. Oil and a container equals a lamp, so I assume you are going to explore some of the tunnels which have been out of bounds to us because there's no gas lamps in them. If you are, and you need someone to carry anything, I'm your man.'

Sandy liked the man's forthright attitude, and tenacity.

'All right, if we need you, we'll let you know.'

Turning aside to Ben a few moments later, Sandy asked,

'What's his name?

'Greg,' Ben replied, 'and he's a good sort, a bit quiet normally, but he gets things done with little or no fuss.'

'OK, we'll include him when we get going, but first I'd like to take a look at the tunnels which go down below the digester room.'

'That's one place we're not supposed to go,' Ben quietly said, 'I've heard that someone went down there a long time ago, and they didn't return.'

'Well, let's find out why, there may be something we should know about the place. I'm damned sure it's not quite what it appears to be, by a long way.'

The meal over, the two went down to the work room as they now referred to it, and lit two of their lamps, trimming the wicks so that they gave a clear flame and no smoke.

'What do we do if the lamps get blown out?' asked Ben, trying to foresee every possible eventuality.

'Good point, but they should be all right with the transparent cover around them, but just to be on the safe side, we'd better get that covered.'

They tried to set fire to some coarse cloth, using the sparks from the spark stone they had discovered earlier. It failed to work, so they settled for a length of smouldering string and some very fine dry plant fibres, obtained from Bell.

When a small bunch of these fibres were placed around the end of the glowing string, and gently blown on, it was just possible to get the fibre to burst into flame.

Sandy was not happy at the unpredictability of the arrangement, but it was all they had at the moment.

'I've got a couple of the dried meat strips, and a small container of water, just in case.' said Ben. 'Always better to be on the safe side.' Sandy grinned to himself, he had chosen well to have Ben as a partner, but then realized that Ben had chosen him.

They went down to the digester room, where all their waste was broken down into compost for Bell's plant growing in the pseudo gas plant.

'What's that smell?' asked Ben as they neared the twin cylinders of the plant.

'Probably from the remains of our old clothing.' Sandy replied, pointing to a small heap of rags. 'I asked Jez to add it a little at a time to the rest of the rubbish, we may as well break it down for compost.'

'Good God, and we wore that!' exclaimed Ben, hardly able to believe his eyes and nose.

'I still don't understand this gas plant,' Ben continued, 'why try to fool us that it produces our gas?'

'I haven't worked that one out fully yet,' Sandy replied, 'either it was put in by our predecessors, or the people who set this place up in the first place, and then dumped us here.

'We may get some clues when we explore the tunnels and other caves we've not been in yet. I'm certain of one thing though, this place is not what is seems.' Ben just nodded.

In the far corner of the cavern, hidden from normal view by a buttress of rock, a tunnel sloped gently downwards.

After checking and adjusting their lamps for maximum light, the pair entered it, Sandy pointing out that the walls were definitely man made, because when looked at closely, the tool marks were still visible.

'Aren't all the passages man made then?' asked Ben, who had never given it much thought.

'No, if you look closely, you'll see some are almost smooth, where liquid rock must have flowed through at some time when this volcano was active, others are like this one, tool marked, and the one leading down to your storerooms has been cut using a boring machine of some sort. The surface is smooth, until you examine it close up, and then you can see very fine marks where something has cut the rock consistently, not with random cuts like these.' He illustrated the point, by holding the lamp up against the wall.

The incline got steeper as they went along, traces of moisture glistening on the walls every now and again, but not enough to warrant collecting for use, not that they needed to now that they had the condensing room.

The passageway ahead branched into three, one branch only going about four metres, as if someone had changed their mind about the direction, or hit a particularly hard section of rock. Of the other two, one had a dank stillness about it, which neither of them felt tempted to enter.

'Looks like we go down this one,' Sandy said, 'there's something about that other one which makes me feel uneasy.'

They had only gone a few metres, when it became apparent that the passageway was curving off sharply to their right, the spiral tightening as they went along.

'This reminds me of something,' Ben said, his voice suddenly acquiring a strange echo effect, 'it's like going down a spiral staircase, except we're on a slope.'

'And it's getting steeper,' Sandy added, 'watch out for any damp patches on the ground, if we slip and lose our footing God knows where we'll wind up.'

The curve of the tunnel was now such that they felt they were walking directly above the section underneath, only a thin layer of rock on which they trod separating them from the passage below.

Sandy was on the point of calling a halt to their journey and returning to the sanity of the digester room, when the tunnel opened out into the biggest cavern they had ever seen.

It stretched off in all directions, the light from their feeble lamps unable to reach the far walls, the roof of the cave a black ominous hole above them.

'The only way we can explore this cave is to go around the outer walls until we come back here.' Sandy suggested.

'What if there are other openings like this one, and we can't tell one from the other? We could be stuck down here for ever trying to find our way out.' Ben was rightly worried.

'How about leaving your water bottle by this one as a marker?' Sandy said after a few moments thought.

Placing the water bottle to one side of the opening, they set off, going around the vast cavern a few metres away from the towering black walls, looking for any sign of other tunnels, but there were none.

They both began to worry as the featureless walls seemed to go on for ever, just a gentle curve indicating that they were in what appeared to be a very large circular chamber.

By the time they had come full circle, they were almost on the point of panic, and then they saw the glint of the metal water bottle shining in the lamp light.

'God, am I glad to see your bottle,' Sandy gasped out, 'that was unnerving, to say the least of it. One thing puzzles me though, why make a tunnel all the way down here to just finish in this bloody great cavern with no other exits? There must have been some reason for doing it, surely.'

Ben could find no sensible reason for the tunnel either.

'We could walk across the middle, to see if there's anything out there.' Ben then suggested.

'OK, but how the hell are we going to maintain a straight line? Without bearings, people always curve off to one side, it's a natural quirk we have.'

'How about I go out towards the middle, and put one of the lamps down, then walk on again. You can call out, keeping me in line with yourself and the lamp on the ground. You then come forward and pick up the lamp and join me. If we keep doing that, it should keep us fairly straight.'

'That's a good idea.' Sandy was impressed with Ben's logical approach to the problem. 'But I expect you'll find wandering about in the middle of this cavern, surrounded by nothing but blackness, an unnerving sensation. Are you sure you want to try it?'

'Yer, what the hell, we're down here, may as well.'

They had reached what they thought must be the middle of the empty blackness, taking it in turns to go forward with the lamps, when a large dark shape loomed up ahead of them.

'What the hell's that?' exclaimed Ben, who was in the lead, and had now stopped. 'It's huge.'

Ahead of them was a twenty metre high round dome of rock, its smooth curved surface glistening in the flickering light from their oil lamps.

'I suppose it's what it looks like,' Sandy answered cautiously, 'a massive great dome of rock. But look at the surface, it's been machined smooth, that's not natural.'

'It's certainly different to the floor of the cavern, that looks as if it's been chewed flat by something,' Ben observed, 'it's covered in tiny grooves. Do you think it's the same material?'

Sandy went to run his hand over the glistening surface of the dome, and withdrew it immediately, looking puzzled,

'The damn thing's warm, or seems to be, what do you think?'

Ben put his hand flat on the floor of the cavern, and then gingerly on the dome, and then repeated the process again.

'I don't think it's warm so much as giving the illusion of being warm, but how it does that beats me. Let's take a look around the other side of it, there may be something different there.'

Keeping their lamps trained on the shiny surface, the pair slowly walked around the huge stone block and nearly bumped into something else in the darkness. They cannoned into each other, Sandy nearly dropping his lamp and swearing as he tried to regain his balance.

'Well, that's different, and it's not made of stone. Seems to be some kind of machine, although I've never seen anything like it before.' Sandy brought the lamp up close to the surface of the machine, noticing several narrow grooves which ran from end to end of the four metre block.

Four:
New Lands Beckon

'THESE ODD LOOKING grooves run all around it, and on the ends as well. I think it opens up to become something. At the moment it's all folded up, possibly ready to be moved off to another job, maybe. We could come down here again, and see if we can get it to open up, and possibly make it work. That's if we can figure out what it's supposed to do.'

'I don't think we should fiddle with it just now.' Ben didn't like the idea of starting something they may not be able to control or stop. 'I think coming down later is a good idea.'

They left the machine, Sandy reluctantly, and moved on around the dome, but had only gone a few metres when Ben stopped again, pointing to a large black hole in the mound.

'That looks like another tunnel going downwards, do we chance it?'

'That's what we're here for,' Sandy replied brightly, 'lead on, but carefully, I've got a feeling about this one.'

The passage began to curve, tightening into the spiral like the one which had brought them into the huge cavern above, and then it straightened out again, and began to widen.

'Slow down a bit.' Sandy called out to Ben, who had hurried on ahead, and was some five metres in front. 'We don't know what's down here, or what this place is for.'

The slope increased sharply, and then in the distance, could be seen to flatten out again.

'It looks as if there's some white sticks on the ground in front, I'll move up a bit and see what they are.' Ben went quickly on ahead, despite Sandy's earlier words of caution.

'Good God, it's a bloody skeleton. Some poor sod's come down here and died, by the look of it.'

Then his lamp burnt a deep red colour, flickered twice, and went out.

'Back up,' Sandy called out desperately, 'now, do it NOW.'

Ben turned, and staggered back towards the only remaining light, Sandy was reluctant to go forward to help him in case he too got trapped in the gas filled tunnel.

'God, I can't get enough air into my lungs,' Ben gasped, 'I feel dizzy and faint, what happened?'

'I think I know,' Sandy replied, helping a wobbling Ben back up the tunnel, 'it's to do with oxygen, or the lack of it.'

'What's oxygen?' asked Ben, still panting for breath.

'It's a gas in the atmosphere, which we need to breathe to stay alive, and anything that's burning, needs it also. That's why the flame in your lamp went out, there's no oxygen down there, and that's probably why that poor sod died in the first place, he couldn't breathe either, and just collapsed.'

Ben sat down, leaning against the tunnel wall, while Sandy opened the top of the two lamps so that a flame could be transferred to the unlit one.

With both lamps now lighting the tunnel with their cheerful yellow glow, the place seemed less frightening, and the feeling of panic eased away.

'Do you think it's a trap to stop anyone from going any further?' asked Ben, his breathing having returned to near normal.

'I doubt it, they'd have just blocked off the passage if they wanted to stop anyone. No, I think it's a natural phenomenon, volcanoes generate carbon dioxide, and other noxious gasses, so it's quite likely it drifted up from below somewhere.'

'Won't it gradually fill up the cavern, and then come up to our level?' asked a worried Ben, who could see them all having to move into another cave complex, if they could find an unoccupied one.

'I don't think we need to worry about that. If you noticed, the flame of your lamp went out at about the same height that man's head would have been when standing up, so the gas level hasn't gone up much since he died, and that must have been some time ago as there are only bones left. We've heard about someone going 'down below' and never returning, but that happened a long while ago, so I'm told.'

'I'd like to take a closer look at him, but how can we do it safely?' asked Ben, having now fully recovered.

'You really want to?' asked a surprised Sandy, and then paused to think, while Ben just nodded in the dim light.

'We could use one of the lamps to show us where the gas level is. It'll go reddish before it goes out, due to incomplete burning of the oil. If you then take a deep breath and run forward you should have a few seconds to reach him and then get back to clean air again. I'll bend the reflector on my lamp to focus the beam to give you maximum light on the skeleton.'

When the little flame on his lamp flicked and turned red, Ben hesitated for a moment. He then backed up a couple of metres, put his lamp on the floor of the tunnel, took a deep breath and rushed forward.

He was beside the untidy scatter of bones in seconds, and noticed a silver coloured object lying next to the remains of what had once been a hand. He picked it up, looked around quickly to make sure he had not overlooked anything else interesting, and ran back to Sandy.

'Pick up the lamp on your way,' Sandy called out calmly, 'or you'll have to go back again.'

Ben scooped up the lamp as he passed, letting out the breath he had been holding with a great whoosh, and nearly knocking Sandy over as he drew level.

'Good God man, what's the rush? You should be able to hold your breath longer than that.'

Ben took up his sitting position against the tunnel wall again, while he tried to get his breathing under control.

'What's that thing you picked up?' asked Sandy, sitting down beside the still panting Ben. 'It looks metallic from here.'

Ben handed over the object he had found without thinking, his head still spinning from lack of oxygen.

Sandy turned the shiny metal object over in his hand, examining it carefully in the soft light of the oil lamps.

'My memory is coming back in big chunks, I think I know what this is,' he exclaimed excitedly, 'it's a gun!'

'What's a gun?' asked Ben, not showing the interest he would normally have done.

'It's a thing for shooting with, like the gas guns you have up top. It propels a missile out at high velocity. I wonder why anyone down here would need one of these?'

'Don't suppose he lived down here,' Ben commented, 'he probably came from up top, as we do.'

'Probably, as you say, but what's he doing with a weapon like this? We don't have anything like it, nor do any of the other groups, or we would have found out about it long ago.'

Sandy pointed the gun down the tunnel, and gently squeezed the firing stud. A thin beam of red light made a tiny red dot on the tunnel floor, just past the scattered bones of its previous owner.

'Don't think that would stop very much,' said Ben, not in the least impressed.

Sandy increased the pressure on the stud without really meaning to, and a section of the tunnel floor exploded in a mist of fine particles, leaving a quarter metre hole.

'Now I'm impressed, said Ben, 'but how does it do that? There was no bang like our guns.'

'Not sure yet, but I think the red light is used for finding the target, and when I pressed a little harder on this stud, the floor blew up. As you said, there was no bang, and certainly no kick back, so it must be some form of energy beam. It would have been a little more humane, and definitely more effective than our flame-thrower, had we had it earlier.' he added thoughtfully.

As there was little else they could do with regard to exploring the tunnel system, because of the gas pocket, it was decided to return to the surface, neither of them realizing just how much time had gone by since they began their exploration that morning.

Halfway up the long spiral slope leading to the digester room, Sandy called a halt, as both were out of breath.

'Still got your container of water?' he asked an equally exhausted Ben.

'Yes, and a couple of dried meat strips, want one?'

After a much needed drink, they both began to chew on a meat strip, leaning against the tunnel wall for support.

As the strips softened, they were able to break bits off and swallow them, easing the emptiness of their stomachs.

'God, it's tough, but it tastes good, and is probably nutritious.' Ben said, Sandy nodded, his mouth too full to speak.

Another drink of water meant their supplies were all spent, and the long haul up the seemingly never ending spiral slope was continued.

Reaching the digester room, they both paused for a rest before the last short climb to the domestic section of the complex. They wondered how much time had passed, and if they had been missed.

As there was no sign of life in the tunnels, they assumed rightly that the group had assembled for a meal, but which one they had yet to find out.

As the pair entered the main cavern, a few weak cheers went up, but these soon faded away as Nan drew himself up to his full height, with a face as black as thunder said,

'And where have you two been? We've been searching for you ever since mid morning.'

Suddenly realizing the trouble they had caused by not advising any one of their intentions, Sandy decided a contrite response was called for, along with humble apologizing,

'I'm sorry, Nan, we should have told someone what we were up to. We just didn't realize how long it would take us, and we have no means of measuring the passage of time.'

'You still haven't said where you were.'

'We've been down the tunnels below the digester room, and you'll be amazed what we found there.' Sandy added quickly, hoping to divert some of Nan's anger.

'That area is forbidden. You have no right to go there, it isn't meant for us to use. That area belongs to the Great Light, that's why you die if you trespass on its sacred ground.'

'There's nothing sacred down there,' Sandy's patience was beginning to falter, 'just a mass of tunnels, and a cavern the size of which you wouldn't believe, in the middle of it

'You have no right to go there, it is forbidden.' Nan thundered, his face going an even darker shade of purple.

It was too much, Sandy was tired, desperately wanted something to eat and drink, and his patience finally snapped.

'For Gods sake, Nan, grow up,' he shouted back, 'get into the real world, such as it is. There is no Great Light lording it over us, there are no sacred caves or ground, and nothing is forbidden, there's just this bloody crater, and us.'

All heads turned to look at Sandy in the deathly hush which followed his outburst, 'I agree.' someone said, but it was impossible to see who the heretic was.

'I shall confine you to your cave, until I can find another group who will take you in, and that will be difficult. Ben has been contaminated with your heretical views, and he must go too. After this meal, we will all wrap ourselves up well, endure the cold, and pray to the Great Light to forgive us for this trespass on their holy grounds.'

The others around the table looked as shocked as Sandy felt, hardly able to believe their ears.

'For God's sake, shut up, you stupid old fart.' Sandy could no longer constrain his feelings, and released the pent up frustration which had been building over the last few days.

This time the silence was even longer, except for the soft rustle of clothing as heads turned this way and that, wondering who would release the next verbal blast.

Slowly, a series of quietly muttered comments grew in volume, until there was a loud bang from the other end of the table. Greg had risen to his feet, lifted his feeding bowl, and brought it down hard on the table top. Everyone jumped, releasing the tension which had built up.

'The time has come for us to make a decision which will affect the group into the foreseeable future.' He paused, to make sure he had everyone's attention, which he had.

'Nan has done a great job of leading us in the past, but unfortunately his wheels have finally dropped off, and is no longer capable of making rational decisions any more. We must have a sane, strong leader, in order to survive, and I propose we elect Sandy to take his place. All those in favour, please raise a hand now.'

Nearly everyone raised a hand, some raised both.

Greg did not even bother to count the raised hands, so overwhelming was the result, but being fair to Nan he asked,

'Does anyone disagree?'

All hands fell as one, and no others were raised. A few had not shown their wishes, abstaining from the vote just in case Nan did manage to hold his position, and seek retribution in the future.

Nan had sat down, his head buried in his hands, mumbling something about the Great Light, but no one took any notice of him.

'So that's decided then, Sandy is our new leader,' Greg made it sound like an order rather than a question, and turning to him asked, 'do you accept?'

'Yes, if that's what you wish. I don't want to change anything, just improve some things, so that our life is a little better.'

'I understand,' said Greg, who was still standing, 'that you have some views on this place, and us, and why we are all here. I think we would all like to hear them.' A chorus of 'yers' and other affirmations gave Sandy little chance to avoid the issue.

'All right, you may not like what I have to say, and it may not be the whole truth, but it is based on what I have observed and reasoned out.' He paused to gather his thoughts, and decide just how much to reveal to his attentive audience.

'This business about the Great Lights. There's nothing mystical or holy about them, they're just the lights on a vehicle which can travel through the air, and is responsible for dumping us here. Why we are left here, I'm not totally sure, the only reason which makes any sense to me is that we have been a nuisance, to a greater or lesser degree, to someone or something, who wants us out of their way.'

If he had said anything to shock his audience, it was not apparent, all eyes were on him, giving him their undivided attention, and he felt uneasy at the deference shown.

'Why we have been sent to this desolate place, I can only guess at. Maybe it was all they could find, or perhaps their thinking was that we would be so preoccupied with survival we wouldn't have the time or inclination to try to do anything about it. One thing is for sure, all our minds have been tampered with, such that we can't recall anything from the time before our arrival. I, and a few others are fortunate, or unfortunate, depending upon your view point, in that a little of our past is leaking through the barrier they have created, and our memories are returning, bit by bit. The more we try to remember, the better it gets, so don't be afraid to try to recall the past, it could help in our survival.

'I suspect that Nan's theory about the Great Lights may be implanted, just to cause confusion, so please don't blame him totally for his ideas, I'm sure he meant well. Do you have any questions?'

After a very long silent pause, someone hesitantly asked,

'Where is this place, I mean, what is this place?'

Sandy took a deep breath, marshalling his racing thoughts,

'It's the crater of a vast volcano, far bigger than any I have ever heard of, so I assume it must be on another world to the one I came from. Why it is filled with sand, I don't know, that too is something I've never heard of before. I think there is a way out of this hell hole, and that is what Ben and I have been trying to find out. If we can find a means of escape to a better place, you will all be given the chance to join us.

'From the things we have found out so far, I think this place has been modified to accommodate us, like a prison.'

Comprehension could be seen dawning on several faces as they digested what Sandy had just said, adding it to what some of them had worked out for themselves.

'What I find most astonishing,' Sandy continued, 'is the high level of population in the crater. If the whole rim is as densely populated as the area around this part, and we have no reason to suppose otherwise, then it amounts to a very large number of people, and if that is the case, then the probability of this being a prison complex of some sort, is reinforced to the degree of almost being a certainty.

'This raises another point, they, whoever they are, will have made it very difficult for us to get away from here, so don't expect to escape immediately, it will take time to find an escape route, and probably longer to find somewhere to go to. If you have no further questions,

I suggest we finish our meal. You are all welcome to come to me at any time if you have questions, and I will keep you informed of our progress.' Sandy sat down, to a round of applause, which made him feel even more uncomfortable.

Mop came to the rescue with a bowl of hot stew, the aroma from which reminded him of how hungry he was.

'Ben, perhaps you could find someone who would be suited to looking after Nan, we can't just leave him to his own devices. The poor old sod's cracked up at last, and we owe him at least that.' Ben agreed to attend to it right after the meal, as Nan was now tucking into his food as if nothing had happened.

'What's next on the agenda?' asked a bloated Ben, who had cajoled Mop into giving him a generous second helping.

'I think the tunnel in your storeroom, the one we found today won't get us anywhere, as interesting as it is.' Sandy was more concerned with a good night's sleep after his meal.

Word about the group's new found fame must have spread around the crater faster than the proverbial bush fire, for by next morning they had received three requests for flame-throwers, five for new clothes, and Mop had two suitors from a neighbouring group who could not even speak her language.

This caused a great deal of amusement to those present, as the overtures had to be passed to her by way of an interpreter, who found the whole thing a great embarrassment.

She declined the offer as gracefully as she could, being quite content with her relationship with Sandy, although it was a little one-sided.

The rejected suitors were astonished at her rejection, as within their group they were considered to be the most desirable of men, despite their ragged clothing and the accompanying aroma of unwashed bodies.

Nan seemed his old self again, much to everyone's amazement. He went about the complex issuing orders which no one took any real notice of, but what was more surprising, he seemed oblivious to the lack of compliance.

Once the morning meal was over, Sandy and Ben went down to the storeroom to continue their exploration of the tunnel they had discovered in one corner of the cave.

Ben had enlarged the entrance a little, so that they were able to enter the passage with ease, and now they had the oil lamps, further penetration of the upward sloping tunnel could be attempted.

They had left word with Mop of their intentions, just in case anything went wrong, being mindful of the upset caused on the previous day by not doing so.

With the lamps refuelled, a spare container of oil, one of water, and some strips of dried meat, they were ready.

On their last exploration of the tunnel, they had only been able to go up the slope for a few metres, as the light from the gas lamp in the cave soon faded out. Now they could clearly see the surface of the walls, and both agreed it was a natural tunnel, caused by the flow of molten lava.

Some twenty metres in, and the tunnel began to shrink in size, causing them to bow their heads, and then the surface texture changed.

'Look at that,' Sandy said, pointing to obvious tool marks on the wall, 'someone has enlarged this section, so there must be something of interest here to go to all that trouble.'

Their enthusiasm was soon dashed, when they were faced by a blank wall a few metres ahead.

'It can't be completely blocked off,' Ben ventured, 'otherwise there wouldn't be that faint draft we noticed earlier, so the air's getting through somewhere.' They searched for the suspected hole, but found only solid rock.

'This whole thing is artificial,' Sandy announced confidently, 'it looks as if a wall has been built across the tunnel, and the surface of the blocks fused to make them look like natural rock. We should be able to break through.'

They had to return to the storeroom to retrieve a metal bar and something to hit it with, and it was two days later before they managed to break through the barrier completely.

It took them only a short time to find a weak spot in the wall, the metal bar suddenly going through into free air, and as this indicated the continuance of the passage, it supplied the necessary encouragement to drive them on.

Sandy later admitted, if they had not made the early break- through, he would probably have given up after the first day, as the wall was so difficult to break into, appearing to be solid rock, and therefore the natural end of the tunnel.

It took a little time to distribute the rubble evenly along the tunnel, as the blockage had been thicker than they expected and there was little room to spare in this cut section of the tunnel anyway.

At the evening meal, they casually announced that a new passage had been found, and was in the process of being cleared. No one seemed particularly interested in the discovery at the time, and they hoped they would be left on their own to continue the exploration.

Having cleared the blockage, the passage continued on in a straight line for some distance, gradually rising, and then gently curving away to the left and levelling out.

The pair trudged on for some time, and Ben had just announced that it was getting a bit boring when a split appeared up ahead. One branch turned sharply to the left and went downwards, the other continuing straight ahead.

'Let's go ahead,' Sandy suggested, 'and if we find nothing of interest, we'll come back and try the other one.' Ben agreed, and they continued, the tunnel now having widened considerably, giving them room to walk side by side.

As they strode along, looking for any abnormalities in the passage walls, they talked about Nan, and the strange attitude he had adopted once Sandy began showing an interest in the complex, Ben pointing out that it had all happened only when Sandy had appeared on the scene.

So engrossed were they in their conversation, they failed to notice the patch of light ahead of them.

'Stop,' Sandy whispered, placing a restraining hand on Ben's arm, 'there's something glowing up there.'

'It's not like our lights, it's too white.' Ben said softly, and Sandy could feel the tension grow in Ben's arm as his imagination ran riot.

'It's not moving, so perhaps it's not a lamp like ours,' Sandy added, trying to remain calm, 'let's go on a bit further, carefully.'

Another twenty metres and it became obvious that it was the wall of the tunnel which was awash with light, a slight bend obscuring the source.

'I think we've reached the other side of the rim,' Sandy announced, relief clearly sounding in his voice, 'it looks like sunlight, it's far too bright for a lamp.'

Slowly the pair rounded the bend, and had to shield their eyes against the brilliant glare which confronted them.

The tunnel opened out onto a wide ledge, and ahead was the open sky, the harsh glare of the naked sun had warmed the rock, and they could feel the radiated heat washing over them as they squinted their eyes, trying to get used to the sudden increase in light level.

The ledge protruded from the side of the volcanoes outer wall like a huge lip, giving the pair a good view of the surrounding rock walls, and the towering cliffs above them.

'Why aren't we being burnt by the sun?' asked Ben, hesitant to go too far out onto the ledge. 'By now it would be lethal in the crater.'

'If you look up, you'll see the rim of the crater shields us from the direct sunlight, otherwise we'd be cooked.'

As their eyes got used to the unaccustomed glare of pure sunlight, they looked down, and were in for another shock.

'Good God, what's that?' exclaimed Ben, looking down over the ledge to a great sea of white mist.

'Those are clouds, which makes me wonder just how high up we are.' answered Sandy, awe struck at the magnificent sight of the cloud covered world below them, the occasional rocky up-thrust looking like black fingers pointing skywards.

'What do you think is down there,' asked Ben, 'beneath all that cloud?'

'Don't know for sure, but it could be a world like the one I can remember bits of sometimes. You know the plants Bell grows? I get a hazy memory of plants like that, only much, much bigger, and covering the ground for as far as you can see. There are things called trees, which grow up to a height of twenty metres or more, and some of them have fruit on them, like the berry bushes Bell grows.' Sandy looked wistful, recalling shadowy fragments of a better life from long ago, but unable to hold the pictures long enough for them to become real.

'Do you think it might be worth trying to get down there,' asked Ben, 'and if so, how? There's no track leading off this ledge, and it's a hell of a long way down just to the clouds, so I doubt we'd be able to climb down.'

'I think the only way down to real ground level is through the tunnels within the volcano. If we can't make it that way, I doubt we'll ever get there, we're just too high up.' Sandy sounded disappointed that the opening into the world he suspected of being there only gave a frustrating glimpse of what might be, and certainly no easy access. 'We'd best get back and try the other tunnel, at least it's going downwards.'

They refilled their oil lamps, took a drink of water, and when their eyes had got used to the gloom of the tunnel, made their way back to the junction they had passed earlier.

'We'll go down for a while, just to see what's there, and if it looks promising, we'll return again tomorrow for a full exploration.' Sandy announced.

'Sounds good to me,' Ben answered cheerfully, 'we'll need a lot of supplies if we are going right down to the bottom, that's if it goes that far.'

The slope down was quite gentle to begin with, and then it steepened considerably, the tunnel walls glistened in the flickering lamp light, indicating that it was a natural passage formed by lava flow, long ago. Every so often, there were cut marks, evidence that the natural tunnel had narrowed, and had then been enlarged to accommodate whatever it was that had needed to travel this way.

Going downwards was relatively easy, and the pair quickly covered a considerable amount of ground. Realizing that it would be a long haul back up to the junction, Sandy called a halt to their exploration, suggesting they return to base, and perhaps put together a team for the next day.

As it might take a long time to reach the bottom and return, a considerable amount of provisions would need to be taken, Ben reasoned that once half the supplies had been consumed, they would have to turn back if they didn't want to die from dehydration or exhaustion.

It was a very tired couple of travellers who finally stumbled into the main cavern, just before Mop came bouncing in with her latest offering for the evening meal. What surprised them was the amount of time which had passed since they had set out that morning.

Everyone wanted to know what had happened, until someone said, 'Let 'em eat first, for God's sake!'

Nan, sat at the table staring straight ahead with a bemused look on his face, his eyes completely out of focus. A minder had been appointed to attend to his daily needs, as he seemed incapable of doing anything for himself now, which included feeding him at meal times.

Once the meal was over, and Mop's cooking pot had been emptied, everyone looked at Sandy and Ben expectantly, none daring to ask after the initial rebuke.

Sandy arose to his feet, and total silence fell on the cavern, except for a muted burp, the originator receiving several dirty looks from those near him.

'We have found a way out to the other side of the crater rim, which proves that another world awaits us, if we can get down to it, that is.

The tunnel we explored comes out higher up than we are now, and we looked down on clouds, which means the actual land itself must be much lower. Another tunnel leads downwards, and we followed it for quite some way, but not far enough to reach the bottom. We think it might take us to this new land, but we can't be certain, so we'll try again tomorrow. This might take several days, so don't get worried if we don't return for a while.'

A chorus of cheers went up, together with much hand clapping and banging of the table top. When it had subsided, a lone voice asked, 'Do you think there'll be any women down there?'

'Ben and I get first choice, if there are!' Sandy retorted quickly, and Mop gave him a filthy look, grabbed her cooking pot, and stormed out of the cavern.

The rest of the evening was spent trying to answer the inevitable innumerable questions posed by the rest of the group, which illustrated their keenness to find a new home.

When Sandy finally retired to his cave, Mop had got over her fit of peek, and welcomed him with open arms, literally.

Early next day, before the morning meal, provisions were being put together, and an extra two personnel were added to the exploration team. Greg was the first choice, although Sandy really had little option other than to ask him, as he had been following them around the previous evening like a well trained gun dog, and certainly did not intend to be left out of the venture, if he could help it.

The other newcomer to the team was Kel, his general handiness qualifying him above all others, although Ben was a little doubtful of his quiet and sometimes truculent nature.

Karry volubly expressed her opinion as no women were included in the project, and was pacified to some extent by the argument that women were in short supply, and considered to be far too valuable to risk on such a venture.

The level of excitement and anticipation had risen to fever pitch by the time they had all assembled for the early morning meal, and for once voices enthusiastically overwhelmed the normal clatter of spoons on bowls, and the usual ribald comments on Mop's cooking, although of late it had improved greatly.

The meal over, everyone crammed into the passage outside Ben's store cave to give the adventurers a good send off, while Mop did her best to hide the odd tear, fearful that her chosen man may not return.

As the heel of the last person to enter the small opening into the tunnel disappeared, someone gave a cheer, and everyone else joined in, feeling that something should be done, and not knowing what else to do.

Once inside the main tunnel, Sandy gave orders that they would go in single file, everyone to be on the lookout for anything unusual, which left the two new members of the team a little confused, as to them the whole thing was unusual in the extreme. Each member had been supplied with an oil lamp, spare oil, water, and dried meat strips, and each carried a coil of cord and a metal rod to use as a defensive weapon, should the need arise.

Mop had assembled a mixture of plant based food for their first meal, but she only received a perfunctory thanks for it, as they were all too preoccupied with the coming adventure.

They made speedy progress to the point where the passage split in two. Sandy suggested that they all take a look at the cloud layer below from the ledge, as they were unlikely to see anything like it again if they ever managed to reach the new world he felt so sure existed below.

'We'll stand in the bright light just inside the opening, until our eyes get used to the glare, it's very bright out there.'

The two new members of the team experienced vertigo for the first time, and Ben was not the happiest of men as he bravely stood on the very edge of the precipitous drop to the swirling silver mists below.

'Below that cloud is what I think will be a world in which we could live, if we can get to it, and that's what this expedition is all about, finding a way down through the crater rim. As you can see, there's no way we could climb down, it's too sheer in places, and where it's not, the rocks look slippery. Our only chance is to find an internal route that's safe, and we've found one which takes us quite a long way down, but we didn't have time to complete it.'

They had to wait for a while back in the tunnel for their eyes to get used to the feeble light from their lamps before going on to the junction, and then they began the long journey downwards.

The steepness of the incline varied as they went along, and Sandy pointed out where the passage walls had been cut at some time in the past to make them the same width as the main natural passage, which had been brought into existence by molten lava flow, when the volcano was active.

Greg asked for an explanation of what lava was, and how the tunnels had been formed, which caused Sandy to dig deeply into his past for the answers, and in doing so, released large amounts of blocked off memory.

Judging time was difficult, so they let their stomachs indicate when a meal break was called for. This of course differed for each individual, and so Sandy had to make an arbitrary judgement when they would stop for food.

A little later, they came to a section where the tunnel had been opened out to form a small cave, part of which was like a natural bubble in the surrounding rock.

'Time to eat, and take a little water. Everyone feeling fit?' Sandy asked, as any sprain or injury could jeopardize the project at a later time. All reported feeling well, but Sandy suspected that any little injuries sustained would easily be masked by the general enthusiasm to get on with the journey.

It was a pity Mop had not been present to hear the acclamations for her food packages, spiced as they were with the new sweet herbs, only recently grown large enough to be harvested from the seedlings Bell had acquired during an exchange of goods.

Ben made much of the fact that Sandy's portion was much larger than anyone else's, which brought forth the usual ribald comments, and laughter echoing up and down the tunnels, dissipating the tension which had quietly built up.

The meal break over, they continued their journey ever downwards, some sections being very steep and long. This caused the travellers to become more tired than they expected, largely due to the excessive use of muscles which normally only had to cope with short periods of the downward slopes in their home tunnels.

It was at the end of a particularly long downwards incline that Kel announced 'the journey back up was going to be a right pain in the basic orifice.' This caused Sandy to reassess the point in their rations depletion which would indicate when they should begin the return journey.

His original decision had been to return when nearly half the rations had been consumed, irrespective of whether they had achieved their goal or not, but now this was changed to a return when one third of the rations had been consumed, so allowing a small safety margin for unforeseen circumstances.

A level section of the tunnel cheered everyone up, although it added little to their objective of reaching the bottom of the crater, but was a welcome break for aching muscles.

Rounding a bend in the passage, Ben, who had been leading for a while, raised his hand, and they all stopped. Ahead, the tunnel walls had changed from the familiar rock to one of metal; a long dull grey tube stretched off into the distance.

The lamps were too feeble to show how long the tube was, but all agreed they felt more than a little uneasy about it.

'It has obviously been constructed to transport people over something they could not otherwise have crossed,' Sandy said, to allay the fears they all felt, 'so it should be safe enough. I suggest we go across one at a time, and signal with a lamp when the other side is reached.'

No one volunteered to be the first to attempt the crossing, so Sandy took the lamp with the flexible reflector, and walked out onto the metallic floor of the tube, dramatizing a bravery he did not feel. The sound of his footsteps echoed loudly, adding a surrealistic atmosphere to the already strange scene, the light from his lamp gradually fading until it was only just visible in the distance, and then it was gone.

Everyone waited with bated breath for the light to reappear, signalling that he had safely reached the other end, but it failed to show. Ben suggested they wait for a while, and then someone else should go across to see what had happened, but there was no consensus for his proposal.

Ben was just about to announce that he would go across next, when a faint glimmer of light bobbed up and down in the far reaches of the tunnel.

'There you are, he's safe and signalling us, I'm going over now.' And with that he strode off, disappointed at the lack of feeling the others had for their leader.

Sandy met him about halfway across the long echoing tube,

'What happened?' Sandy asked, 'I've been waving my lamp for ages, thought you'd all gone home.'

Ben explained, but Sandy made light of it. 'I'll leave my lamp here,' he said, waving it up and down, 'and we'll go on, there's something I want to show you.'

Ten metres further on and Sandy slowed his brisk pace,

'There's a section of the tube floor which is transparent, and you'll not believe what's below us. Don't worry, we're quite safe, it just looks worse than it really is.'

A section of the floor had been replaced with a glass like substance for some two metres, and a dull red glow could be seen lighting it up from below.

'Bloody roll on,' exclaimed Ben, who had dropped to his knees, and crawled forward to peer into the transparent section of the floor. A fiery lake of molten rock bubbled and boiled some hundreds of metres beneath them, sending long streamers of liquid rock high into the air, which then fell back to create yet more splashes of fluid light.

'You can see why they built this tube,' Sandy said, not at all fazed by the incredible spectacle below, 'it's the only way to cross this huge pit. If you look at the sides, you'll see great cracks going back a long way into the surrounding rock, so a curving passage around this lot would be too long.'

Ben knelt there, seemingly hypnotized by the awesome spectacle of nature in the raw.

'Come on,' Sandy said gently, 'the others will be along soon, that's if they can get the nerve up to enter the tube.'

'That's the most incredible sight I've ever seen,' exclaimed Ben, still reeling from the shock of seeing so much raw energy below him, 'why doesn't the tube melt in such tremendous heat?'

'For one thing, notice the air flow through the tube, that will take away a fair amount of heat, and I expect it is made from material which is designed to withstand it anyway.

'Quite something, isn't it? There must have been a very good reason to construct such a thing in the first place, that's why I'm sure we can reach this other world below the volcano base, there has to be something important there.'

They waited at the tube end for the others to come across, and in time they did, visibly shaken from having to walk across the transparent section with the molten fires below.

'Come on, gentlemen, we've a long way to go yet.' Sandy set off again down the tunnel, his lamp sending sparkles of light back from the crystalline structures in the fused rock of the walls, reminding them of the enormous powers the volcano once had, hoping it was now in its sleeping stage.

Another meal break, and the rations were looking sadly depleted, but they had not yet reached the critical quantity which would herald a return to the world above.

A rock fall held them up for some time, as the rubble had to be passed back along the passage to be distributed evenly along the walls, so as not to impede the progress of those who would hopefully follow them in time.

The tunnel suddenly swung to the right, and a patch of light shone on one side of the wall. They slowed down, not too sure of what to expect, so Sandy took the lead once more, guessing what it was, but saying nothing.

As they neared the light, Ben suddenly remembered the external ledge they had found earlier, and eagerly joined Sandy as he strode ahead towards the outside world.

This time, the lip of rock was of immense proportions, jutting out over a forest below, and giving a good view of the vast towering cliffs of rock which disappeared into the clouds above.

As the four of them stood there, gazing out over a sea of greenery, something brightly coloured glided down past the ledge and into the trees below.

'What was that?' asked Greg, stepping back from the edge.

'That's a ... Bird.' Sandy replied, not too sure if he was right, and then the pictures from his past came flooding back in. 'Yes, it's a bird, a creature which can fly through the air by flapping its wings. That means there are insects down there, and probably other creatures too. I knew I was right, there had to be something other than that bloody crater, and this is it. Somehow, we must get down there.'

Sandy went to the edge of the lip, and dropped onto all fours to safely peer over at the tangle of growth below.

'If we have to, we could get down using ropes, although I don't think those we have would be long enough. We may be able to get down to a ledge as a group, and then go on down in stages. Trouble is, I can't see the ground, and I've no idea how tall those trees are.'

'The tunnels may go on down to ground level,' Ben suggested, 'and that would be a lot easier for the others. I can't see some of them shinning down a rope, no matter what's at the bottom.'

'Right, that's settled then, we go on down. It doesn't look too far, so we should be able to do it before the food runs out and we have to turn back.'

They all trooped back into the tunnel and waited for their eyes to get used to the gloom before beginning the last stage of their journey to a new life.

They had gone but a few metres, when Sandy stopped.

'Just realized something. The tunnel didn't split in two as it did up above, so where's the one we need leading down?'

In the dim lamp light, they looked at each other in horror, neither wanting to admit they had been thwarted, as the tunnel they had just come down was the only one in sight.

'There must be a way down,' Sandy said in desperation, 'it's just that we haven't found it yet.'

They stood there for a while, undecided what to do, all looking at Sandy to come up with a solution to the problem.

'There's nothing for it, we'll have to go back up again, and then use ropes from the ledge if we want to reach ground level.' Sandy was more disappointed than he let himself sound, suspecting that the drop down from the ledge using ropes was likely to be more difficult than it sounded.

They had gone but a few metres, with little enthusiasm, when Ben let out a yell, and everyone jumped.

'Look there, a tunnel has been partially blocked off, and it's coming in at an angle, that's why we didn't see it on the way down.' Ben was jubilant at his discovery.

Sure enough, there was another tunnel, cutting in at an obtuse angle, and the entrance was partly blocked with broken stone, not sealing it off, but disguising its presence from anyone coming down the main tunnel.

Eager hands removed the stone blocks, laying them in neat rows along the passage walls until the opening was fully exposed.

'Do we go down there? asked Kel.'

'You bloody bet we do!' Sandy instantly responded.

The passage curved around, so that before long it was evident that it was in line with the main one they had come down earlier, although no one could suggest a reasonable explanation for the deceptive junction.

The incline was not so steep that a safe fast walk could not be maintained, and the group marched on, chatting and making the odd joke as the metres sped by.

Sooner than they expected, a change took place. The tunnel opened out into a large square cavern, around the sides of which a stone ledge ran, encompassing a large pool of water.

They went all around the cavern looking for a continuation of the passage, but found nothing. The side facing the tunnel entrance had no ledge, so their attention was drawn to this as it was different to the other three sides of the chamber.

'I think we've reached ground level,' said Sandy, confidently, 'and this looks like a dock, something a ship goes into to discharge its cargo.'

The others looked puzzled at the strange words, so he explained, and in doing so, his memory of docks and ships came back from the deep past.

'Do you think that end wall without the ledge, is a kind of door,' asked Ben, trying to rationalize the scene, 'something which could be lifted or moved to one side?'

'It looks like solid stone to me,' Greg answered, 'but I see what you mean. If the water continues on the other side, then I would expect there to be some means of opening it.'

'We don't know if it does.' Kel added, sounding nervous, as he wondered what they would be asked to do next.

'I've got an idea,' said Sandy, 'put all the lamps in a group facing up the tunnel, and then carefully make your way back to the ledge here.' A tinkling clatter echoed around the chamber, and the light dimmed to a pale glow.

Scuffles and grunts indicated that the various members of the team were moving towards the ledge on their hands and knees, none wishing to unsuspectingly step off into water of unknown depth. Not that they could exactly remember what might happen to them if they did, but certain survival instincts were well able to survive the mind blocks which had been imposed on the unfortunate inhabitants of the crater.

'Let your eyes get used to the dark, and if I'm right, you'll be in for a surprise.' Sandy made it sound more like a children's outing than one of survival, realizing that his men would respond far better to an emergency if tension was kept to a minimum.

Greg was the first one to notice the light seepage coming in under the end wall of rock, a very pale glow of green adding an eerie touch to the jet black of the main body of water.

'So it looks as if the water continues on the other side of that wall,' said Sandy, a satisfied tone in his voice, 'who's going to volunteer to swim under it and find out?'

The ensuing silence was only broken by the occasional drip of water from some place high up in the roof into the pool below, there were no volunteers, not that he really expected there to be any. The longer they stood there, the more their eyes got used to the darkness and the brighter the glow from the outside world grew.

'There must be some way out,' Sandy stated, returning to the lamps, 'all we've got to do now is find it.'

They scoured the walls of the cavern for clues, but they were just solid rock, cut smooth and square by some machine they could hardly imagine. It was Kel who solved the mystery, by tripping over a bar of stone and falling flat on his face, emitting some expletives which made Sandy wince.

They had to re-light his lamp, which had gone out in the tumble, and then attention was turned to what had caused the accident.

Although it looked like stone, Greg insisted it was metal made to look like it, the ensuing argument being purely academic, although somewhat heated. It was when Ben tried to lift one end of the block that they were all in for a surprise. It was hinged at one end, and came up quite easily, accompanied by the sound of rushing water, and the whirling of gears.

Slowly the level of water in the cavern dropped, only just perceptibly at first, but quickening as the gears ground out their music.

Several minutes later, the gears were still, the water all but gone, and strong sunlight flooded into the boxlike recess in the cavern floor.

'Well I'll be ...' Sandy never got to finish the sentence, as the scream of some creature in its death throws shattered the silence, making them all jump.

'Well, there's life out there.' said a nervous sounding Kel, not at all sure he wanted to join it.

Now that the water had gone, they could see a ramp, and next to it a flight of steps cut into the rock leading to the bottom of the pool. Sandy was the first down, warning the others that it was a bit slippery, and then he walked across the floor of the pool, shielding his eyes as he entered the blaze of light which flooded in under the end wall of the cavern.

Soon, all four were outside. The light level, while bright, was considerably less than what they had experienced on the high ledge on the crater rim, and they stood staring in disbelief at what they saw.

The water had drained away through a hole in the base of the vast trough, exposing another flight of steps and a ramp leading up to the level ground beyond.

What Sandy referred to as grass, fringed the now empty pool casement, and continued for some distance before it was supplanted by low bushes, and behind them tall trees gently waved in a light breeze.

'Bell wouldn't believe this,' Kel remarked, turning this way and that, trying to take it all in, 'it makes her little growing tubs look a bit puny, just look at the quantity of greenery.'

'I think I know what that pool was all about,' said Sandy after a while, 'it's a water trap, a means of stopping anything out here getting into our world, although I can't think why they bothered. No creature with any survival instincts would venture very far up those tunnels, not in complete darkness, and with no food.'

Just then, another screech rent the still perfumed air.

'We must stay together, in a close bunch until we know what is making those noises.' Sandy said, a slight shake in his voice.

'I think we should be more aware of the creature which is causing the other one to make those noises.' Ben corrected, and they nervously giggled at his quick riposte.

'Careful as you climb these steps, they're slippery, and we don't want any broken bones.'

One by one they mounted the steps out of the trough, and stood for the first time on the soft springy grass of a new world. It seemed quiet and peaceful enough, but the ghostly echoing screech of a creature in pain still rang in their ears, prompting caution as they spread out a little, taking in the unbelievable view of paradise.

'One thing's for sure,' Sandy noted, 'the temperature down here is reasonably stable, otherwise the plants wouldn't survive, so it'll be a lot more comfortable for us.'

Kel had moved away from the rest of the group, and was looking down through an avenue of small trees, craning his head this way and that, as though something had attracted his attention, but he did not wish to get any closer to it.

'What have you seen?' asked Ben, trotting over to him, his pointed metal rod held at the ready.

'Looks like something on four legs, eating the grass or small plants at the base of that ... tree, I think Sandy called it.' The plump grey elongated shape looked up, sniffing the air with its trunk-like nose.

'It's seen us!' Kel said, louder than he intended, and the creature immediately swung its head in their direction, fixing its gaze on the pair with its two large brown eyes.

By now the other two had joined them, pointed rods at the ready, wondering whether to fight, or run to the sanctuary of the water trough, not that it would give much protection now the water had drained away.

Slowly, as if it had all the time in the world, the creature ambled towards them, its long snout waving from side to side, sampling the air, trying to make sense of the strangers in its domain.

'I don't think we need to worry,' Sandy said calmly, 'it's a herbivore, something which eats plants, so it's not likely it'll try to make a meal of us. If it was going to attack, it would charge at us. I think it's just curious, so if we hold our ground, it'll probably have a look, and then walk away.'

As the creature drew nearer, they realized it was a lot bigger than they had first thought, the body standing at their shoulder height, and nearly three times as long.

'Are you sure it's harmless?' quavered Greg's voice, faintly from behind the group.

'Yes.' Sandy replied, but he was beginning to doubt his own judgement as the creature came even closer.

Ready to stab with their pointed rods and then flee, the group stood firm, more from indecision than reason, while the grey beast with the long snout lowered its cropping and sense organ to gently brush against Sandy's hair, inhaling as it did so.

Taking one more step forwards, the creature gently rubbed its head against Kel's shoulder a couple of times, and then backed off two paces, its soft brown unblinking eyes watching them all the time.

'It's either got an itch, or it's making overtures to you,' Sandy whispered, trying to lessen the tension, 'I don't think it'll harm us.'

Much to the surprise of the others, Ben stepped forward and ran his hand up across the creature's face, and down the long nose, using a scratching action when he felt the creature lean in his direction.

'You're right,' he said quietly, 'it just wants a scratch.'

The docility of the creature had lowered their guard, but not for long. A rustling in the bushes just ahead caused them to tense up again, as a pear shaped nightmare on two sturdy legs crashed through into the clearing. Two short clawed arms reached forward from below an elongated head equipped with an impressive double row of teeth, emitting a deep hiss.

The group would have stood little chance against such a large and ferocious carnivore, and luckily for them, they had no need to, as the grey herbivore swung around and placed itself between the group and the attacker.

As the attacker advanced, the herbivore straightened its long trunk, pointing it straight at the hideous fanged face.

A series of ripples raced up the herbivore's body, culminating in one huge convulsion, and a jet of steaming liquid left the trunk, hitting the attacker square in the face, some of the liquid going down its throat.

The attacker skidded to a stop, convulsed, and brought up a huge quantity of red meat which lay steaming on the bright green grass.

The body heaved several more times, but there was nothing else to bring up.

It then staggered a couple of times, trying to regain its balance, turned, and headed back the way it had come, throwing up earth and sods of grass as it accelerated away.

The herbivore had already begun to eat again, the long snout selectively picking out the choicest morsels from the mixture of plants which fringed the grassy glade.

'God, what a defence mechanism.' said Greg, still shaking.

'And bloody effective, too.' Sandy added.

Ben had left the group, and walked up to the herbivore, lightly stroking it's smooth grey head. The trunk swung up and around, gently touched Ben's head, and returned to plucking up its food.

Sandy sensed that Kel was about to make one of his usual quips, and put a restraining hand on his arm, noting the glint of a tear in Ben's eyes as he left the creature. Ben had been more deeply moved by the incident than any of them had realized.

'I think it's time we had a break too,' Sandy said, to ease the tension which had built up again, 'I'm hungry enough to try some of those plants myself.'

They moved back to the safety of the water trough, and sat down on the soft grass verge.

After chewing on the dried meat strips and several drinks of water later, they all felt better. Ben suggested that they try to find a supply of water to replenish their much depleted containers for the journey back.

'I think we should explore a little more before we bring the others down here.' Sandy said. 'Although we can bring the rest of the meat strips with us, we'll need to supplement them with local food, and so far we haven't found any.'

The grey herbivore was still on the edge of the clearing, chomping away at the vegetation when they set off, and Ben somehow persuaded it to follow them, or perhaps it just wanted to go in their direction anyway.

A well worn path led upwards from the clearing towards a rise in the ground. This was adorned with a stand of tall trees, growing out of a jumble of rocks, and as this would give them a view point to survey the local area, they headed for it, crossing a small stream on their way.

Kel knelt down and sampled the water before anyone could stop him, pronouncing it to be very good and sweet in taste. Sandy resolved to refill their water containers if nothing untoward had happened to Kel in the meantime.

When they reached the top of the rise, Ben climbed one of the trees to get a better view of the surrounding land, and returned to describe what he had seen, a little scratched for his troubles. 'It would seem we're in a valley, one end of which is blocked off by the high cliffs of the volcano, and the other by a sudden drop in ground level, and hemmed in by thick forest on either side. There are several rises in the ground like this one, some have rocks on them and they all have a clump of trees. Anyone else want to go up?' The cuts and scratches he had sustained in his climb, put the others off for a time.

Although several trees sported fruits dangling from their branches, and most bushes had berries of one kind or another, they were unable to tell if any were safe to eat, as they bore no resemblance to anything Bell grew in her boxes.

Kel said he would try to devise a means of testing the fruits and berries, but at the moment could not think of a way other than to try them, albeit in small quantities. Sandy forbade eating anything which they had not brought with them, until some method of safe testing could be devised.

After some examination and discussion, it was agreed that the tracks were made by the local animal life, and not by invisible human inhabitants, as there were no signs of human activity, such as cut trees or signs of cultivation.

Accompanied by their newly found friend, they eventually made their way to the edge of the valley floor where it dropped away sharply to another valley below, clothed in much the same vegetation, but much larger in area.

'We could get down there if we tried,' said Ben, 'there are one or two places where we'll have to use ropes, but it's not too bad.'

'Don't see the point, at the moment.' Sandy replied, looking out over the vast expanse of forest below. 'All we need to do at the moment is to establish that this area can support us for a while, and that we don't get eaten in the meantime. Anyway, have you noticed it's getting a bit duskish? I think we'd better retire to the area of the water trap for the night, and get some rest.'

They made their way back to the haven of the water trap, followed by their newly acquired friend who stopped every now and again to sample a particularly tasty morsel, and then made the ground shake with its considerable mass as it hurriedly lumbered along to catch them up again.

Greg and Kel found some slate-like stones, and scraped the steps clear of the silt deposit, so making them safe for speedy access, should the need arise, while the other two went inside to recharge the oil lamps, one of which had been left burning.

As night fell, they were surprised to find there was little difference in atmospheric temperature, Sandy putting it down to the protecting layer of cloud. They remained outside with one oil lamp, until it became truly dark, and then had to retire as the lamp attracted so many flying insects, some of which seemed to sting, according to Kel.

Although it was dark, they felt no inclination to sleep, and Ben went over to the stone-like lever which had emptied the water from the trough earlier that day.

'Wonder what would happen if I pushed it back to its original position?'

'Give it a try, can't see what harm it'll do.' Sandy replied, thinking it would do nothing.

There was a clunk, and then the sound of water flowing somewhere, accompanied by the grinding of gears, as before.

Slowly the water level rose in the trough, until it was as it had been when they had arrived, and they were safely sealed in the womb of the crater against all threats from outside.

Their eyes soon got used to the darkness and the light one lamp provided, so another meal was taken, this time with plenty of water, as the stream outside had proved to be wholesome.

'If we leave our cave system, do we tell the other groups of our find?' Ben wanted to know, concerned that their numbers would dwindle in time, until only one would be left alive.

'That's something I've been thinking about for a while now,' replied Sandy, thoughtfully, 'there are pros and cons.'

'What do you mean?' Ben was not used to the term.

'There are things for and against the idea.' Sandy said. 'Have you noticed that we are all adults? There are no children, no little ones. This either means that we have been stopped from reproducing, or the environment of the crater prevents it somehow. If we can produce offspring, there's no need to bring any others into our little haven, although it seems a bit mean not to do so. But if we can't reproduce, then it might be a good idea to have a few more people down here, and leave the door open, as it were, to add others in a controlled manner, later on.'

'We'd have to be very careful how we chose them,' Ben said, remembering the attack on the complex. 'Just a few evil minded sods could wreck everything.'

'I'm well aware of that, it's going to be a difficult decision to make, but we don't have to make it just yet.'

The conversation drifted on for a while, then the stresses of the day caught up with them, and Sandy suggested they get some sleep. The idea was a good one, but they were bereft of the comfort of their rag piles, and so sleep came late that night, and when it did, it was through exhaustion.

Next day, the water trap emptied itself as soon as the lever was returned to its upright position, and they all piled out into the bright light of a new day, eyes half shut with sleepy dust, bruised from the hard rock on which they had slept, and a little colder than they would have liked.

A meal, although it was only the meat strips, cheered everyone up a little, and Ben commented that Mop's morning meal would taste like heaven right now. He received a fusillade of grass sods and small stones for his trouble.

'What do we do today?' asked Ben, when the hail of missiles had stopped.

Sandy thought for a moment, 'I think we should collect one of each fruit and berry we can find, and see if Bell can identify any of them as being safe to eat. We'll also have to find somewhere we can make into a safe place to sleep at night, a cave or rock fissure we can barricade to prevent access by anything dangerous. We could use the water trap, but it's bloody hard in there, and I don't think carrying our bed rags down is a viable proposition, because of their bulk.

'Anyway, we'll have enough to transport, and I don't suppose anyone will want to make several journeys up and down, having done it once.'

'How about if we go along the edge of the cliffs? There could be some smaller caves there, I would think. And if we find some, we could make beds of dried grass, or even some of the softer bushes,' suggested Greg. 'I think it's the size of the water trap cave that makes it so cold.' he added.

By midday, they had a considerable collection of fruits and berries, found a small cave complex, the entrance of which could be closed off without too much trouble, and had begun to clear it out. A collection of leaves, small branches which something had dragged in, and a couple of small furry four legged creatures which shot out so fast they were unable to recall exactly what they had seen, were the only occupants, as far as they knew.

A water supply, which trickled down from a small hole in one of the caves, was diverted, so that by the time they returned, the cave floor would be dry.

As the team continued to explore their new land, roaming from glade to glade, the grey herbivore joined them after a while, suddenly appearing out of the bushes and giving them the fright they needed to remind them to be vigilant at all times in this strange land.

As the day drew to its close, it was decided to spend the night in the water trap cave, as it guaranteed some degree of safety, and begin the journey back up to the crater complex after the morning meal.

The water containers were topped up from the little stream, and the oil lamps checked to make sure they were full. One lone lamp lighted the huge cavern as the team settled down for the night, all agreeing that the smelly pile of rags they normally slept on was far preferable to the cold hard stone of the water cave.

One by one, they drifted off into fitful sleep, not really feeling very refreshed when they awoke next day. A clear patch of sky allowed the sun to blaze down in its full glory for once, the water in the trough transmitting the light into the cave, lighting it up with a weird green glow.

A hurried morning meal was consumed without much interest as the team were eager to get started on the journey, despite the long haul up to the crater. A quick look around to make sure they had left nothing behind, and they began, with Ben in the lead emitting a tuneless whistle.

As they approached the ledge which looked out over their new land, it was suggested by Kel that they take one more look at the amazing sight of so much greenery, before committing themselves to the sterile drabness of the tunnels.

'I still find it hard to believe that all this could exist, and we knew nothing about it.' said Greg, gazing out over the tree tops. 'And we wouldn't have, if it hadn't been for Sandy, so let's not forget that.' Ben added.

They turned as one, and began the long pull up the first really steep incline of many yet to come, torn between staying in their green and pleasant land, and rejoining those they had left behind in the crater far above them.

Passing back through the metal tunnel over the molten lava pit had lost some of its terrors, and the team were a little more nonchalant in their approach to the transparent section which gave a good view of the fiery turmoil below.

They still marvelled at the fact that the tube remained cool despite the tremendous heat below from the liquid rock, the only really disconcerting thing being the huge span of the tube across the pit, with no visible means of support.

The continuous upward pull, especially on the longer steep sections, took its toll, and frequent breaks were called for.

Sandy had hoped to complete the journey in what he thought was one day, as they had done on the way down, but it soon became obvious that they would have to spend the night in the tunnels, if only to rest their aching muscles.

At what they estimated to be the halfway point, although no one was sure, they stopped for a meal and sleep. Even the dried meat strips tasted good, and the water, although it had been sloshed around for hours and acquired a little warmth from their bodies, was pure nectar. There were the usual grumbles about the hard rock, but these soon faded as tired bodies, pushed almost beyond their limits, went into sleep mode. The only sound in the otherwise silent tunnels was the deep snoring of Kel, who was frequently turned over in unsuccessful attempts to abate the nerve rasping noises he emitted due to a defective soft palate.

When they awoke they had no idea what part of the day it was, or even if it was still night. Ben had been the first to arise, and had refilled the lamps, polished the reflecting plates, and adjusted their wicks. They were all a bit grumpy as they set off, dolefully still chewing the remains of their dried meat strips, and looking forward to one of Mop's sumptuous stews.

Two more stops for refreshment were needed before they came to the junction which led out to the first ledge high up on the rim, where they had looked down on the clouds.

'We're nearly home now,' said Sandy, relief sounding in his voice, 'so how about we take one more look at the cloud layer? It will also give us some idea of what part of the day it is.' They turned into the tunnel leading to the ledge, too tired to argue, and caring little, as the long journey was now nearly over.

As they walked out onto the ledge, a chill wind greeted them, indicating that it was either early morning or very late evening. Ben pointed out that it must be evening, as the sunlight was well down below the crater rim behind them, and the clouds were tinged with pink, an evening colour.

They were just about to turn and enter the tunnel for the last stage of their journey, when a flash of light far out over the cloud field caught their attention.

'There it is again.' Ben pointed towards a faint flash of silver which seemed to ascend from the distant haze and then glide along just above cloud level.

'It's not coming in our direction,' Sandy said, disappointedly, 'I'll bet it's one of those bloody vehicles which drop us down here.'

The others exchanged uneasy glances, Ben afraid Sandy might want to take the craft on in a show of force, and the other two afraid he was going the way of Nan, to the land of the confused.

The speck of silver flickered out of existence, and they returned to the more mundane task of tramping the tunnels until they reached their old home caves, and a decent meal.

An undignified scramble down the last incline brought them into Ben's storeroom, and home.

Five:
The Last Exchange

THEY COULD HEAR voices as they went up the passage towards the main cave, and despite the tiredness, broke into a trot for the last few metres, and burst into the cavern.

Mop was the first to react, her ample proportions wobbling as she ran up to Sandy and threw her arms around him, sobbing.

'Thought you'd never come back,' she sobbed out at last, 'thought some awful creature down there had got you.'

The others were greeted like long lost heroes, with much back slapping and hugging, and a few not ashamed to show their tears of joy at the safe return of their comrades.

'How about some food then?' asked Sandy, when he had untangled himself from the overjoyed Mop. 'We're bloody starving.'

Mop left the cavern to fetch the cooking pot she had already prepared, glancing back twice to make sure Sandy was really there, and it was not one of her frightening dreams.

The stew, when it came, was acclaimed the best ever by the team, who received a few sideways looks from the others who had received copious amounts of it over the last few days, while Mop waited for her chosen one to return.

The team took it in turns to recount their adventure in great detail, answering questions wherever possible, but finding it difficult to describe some of what they had seen as some of the others had no recall of the past, and therefore no reference points from which to begin.

Mop disappeared for a while, and then returned with a pot of some steaming green liquid, which she poured out into their drinking bowls. After the first tentative sip, it was downed with great enthusiasm, the sweet aromatic smell of the new herbs lingering long afterwards in their meal cavern.

When they eventually went to bed, everyone fell asleep as soon as their heads hit the rags, with the exception of Sandy.

Mop was so pleased that he had returned safe and sound, that she found it difficult to express her relief, and showed it in the only way she knew how. An exhausted Sandy was totally shattered when he was finally allowed to close his eyes, and began to wonder if a celibate life was preferable after all. But then again, her cooking was very good.

The sun was high in the sky when the first members of the group at last managed to drag themselves up to the main cavern, and to their surprise were greeted by a deputation from one of the other clans from nearby.

'Our apologies for intruding into your system, but no one was about, and we wondered if any harm had befallen you.'

Greg rubbed his sore eyes, and tried to get them into focus.

'Oh, we had a bit of a bash last night, and retired rather late. We're all right, just a bit shattered, that's all. Why have you come to see us?'

'Word is about that you have developed a super weapon, something which annihilated the raiders who have been plaguing the area for some time. We would like one, we have many things to trade with, so there should be something you would like to have.'

Greg thought for a moment, Sandy was the new leader, so it was up to him to make decisions of this nature.

'There are two things I would say,' he began, 'one is that we have destroyed the raiders, and so far we haven't heard of any more, and the other is that we only have the one weapon, and no means to make another one.' He then wondered if he had said too much, and exposed them to an attack in order to retrieve the weapon for themselves. He decided he had better fetch Sandy, and let him sort it out.

Leaving the visitors in the main cavern, Greg hurried down to Sandy's cave and awoke him, shaking him roughly by what he thought was his shoulder.

'Oh, for God's sake, Mop, let me sleep,' the buried head under the rags mumbled, 'it can't be day already. Oh, it's you.' The bleary eyed Sandy raised himself on one elbow, shook his head a couple of times to clear it, and enquired,

'What's the problem?' knowing that no one would wake him up unless there was an impending catastrophe.

Briefly, Greg explained what had happened, and what he had said in response to the visitor's request.

'No great harm done. I don't suppose they would risk trying to take it from us by force, and I doubt very much they have anything we really need now. I'll go see 'em, keep 'em entertained for a while, and I'll be up.'

With that the head retired beneath the rags again, and Mop's happy smiling face emerged.

'Sod off, there's a dear,' she said sweetly, 'we'll be up shortly.' Apart from feeling a little embarrassed, Greg was annoyed that the situation should be taken so lightly, especially when he could foresee the possible dangers.

Some little while later, Sandy staggered into the main cavern, smiled around at those present, and plumped down heavily on the one remaining unoccupied section of bench.

'Greg here, has explained your mission, and my answer is much the same as his. I don't think you need to worry about any more attacks. If you're still really worried, what you could do is spread the rumour that you have acquired a similar weapon to ours, and that should deter anyone with covetous intentions on your cave system and its contents.'

'It's the women we're worried about,' the leader of the visitors said, 'we have a lot of them, and the others don't.'

Sandy and Greg found difficulty in hiding their surprise at the unexpected statement, women were few and far between in most groups, and here was one with a surplus.

'Tell you what,' Sandy said, thinking quickly, 'tell us where you are situated in the crater rim, and in the near future we may be able to do a deal. If you have more women than you feel is comfortable for the size of your group, we could do an exchange for some, that's if they would like to join us. You could sound them out on the proposal, and let us know how they feel about it.'

This satisfied the visitors, and they left feeling they had achieved something, but were not too sure what it was.

'What have you got in mind?' asked Greg, as they sat down again, waiting for the morning meal.

'Well, we don't have enough women to go around, that's if every man wants a partner when we go down to our new land, and I think most will once we get organized and life becomes a little easier. We won't need the gas weapon, and we couldn't get it down those tunnels anyway, so they may as well have it. If we can get partners for our men in exchange, I reckon that's a good deal.'

'How about telling the other groups about our new land, or do you think we should keep it to ourselves?'

'I'd thought about that. They're a mixed bunch, and some are darn right dangerous. The trouble is, most of 'em have developed strange religious beliefs which aren't based on facts or reason, and that could spell trouble. No, for the time being, I think we'll keep our discovery to ourselves, after all, our survival comes first.'

Ben nodded his acceptance of Sandy's judgement on the situation, he was usually proved right, and that was a comfort in itself.

Any further discussion of the matter was halted, as other members of the group came in for their first meal of a day which would change their lives for ever.

When all were assembled, and had had their fill of Mop's new gruel and crushed grain buns, Sandy rose to his feet.

'We had a visit from one of the other groups this morning, and it would seem they have a surplus of women, and would like our flame-thrower. I think we may be able to do a deal with them, but it depends on whether you all want a partner in our new land or not. Think about it carefully, once we are down there, there's no guarantee we will be able to return here to get more women should any of you not want a partner now, and later change your minds.'

Sandy waited for the general hubbub of voices expressing their own thoughts on the matter to die down, and continued,

'You don't have to make up your minds for a day or two, but I'll need to know before we approach the other group. Now, is there anyone who doesn't want to go down to the land we discovered? If any of you decide not to go, then you may have to join another group, just to survive. Let's have a show of hands, who doesn't want to go?'

No one physically moved, although a few pairs of eyes flickered from side to side to see if there were any dissenters.

'OK, that's settled then, we all go. I'm very glad, there are none of you whom I would wish to leave behind.'

With that, the meeting broke up, everyone going their own way to do whatever it was they had to do.

'I suggest we go down to your store and begin to sort out those things we shall need to take with us.' Sandy said to Ben, he was eager to return to the gentle warmth and greenery of the land below the volcano, he had had his fill of dark tunnels and extreme heat and cold.

Anything which could be made into a cutting tool, ropes and cords, containers of any size, and the remains of the roll of cloth, were all considered priority items.

Ben suggested that most things could be dragged along on frames, as this would amount to far more than anyone could carry as a load. Sandy liked the idea, as the frames themselves would then be another source of material.

Slowly the pile of goods selected for the new world grew, Ben being loath to leave behind some of his hard acquired treasures until Sandy suggested that they exchanged some of the unnecessary goods for items of use in their new life.

'What about that gun thing which fires out the red light?' Ben asked, curious why it had not been mentioned.

'I've got it hidden away down here,' Sandy replied, 'it's not the sort of thing you bandy about haphazardly, or others will become too reliant on its use, and thereby become weaker and less able to defend themselves.'

'Not thought of it like that,' said Ben pensively, 'but you could give the Great Lights something to remember you by, that's if they come again.'

'Oh, they'll come again, and I had initially thought along those lines, but now we have found a better life, I feel less inclined to seek vengeance. Don't forget, they're just like us, ridding their society of those who cause them problems, as we have done. At least they didn't kill us, many would have.'

'Are you sure about this 'getting rid of undesirables' idea? It seems a bit unreal to me.' Ben still felt a little uneasy at some of Sandy's ideas.

'Without a doubt, nothing else makes sense.'

It was close to the midday break when one of the group came down to the storeroom, looking tense.

'I think you'd better come up.' he said, solemn faced.

Why? What's the problem?'

'Nan's died.' The man tried to look as one should when bereft of a great person, but failed miserably. 'They are waiting for you in the main cavern.'

'Why do you think that happened?' Sandy enquired, as they left the store. 'He seemed all right yesterday, he wasn't quite with us, but he was walking around and eating.'

'Don't know, that's why we want you up there.'

There were six people in the main cavern, including Bell and Karry, some looking sadder than others. Despite his strange ways, they had known him a long time, and in the early days he had led them well.

'Tell me what happened.' Sandy asked.

'I was doing my plants,' said Bell, wiping a tear from her cheek with a grubby finger, 'when Henree, who had been looking after him, came and said he had died. So that's when I collected the others on the way here, and sent for you.'

'Where's Henree now?'

'Still with him, I think.' Bell rubbed the other cheek, adding a balancing dark streak to the other side of her face.

'Right, let's go see him.' The others stood respectfully aside as Sandy swept from the cavern, closely followed by Ben, the rest of them tagging along behind.

Nan's cave was a surprise to Sandy, who had never had reason to visit it. The walls were adorned with strange but well crafted pictures, drawn and coloured on flattened pieces of metal and pegged to cracks in the rock. Whatever had inspired the artist, it was certainly not of this world, Sandy later confided to Ben, and in his opinion, it looked as if Nan had been heading for a breakdown for some time, if the pictures were anything to go by.

Nan was lying on a rag covered raised platform, a serene smile on his face, and both arms folded across his chest.

'Tell me what happened from early this morning, Henree.'

'I took him in for the morning meal, fed him as usual, and brought him back here. He said the Great Lights were coming soon, and I jollied him along a bit, but he got angry, so I just sat over there,' and he pointed to a crude stool, 'and waited to see what he would do next.

'He just walked around the cave, looking at the pictures and mumbling as usual, and I must have dozed off. When I came to, he had opened that little box over there, and took a pinch of stuff from it, and then sniffed it up his nose. He seemed all right, so I went for a pee, and when I came back, he was lying on his bed, just like he is now,' and he pointed to the recumbent Nan, 'I thought he was asleep, 'cos he sleeps a lot now, and then I noticed he wasn't breathing.

'I lifted an eyelid, but he didn't try to blink, so I shook him, hard, but he didn't wake up, and that's when I called for you lot. I'm sorry if it's my fault, but I...'

'No, it's not your fault,' said Sandy, trying to console the distraught man, 'poor old Nan has been heading this way for some time, there's nothing you could have done to save him. It's called old age, probably helped along by that powder he took.' Sandy went across to the box on the shelf, and picked it up carefully. Gently opening the lid, he looked inside. A fine grey powder flowed like dirty water as he rocked the box back and forth.

'Anyone know what this is?' There was no reply.

Taking a small amount on his finger, Sandy touched it to his lip, letting his tongue slide across the spot. For a few seconds nothing happened, then the room swam and his eyes went out of focus.

If someone had not caught him, he would have fallen to the ground in a helpless heap. They carried Sandy across to the stool and sat him down, Ben holding him by the shoulders to make sure he stayed upright.

After a few minutes, he shook his head a couple of times, put a steadying hand on the wall, and stood up, shakily.

'The silly old sod's been taking drugs,' he exclaimed, 'that's one powerful hallucinogenic, no wonder he died.'

'What's that?' asked Ben, always eager to add to his knowledge.

'It's a compound which makes you see things which aren't really there, a bit like a dream. Trouble is, most of 'em are poisonous in the long term, and this one certainly was. Anyone know where he got it?' No one did.

'What do we normally do with a body?' Sandy asked.

'It's been a long time since anyone's died, I think we put them out on the sands in the early morning, but I'm not too sure.' Henree was visibly shaking, so Sandy put an arm around his shoulder, 'as I said, it's not your fault.'

When they had all gathered for the midday meal, Sandy made the official announcement, although word had gone around long before that, so no one looked too surprised.

'I believe it's the custom to leave the body out on the sands, unless anyone has a better idea?' The total silence indicated that no one had. 'Tomorrow morning we will take our old friend out to the sands, 'till then, he will remain in his cave so that anyone who wishes to see him may do so.

'I know he was a cantankerous old so and so towards the end, but he has led you well in his time, so let's remember him as he was, not as he is now. He was kind and helpful to me when I needed it most, and that's something I can't repay, except by trying to do as good a job as he did.'

By the time several others had stood to say their pieces, Mop was quietly sobbing away at the end of the table, Bell shed a few tears, but Karry held hers back. This made her nose run, and that was an even worse sight.

After they had all quietly dispersed, Sandy and Ben returned to the storeroom to continue their sorting of those things they would soon take down to the new land.

'You really think the Great Lights will come?' asked Ben.

'Probably, at sometime. I think it was that bloody powder he took rather than some ability to foresee the future.'

'But he knew when you were coming, he told us the night before, and next morning in you came.' Sandy just gave him a look, and carried on with the sorting.

Mop did her very best for the evening meal, but everyone was still in a sombre mood, which left her wondering where she had gone wrong.

With the meal over, everyone would normally have retired to their own caves after a while, but this night no one made a move to leave the cavern.

Sandy quietly asked what was going on, and Ben passed the query on down the table. After a bit of subdued muttering, Greg stood up, noisily cleared his throat twice, and said,

'I've been doing a survey, and all us men would like a partner to take with us when we go to our new home, and we are five women short. I know it's a bit soon after Nan's death, but we all feel we would like to make a new start.'

'That's fine by me.' Sandy replied. 'Ben and I will try to do an exchange tomorrow. I'll need two volunteers to help move the flame-thrower over to the other group, so sort it out among yourselves, we leave at first light.'

That ended the evening, and all retired to their sleeping quarters to think their own thoughts on the day's happenings.

Mop was still quietly crying when Sandy entered their cave, and he did his best to comfort her, later realizing her tears had soon stopped once they were snuggled up close.

Mop was also one not to pass up a good opportunity when it was offered.

Next morning, over their uniforms, the team of four put on the best of the now cleaned rags which had been their clothing before the uniforms had been made. Extra wrappings were bound on their feet to insulate them from the still frozen sands, and they set off, two pulling the flame-thrower on ropes, frequently changing with others to keep up a pace. They reached the group who had visited them about the exchange, just as the first signs of the coming dawn lit up the sky in bands of pale pink and orange.

The chief was called, and despite his bleary eyed appearance, it was obvious from the start that a bit of hard bargaining was about to take place, so Sandy asked for seven women in exchange for the flame-thrower.

The chief raised his hands in horror at the exorbitant price asked, but finally agreed, with great reluctance to five, which was what Sandy wanted in the first place.

The women were quite keen about the exchange, partly prompted by the smart appearance of Sandy's men in their uniforms, but mainly because that was the way nature intended things to be. The chief tried his luck again about material to make new clothes for themselves, but gave up when it was apparent there was none left, due to fluent lying on behalf of the team. The women looked more disappointed than the chief, and for a moment Sandy thought the deal might fall through, but hormones proved stronger than fashion, and they all left at top speed to beat the rising sun, and the possibility that the chief might change his mind.

They got back to base just as the first streamers of blazing sunlight cut across the high rim, and vaporized the last of the frost from the now warming sands.

There was no sign of Nan's body, just a few marks in the sand where it had been carried far out, and a disturbance where something had retrieved it. Sandy hoped the something now had crippling indigestion.

The morning meal had been held back for the returning travellers, and apart from a dirty look from Mop, they were given a great welcome as the meal was served.

Sandy grinned at the look of surprise on the new female faces when they saw what was on offer, food wise, that is, and considered they had made a good impression on the new additions to their group.

Ben was asked to briefly explain what was about to happen in the next few days, regarding the new home they would all go to, and that shortly after arrival there, they could partner up, should they wish to.

When the new women were measured up for uniforms, they showed little surprise at the magical appearance of the necessary material, and Sandy wondered why they had been able to convince the chief so easily that there was no more cloth. But Sandy was a little short on understanding women.

Two days later, the sledge frames for transporting all their worldly goods had been completed, and loaded. Ben wanted to take the pair of gas guns, but reluctantly left them behind when Sandy patiently explained that there would be no gas to load them.

The rest of the fat had been rendered down, more oil lamps made, and the rest of the considerable quantity of dried meat strips carefully packed for the journey. All they needed now was a good omen, and they got it next morning.

No one slept too well that night, as the anticipation level of what would happen next day being so high. In the early hours of the morning, Sandy was rudely awakened from his fitful slumbers by an over exuberant Ben.

'Come quickly, I think the Great Lights are coming, there's something up in the sky, and it's too early for the sun.'

They raced up to the entrance of the complex, regretting their imprudent haste when the bitter cold of the crater's air hit them, and threatened to freeze their nostrils solid.

'Look, up there.' Ben pointed to a spot high up in the heavens. Sunlight glinted off something metallic, and it was moving. 'See, I told you.'

'Just shut up and watch.' Sandy retorted, regretting his harshness almost immediately.

The tiny speck of light slowly drifted downwards towards the crater, and then was no more.

'Oh, it's gone.' said Ben, sounding disappointed.

'No it hasn't,' Sandy replied, 'look just below where you saw it last, the stars are being blanked out by something, and it's still coming down.'

The great ship lowered itself into the crater, and fifteen metres from the frozen sands it stopped, hovering, the huge black shape being hardly discernible from the dark rock.

Twin beams of light lanced down to illuminate the sand beneath, and something slowly drifted down from between them, tumbling over and over as it descended.

'My God, that ship's big.' Sandy exclaimed, as the back wash of light off the sand lit up the outline of the vessel.

'Some poor sod's been dumped.' he muttered, recalling his own experience of not so long ago. 'I hope they get to him before he freezes solid.'

'I expect they will if they have a Nan like we had.' Ben said thoughtfully.

Having deposited its cargo on the crater floor, the twin lights went out, and the great ship silently rose up, accelerating away sharply, soon just another moving star, and then it was gone.

'How did you know it would come?' asked Sandy, aware of his shivering for the first time.

'I remembered what Nan said, and thought this would be the last chance to see it.' Ben replied through chattering teeth. 'I'm glad I did, now I know what you said was true.' he added as an after thought.

'I don't think we'll tell the others about this,' Sandy suggested, 'it'll only start another argument, and we don't want that this morning.'

'I agree,' Ben replied, 'they're not scientific like us.' Sandy grinned to himself, yes, Ben was coming along just fine.

They hurried down to Mop's kitchen, the warmest place in the complex, and a chance for an extra portion of food.

'What got you up so early?' she asked, giving Ben a wink which only confused him.

'Ah, things to do,' Sandy answered cheerfully, 'how about a little snack to keep us going?' playfully giving her a sharp slap on her ample rear end.

'You men are all the same, you only think of your stomachs, well, most of the time.'

A generous bowl of Mop's hot gruel and a couple of buns later, and they had almost forgotten the incident in the crater, but not quite.

'Well, the great day has dawned,' said Sandy, wiping his bowl with the remains of a bun, 'and I think you'll like your new home, there's plenty of plants for you to cook, and you wouldn't believe the amount of fruit and berries we've seen.'

He didn't mention the creature who had befriended Ben.

The pair went up to the main cavern to await the morning meal, and put the finishing touches to the planned great exodus. On the way up, they were approached by Bell,

'We've got enough material for the women's uniforms, in fact they're finished, but there isn't a lot left over and we'll need more to replace our own clothes someday. Can you get any more from the other groups?'

'If anyone's got any, we could, but it will mean coming back up again, what do you think Ben?'

'Don't see why not. We've still got a lot of bits and pieces in the store we don't need, we should be able to do an exchange with somebody.'

They walked on to the main cavern, joining others as they too made their way up for the morning meal.

When everyone had had their fill, Sandy outlined the plan.

'We've put all the things we shall need for our new life on frames, which we can drag down the tunnels. It's quite a long way, but we should be there by evening, or perhaps a little earlier. The route may look a bit scary in places, but it is quite safe, we've done it, with no trouble. Everyone should take their own bedding, because if we have to spend the night in the bottom cave for any reason, all you'll have to lie on is rock. Any questions?' There were none.

The event had been talked about so much, that nearly all questions had been covered, one way or another, and now they just wanted to get on with the journey.

The meeting broke up and everyone went to their respective caves, gathered their belongings, and then assembled in the main tunnel leading to the storeroom.

As each person entered, they were allotted a loaded frame on which they were instructed to tie a limited amount of their bedding rags and any other possessions they had.

Four of the stronger members of the group manhandled the frames through the now much enlarged hole leading into the beginning of the tunnel proper, and then the frame was passed on to the allotted 'puller', who took up his rope, and pulled.

How they would manage when it came to the steep down slopes, Sandy had yet to reason out, but he felt sure they could make it, one way or another.

Each frame had its own lamp attached, and this gave just enough light for them to see where they were going, once their eyes had got used to the feeble glow.

Where the tunnel widened out, just before the first ledge, Sandy explained what they had seen there, and offered anyone interested, a quick view. About half the group took up the offer, filing past the others as they made their way up to the front of the column, where Ben lead them out to view the unbelievable vast expanse of cloud below.

They got under way again, those who had viewed the unbelievable trying to tell the unbelieving about it in tunnels which amplified every sound, sending the echoes crashing back and forth, until they ended up as an unintelligible jumble of sound.

Sandy called a halt when they reached the cave they used on their first journey down, although not everyone managed to squeeze in at once. The break was welcome, as few had experienced such steep slopes before, and holding a loaded frame back from crashing into the one in front was a totally new experience. Most difficult of all was judging when to rush around to the back of the frame to hold it back, when an extra steep section was encountered.

So far, there had been no injuries, apart from a few bruised shins, and a wonderful new set of cuss words.

The metal tube crossing the lava pool proved to be more of a problem than Sandy had anticipated. Some had to be gently coerced, others sworn at copiously and then shamed into making the crossing, while a few refused point blank, and had to be physically bundled across, which did little for harmony and good will, especially as someone else then had to go back and drag the protester's loaded frame across.

However, after the next steep downward slope, and a few more bruised shins, the tube was forgotten, as more pressing matters were at hand.

Another break was called when Sandy estimated they were two-thirds the way to the bottom, and that rejuvenated flagging spirits. Getting them back on their feet again was another matter.

At long last, tired, bruised, and a little short tempered, they arrived in the main cavern of the water trap.

'Well done, everyone,' Sandy shouted, his voice echoing around the vast cave and being amplified greatly, 'we've arrived. Take a rest for a few minutes, and we'll open the water trap, then it's out into a land you won't believe!'

The last of the water was drunk, meat strips chewed, and cuts and bruises compared to see who had sustained the most damage, not that anyone really cared. They had made it.

'Now listen up,' it was Ben's turn, at Sandy's insistence, to issue instructions. 'The water trap will be opened in a moment. When all the water has gone, we'll have to manhandle the frames down the slope, and then up the other side. Please stay together when we reach the open, and wait until you are told before moving off. There is a large grey creature with a long nose down here, it is quite harmless and eats plants. It may not be here now, but just in case it is ...' He smiled his widest smile to allay any fears, he hoped.

Sandy nodded at Ben, and he went over to the stone lever, and raised it. They both enjoyed the look on the faces of the rest of the assembly as the water level fell, and was then gone, light flooding in from the green world outside.

'Thank God it's still light out there,' Sandy quietly said to Ben, as the others filed past with their frames, 'otherwise we'd have to stay the night in here, and I didn't like it much last time.'

Soon all had passed through the great trough, and were standing in a close knit group in the grassy glade, mouths open in wonderment at what they saw.

'As we still have some light left, I suggest we carry on a short distance to a cave complex we've found, and make it our home for the night.'

This time there were no hesitations, and the cluster of small caves was reached without incident. The main cavern was kept aside for a general meeting and eating room, the second largest for stores, while the others were for up for grabs, Sandy and Ben having already secured theirs.

After a short rest, they began to construct a crude wall of rocks to close off the main entrance, leaving a small opening which they could easily block with the now defunct frames, should the need arise.

Strict instructions were given concerning the use of the oil lamps. Although there was a considerable quantity of oil left, Sandy knew it would run out one day, and a substitute would have to be found before then.

Two lamps were left burning permanently day and night to act as 'keepers of the flame', the others being lit from them as and when needed.

The light began to fade, and they all withdrew to the main cavern, securely blocking off the opening to the outside.

Mop had produced a hot stew on a fire lit by Sandy, the concept of burning wood being something new to them all.

Most had crowded around Mop's cooking pot to watch it boiling merrily away, and for the first time getting smoke filled eyes into the bargain. Once the principle had sunk in, she had a plentiful supply of wood, the pile growing to a point of embarrassment.

They had tried to make the new eating room as homely as possible, but somehow it lacked the ambience of the old one up in the crater rim. But the stew helped a bit.

The new women who had joined the group caused a little friction, or to be more precise, the men seeking their attention caused those who already belonged, to view the newcomers as a potential threat to any budding relationships which had existed before the new arrivals arrived.

According to Ben, there had been little interaction between the men and women before the new uniforms had been made, Mop's attraction to Sandy being the first really observable and overt partnership. This seemed to act like a catalyst, the group members suddenly becoming aware of their sexuality in a way not previously experienced.

During their discussions on the matter, Sandy thought it might be due to the extreme difficulties they had in order to just survive, or possibly some interference from those who had brought them here in the first place.

Despite their long and arduous journey, they were reluctant to end the evening, and a second pot of soup-like liquid was brewed up by Mop. When they went out to stoke up the fire, Mop came rushing back in, full of excitement, exclaiming,

'You should see the .... stars, I think Ben said they were, little glittering lights all over the sky, they're beautiful.'

Then she rushed back out again.

Few had seen stars, as they were only visible when the sun had passed well below the horizon, and by then the temperature within the crater had dropped well below freezing point, so no one ventured out.

Only Sandy, Ben and Nan had been out early enough in the morning to see the last of the brightest stars fading away as the dawn broke, and they had not bothered to mention it.

What puzzled Sandy was that the cloud cover had disappeared, although during the daytime it seemed to be an unbroken cover, protecting them from the fierce sun above.

Most of the group trooped out to see the new wonder, marvelling at the still warm perfumed air.

Ben got Mop's fire going again, and it shed enough light for all to move around safely in the little glade outside their caves. Then someone started another fire, high up in a pile of rocks, illuminating the whole area. Ben then suggested that it might be a good idea to keep a fire going all night, in case they were troubled by any creatures like the fanged monster they had seen on their first visit.

So far, no one had seen anything of the animal kingdom their new world might have, although there were a few strange noises that night, and one nerve jangling scream just as the soup was being served.

It was very late that night when the barricade of frames was reassembled across the cave's entrance, and the oil lamps extinguished one by one. Seemingly, no one wanted to end their first day in their new world, lest it should all turn out to be a dream, and in the morning the cold reality of the crater would re-impose itself on their lives.

Exhaustion won in the end, and snores echoed around the caves in a fine duet with the night sounds from the creatures of the forest outside.

Next morning, the embers of Mop's cooking fire were still glowing, and she soon had a pot of gruel on the boil. Fortified with dried vegetable roots which Bell had grown, and flavoured with the new herbs, it made a potable and nourishing start for the day.

Sandy put together an exploration party to survey the surrounding area, while those left behind were instructed to rebuild the entrance to the caves, such that a door could be constructed if they were able to fell some of the trees they had seen earlier.

The party set off, Sandy carrying the laser gun hidden in his clothing, as he only wanted it to be used in extreme emergencies. The small stream which ran near the caves eventually fed into a lake of considerable size behind a line of trees, unnoticed in the excitement of their arrival.

Several large swimming creatures, which Sandy called fish, could be seen lazily swimming about, and Ben's first thought was 'food'. They sat on the bank of the lake, their feet dangling in the water while a strategy was worked out for catching the fish.

Greg solved the problem by suggesting that they wove a screen of fine stems, and herded the fish into the shallows where they could be caught.

They moved on, skirting a dark section of forest where little light was able to penetrate, and possible danger lurked.

Occasionally, a clearing in the cloud cover enabled them to see the deep blue of the sky above and feel the heat of the naked sun, which, whilst hot, was far removed from the blazing heat experienced when up in the crater.

Bell had been unable to identify the fruits and berries brought back with them from their first visit, so as tempting as they looked, the party refrained from trying them.

As the supplies they had brought with them would not last for long, it was decided that on the way back to the group they would gather a few samples of fruit, and very carefully test them for edibility, although no one had figured out how this was to be done.

A movement in the bushes up ahead brought the party to a sudden halt. Sandy slipped his hand beneath his tunic, ready to produce the gun. With a loud snort, the grey creature with the long snout emerged, looked around, and then fixed its eyes on the tableau of frozen figures.

'It's my friend,' whispered Ben, 'or one like it.'

'Keep still,' muttered Sandy, 'we can't take any chances.'

Slowly the creature approached the group, its long nose swinging from side to side, trying to pick up the scent of the strange objects ahead. It must have recognized Ben's body odour, for with a little grunt it hurried forward, and rubbed its snout up and down the now shaking Ben.

Satisfied that the strangers posed no threat, they were each in turn subjected to the snout inspection, Kel nervously reaching out to stroke its head.

Sandy explained what had happened on their first visit, when the creature had repelled another which could have killed them all, and that eased any remaining tension.

The creature followed them, as before, until they reached the lip of the valley, where it fell away steeply to the next level below.

'It looks as though the underlying substructure has faulted and slid forward,' Sandy announced, 'resulting in a series of cascading plateau, right down to the intersection with the main continental plate below.' It was Ben, in plain language, who explained to the other baffled members of the group what Sandy meant.

Pangs of hunger indicated that it was time for the midday meal, and the party began the long trek back to the caves, passing on the way a large area of high grass.

'Hey, look at this,' Kel pointed out, 'these grass seeds look just like the stuff Mop grinds up for her gruel.' Several stems of the reed like plant were gathered for Mop to compare with the grain she had obtained in an exchange with another group in the crater.

When they returned, and had ravenously demolished the meal Mop had prepared for them, they showed her the grass samples. The seeds looked the same, although they were a little plumper than those Mop had brought with her.

It was decided to grind some up, and try to make a bun with the resulting powder, baking it in-between the hot stones which encircled the cooking fire.

While they had been away, someone had discovered an area enclosed by rocks which would be protected from grazing animals, if any existed. With Sandy's approval, quantities of earth were laboriously transported to the enclosure to form a growing bed for the herb seedlings which Bell had brought with her.

Slowly but surely, they were establishing a self sustaining community, in idyllic surroundings, and with little threat from outside forces. The memory of the heavily toothed creature was never far from their minds though, and Sandy toyed with the idea of hunting it down to eliminate any possible future dangers. Ben pointed out that there could be many of them wandering around, otherwise where did the one they saw come from? The hunt was postponed.

Lots were drawn for the bun tasting, Jez getting the short straw, and the bun. He pronounced it to be delicious, and there were no serious side effects, except for one.

Jez entertained, or horrified, depending on one's view point, the rest of the group that evening with repeated and copious amounts of loudly vented wind. Mop commented that the ambience of the setting was not really enhanced or conducive to such musical accompaniments, only she expressed her opinion a little more succinctly.

Jez tried to blame the bun for his problems, but repeated trials of the bun on others failed to produce the same results.

As the new seed grains had proved edible, it was decided to keep a watchful eye on the crop, and harvest it when the majority of the grass grain was ripe and dry.

In the following days, the fishing project got under way. They had to make several lengths of woven hurdle for the trap to be efficient, and three of them had to go into the water to sweep the fish into the shallows.

The first problem was convincing the fishers that they were unlikely to drown, as the hurdles were quite buoyant and would help keep them afloat. Then someone wondered if there were bigger fish in the waters, like the sand creatures up in the crater. The three fishers, who by now had been coerced to go in up to their waists, left the water at a speed which was unbelievable, and refused to go back in.

In a show, which was more bravado than conviction, Sandy, Ben, and Greg plunged in, grabbed the hurdles which were about to float out of reach, and began the sweep.

They caught five large fish, more than enough to feed them all, the next problem was how to cook them. Because of their size, the outside would have been burnt before the inside was cooked, so they split them down the middle, and cooked them using hot stones.

After the meal, and because no one was eaten by an imagined lake monster, there was no shortage of fishers.

A small leat was built, diverting a portion of the stream so that it ran by Mop's cooking area. This supplied water for Mop's use, and a little further down, a washing facility, Sandy insisting that they all washed every day.

The long snouted grey creature was never far from the settlement, seeming to enjoy human company, and one day there were two. Both were equally friendly, which got Sandy thinking there might be some sort of telepathic link between them.

Augmenting their fast dwindling food supplies was of paramount importance, Kel reasoning that if the native life could eat it, then it should be safe for them. Sandy's caution was based on the fact that they were alien to this planet, and therefore their body chemistry would be different, as would their reaction to anything eaten. This was not real to some, and caused a great deal of friction.

One by one, the fruits and berries were checked for edibility, very few proving unusable, and those that were had unpleasant tastes or were too tough to eat. Fortunately, only a few fruits and berries were actually toxic, and they were usually black or very dark in colour, making them easy to identify.

Two things put a stop to the fishing project. A big bow wave was seen far out in the lake, which could only have been caused by something considerably larger than the fishers; and the hurdles had become waterlogged, and would no longer float. Both problems were eventually solved by attaching log floats to the top of the screens, which could easily be replaced, and a crude sail of large leaves to take the whole contraption out into the lake when the wind was favourable. It was then only a matter of hauling in the attached ropes, and fish were back on the menu.

Over the following days, various members of the group coupled up. Ben suggested some sort of ceremony would be a good idea, as he had a vague recollection of something like it from the past. When put to the vote all agreed, and Sandy, as their leader, was asked to perform the ceremony.

'What the hell do I do?' he asked Ben, when they were alone. 'It's your idea, so you'd better come up with something.' After much discussion, they arrived at a simple form of bonding, which as it turned out, proved acceptable to all.

Ben, and one of the new women seemed to have found soul mates in each other, and he volunteered to be the first to sample the new bonding ceremony. It was conducted after their evening meal, when everyone felt in a good mood, and appetites had been satiated.

'Do you Ben, and you Kyle, agree to live together, supporting each other come what may, and stay true to each other until death or mutual agreement between you shall break the bond?' They both enthusiastically answered 'Yes'.

'Then I do hereby declare that you are a bonded couple, and no one, for any reason whatsoever, shall try to break that bond on pain of expulsion from our group.'

A great cheer went up, and Kyle stepped forward to plant a wet kiss on Sandy's cheek. Fortunately Mop missed the planting, as someone moved in front of her at the crucial moment.

As the days went by, there were many more bondings, until only Sandy and Mop remained 'unbonded'.

After repeated hints and suggestions, which were carefully evaded by the ever wary Sandy, Ben's help was enlisted by a frustrated Mop, and a scheme was hatched among the rest of the group to legalize the long standing relationship of their leader and head cook.

Sandy sensed that something was afoot that day, but was unable to find out what it was despite several trick questions and a lot of probing. By evening, he had given up, and was totally unaware of what was about to happen.

They had finished their meal, and Sandy had made his short report of the day's happenings for the benefit of those who were not involved, when Jez arose and made his announcement,

'I propose we have a change of leader, and I suggest that Ben be given the job. All in favour, raise a hand.'

A sea of hands went up, accompanied by several verbal comments about youth to be given a chance.

Sandy was dumb struck, and just sat there in disbelief.

'As your new leader,' Ben began, 'it has been brought to my notice by various astute members of our group, that a long standing illegal relationship has been going on between our deposed leader and the plump one who does our cooking, and gives him a double portion when no one's looking.

'So, by the powers invested in me, I do now solemnly declare that these two aforementioned people shall be bonded in a lifelong partnership, whether they like it or not.

'And I do further declare, that no one shall make any attempt to break the bond between the bossy one and the plump one, no matter what.' The caves echoed with cheers and clapping hands for quite some time.

'Due to extreme incompetence on my part, I now resign from the lofty post as your leader, and ask you to vote for the bossy one to be reinstated into that exalted position.'

Another round of cheers, and much back slapping of a shattered Sandy and a moist eyed Mop, concluded the evening's entertainment.

That night, something tried to remove the frame barrier to the caves.

An icy river of fear ran through the group next morning when they found the frame barrier lying scattered around the entrance to their caves.

After a hasty meal, Ben and several others set about felling trees, which they later split into thick crude planks.

Using hard wooden pegs, a door of substantial proportions was constructed, and hung from a massive tree trunk they had now built into the wall surrounding the entrance to the caves.

The oil for their lamps was causing some concern as they had not found a means of replenishing it, when someone noticed a strange smell coming from one of the caves further up the valley, and a trickle of black sticky stuff seeping from a crack in the nearby rocks.

Armed with the laser gun and a lamp, Sandy and Ben with two others set off to see what it was, having an idea that it might be tar. The smell in the cave entrance was almost overpowering, and the lamp burnt with a red tinged flame, a warning that petroleum gas was present.

'We'll have to get rid of that gas,' Sandy explained, 'or we'll blow ourselves to bits if it explodes.'

'Why not lay a trail of dried grass into the cave as far as we can, and then light it?' Ben suggested. 'That should ignite the gas, and once it's burnt off, we can go in.'

Eager hands gathered the necessary grass, and Ben laid it in a line from just outside the cave entrance to several metres into the tunnel like cave by holding his breath and running.

As he had done most of the hard work, Ben was invited to light the grass, which he did from a lamp.

A little ribbon of fire slowly crept into the cave and disappeared, a faint wisp of smoke curling up from the top of the cave's entrance indicated that it was still burning.

Nothing much else happened for several minutes, and they thought the fire trail had gone out, when there was a deep throated roar from within the cliffs and a tongue of flame lanced out several metres, followed by billowing black smoke. Seconds later, there was another thunderous roar, smoke and flame gushed out of the rocks fifty metres above them, and a shower of rock fragments cascaded down all around.

Luckily, no one was severely hurt, although Ben sustained a bruised shoulder from a descending chunk of rock he failed to dodge. When all the smoke had cleared they went into the cave, and apart from the smell of burnt oil, the previous smell of petroleum gas or anything else was absent.

'I think that last explosion blew a hole in the cliffs, and now any gas that's left will be drawn upwards and out through the hole, so it should be safe to take our lamp in.'

They had gone in nearly fifteen metres, when the gentle glow from their lamp glistened on something black and shiny on the ground.

'This looks like tar,' Sandy explained, 'I seem to remember a little about it. If you heat it, it will give off a vapour, which if cooled, turns into an oil, leaving behind thick black sticky stuff, like this.'

'Surely that's no good then,' said Ben, 'all the oil has gone.'

Sandy gave the shiny black surface a poke with one of the pointed rods they all carried. The crust on the pool broke, revealing a much more runny liquid beneath.

'That's what we want,' he exclaimed, 'that'll give us all the oil we want, but we'll have to process it first.' A sample of the thinner tar oil was scooped into a container they had brought for that purpose, and they set off home.

The tar oil burnt quite readily, but with a smoky flame, making the need to refine it more than obvious. During the evening, Ben wanted to know how the tar got in the cave.

'As far as I can remember, tar and a substance called coal, all come from the same source,' Sandy had to dig deep in his memory in order to continue, 'thousands, or maybe millions of years ago, this area must have been covered in a massive dense jungle.

'As the plants died, more grew on top, building up a thick layer of dead plant material. In time this got overlaid with sand, rock or whatever, due to upheavals in the land mass, until it was buried deep in the planet's crust. Heat and pressure converted the dead vegetation into a hard substance called coal, which also burns, or this black sticky stuff.

'If we heat it, the lighter oils boil off and can be condensed into burnable oil, like our water cave condenses the steam from the vent in Mop's old cooking cave.'

'Can we make the necessary equipment to do this?' asked Ben, always ready to try his hand at something new.

'Don't see why not,' Sandy replied, 'but we shall need some tubes to run the hot vapour through so that it will condense. Do we have any up in your store?'

'Think so, but if we don't, we could do a trade for some.'

Two days later, a group of six led by Ben, set off for the crater. They would trade for cloth, if there was any available in the near groups, and locate as much metal tubing as they could find. New frames would be built to transport their goods, the frames themselves providing more raw material for future use in the new colony.

Sandy was surprised to find he felt quite lonely with Ben not present, as they had shared so much in the past, and to some extent, thought along the same lines.

The days rolled by, and after eight had passed with no sign of the team returning, Sandy began to worry. Greg thought they should send up a rescue team, and there were no shortage of volunteers for that, including some of the more robust women folk.

Sandy chose five others to accompany him on a rescue mission, and was about to leave when Ben and his men returned with their laden drag frames.

'What happened?' asked Sandy, relief showing clearly on his face, 'we thought we'd lost you lot, and were about to come up.'

'Sorry about that, but it took a lot longer than we had anticipated. It took two days just to get up to the top, and then none of the near groups had anything we wanted, so we had to stop over with one lot for the day, and then go on next evening. God, what a journey.' Ben looked as if he would collapse at any moment. 'Anyway, we've got most of what you wanted, including the tubes and more cloth.'

After a wash, which they'd been unable to do while up in the crater, and a hot meal, Ben and his team felt better, entertaining the rest of the group with unbelievable stories of what had happened to them.

'If you thought we were weird, you should see some of the others. We got a very useful box of tools from one lot who thought such things were a blasphemous insult to their God, although they were hard put to tell us who or what their God was. Anyway, they almost gave them to us, but we had to go through a special 'protective' ceremony first, to guard us from the evil influence the tools would have on us if we opened the box.'

Sandy noticed what a close knit group they had all become, the safe return of the team emphasizing the fact.

The tool box proved to be more useful than any of them had ever dreamed of, containing a heat torch for welding metal, although they were unable to fathom out how it obtained its power. A good mix of cutting tools, files, and assorted drills made up the main contents, plus a few odd items which they were to puzzle over for months to come.

With the new supply of metal pipes, oil distillation got under way, the stream providing the necessary cooling water for the condenser tubes. The oil they produced was a little thin compared to what they had obtained from the creature up in the crater, but it burnt cleanly, giving a better light, and the supply seemed limitless.

The herb garden was extended to grow a root crop, which someone had discovered quite by accident.

One of the women had pulled up a reed like plant just out of curiosity, and noticed the large bulbous root. It reminded her of something but she was unable to remember what, so she took it back to the group. Mop cleaned it, sliced it up, and cooked it. Small samples were eaten, and no detrimental effects were noticed by those brave enough to try it. The root soon became part of their staple diet, the plant growing prolifically in just about all soil conditions. It had a sweet nutty taste, being filling and nutritious into the bargain.

Once a set routine had established itself, life for the group became a little too easy, there being plenty of food, comfortable shelter, and no return of the multi-fanged creature they had seen on their first visit to the valley.

Such was Sandy's nature, that he soon got itchy feet when there were no problems to overcome, and a survey of the land to the South was proposed. This meant going down the steep escarpments at the end of the valley, and into the unknown beyond.

Two days later, and they were ready, the team comprising Sandy, Ben, Greg, and three others. The women complained bitterly at being excluded from the adventure, and were only partly mollified when a promise was made to include them next time.

Armed with pointed rods, and the hidden laser which few knew about, they set off down the valley to the first steep drop to the cascade of escarpments which would take them to the plains below.

Their view of the lands beyond the valley was obscured to some extent by the steep valley walls, only giving a narrow view of the lower plain straight ahead.

The climb down the first drop proved more arduous than expected, ropes having to be used several times as they were confronted by sheer rock faces with no means of getting a foothold. By the time they had reached the edge of the plain below, they were exhausted from their efforts, and took a break for food and rest.

Looking back, they could see the massive body of the volcano reaching up into the cloud base, and then the clouds parted for a moment to show the true size of the monster volcanic cone.

It seemed to reach up into the very sky itself, the top appearing indistinct because of its height and the faint haze shrouding the uppermost jagged pinnacles of the black rim.

'To think we used to live up there,' Sandy mused, 'and the other poor sods still do. God, what a place to spend your life in.' The others solemnly nodded.

'Where to now?' Ben asked, looking out over the vast expanse of the rock strewn plain. 'There's not much of interest out there, it's just sand, rock, and a few scrubby bushes for as far as you can see.'

'We'll swing around to the left,' Sandy said, 'and follow the base of the escarpment, that way we'll be in easy reach of something to climb up if we have to retreat from anything, and there's more chance of a diversity in the landscape.'

Ben glanced at Greg, who just shrugged his shoulders in non comprehension, smiled, and fell in behind the others.

'I've been thinking,' said Ben, as they strode along, 'bearing in mind the difficulty we had in getting down to this level, how the hell did the grey creature with the long snout get up to our level?'

Sandy stopped, Greg bumped into Ben, and the others gathered around, not quite knowing why.

'That's a point,' Sandy said, 'the area isn't big enough to sustain a large herd of 'em, and we only saw two anyway, so they must have found a way up. We'd better look into that when we get back. If we can block it off, and get rid of the long toothed thing, we should be safe from predators.'

They resumed their march along the volcano base, marvelling at some of the more grotesque rock formations which had been caused by molten lava reacting with some of the softer native rocks.

Many caves or tunnels ran back into the hillside, most of which were old lava tubes where the liquid rock had chilled and hardened on the outside as it flowed, leaving a hollow tube behind when the flow ceased.

'Don't fancy poking about in there.' Greg said, giving a particularly dark opening a wide berth. 'God knows what might be lurking within.'

'I doubt if anything's in there now.' Sandy observed. 'Look at the ground and the edges of the hole, they're smooth, and look as if they've been coated with something shiny. That's probably a vent which gushes steam every now and again.'

'You mean like the steam vent in Mop's old kitchen?' Ben suggested. A deep rumbling could be felt rather than heard, and the group split, racing for either side of the cavernous hole. Seconds later, the hole coughed, and a blast of steam, interspersed with streaks of scalding water, spewed out from the tunnel, drenching the ground ahead for many metres and sending a curling white funnel of water vapour spiralling skywards.

'God, you could do some cooking on that.' someone said.

'That's if you could find the cooking pot afterwards.' came back the rejoinder.

They treated dark holes with a little more caution after that, and then the landscape changed as they rounded a promontory.

A deep gorge ran back into the towering cliffs which formed the foot of the volcano, and was filled with a dense forest of enormous trees, some of which had spread out onto the plain. The air was filled with shrieks and calls from the wildlife within the forest, and Sandy suggested that they go in a little way, as the sounds were calls, not cries of pain.

No one looked very convinced at Sandy's explanation for the raucous sounds, but neither could they summon up the courage to say so.

As they entered the forested area, the air became full of the sounds of humming insects. Some crawled, some flew, others hopped, while a few hitched a ride on the backs of larger ones, all adding to the overall cacophony of sound produced by the larger life forms, as twigs broke under a foot and branches rustled.

'Noisy place isn't it?' Greg felt a little uneasy with so much random sound, mainly produced by things he could not see, let alone avoid, should he need to.

The ground between the mighty trees was covered by a short tough grass, the shorn ends of the grass blades indicating that it was heavily cropped by something with sharp chisel shaped teeth. There was little sign of the copious amounts of fruit they were used to, except very high up in the branches and well out of their reach. But something was reaching it, as evidenced by the skins and fruit stones scattered about under the trees.

A series of small grassy glades formed a linked pathway through what would otherwise have been an impenetrably dense mass of vegetation, the gaps between the larger trees being taken up by smaller ones of different types, and clumps of bushes.

The further they went, the taller the trees became, until they came to the actual cliff face where the huge trunks were ten metres or so in diameter.

'I had no idea trees could grow so big,' commented Sandy, gazing up at the forest giants, 'it must be due to something in the soil. I know volcanic ash is very rich in nutrients, but this is amazing.' As all six stood gazing up at the massive trunk which disappeared into a huge umbrella of green leaves, a slight movement high above was noticed by Greg.

'There's something moving up there,' he observed, 'and I get the feeling it's looking at us.'

Before anyone could comment on Greg's remark, a round shape came crashing down through the lower branches to land at their feet with a thud. The impact split the huge nut open, exposing a glistening creamy white flesh inside the two halves of the dark brown shell.

As Ben stepped forward to pick up a piece of the broken nut, another came whistling down, just missing him by a few centimetres as it tried to bury itself in the ground.

They instinctively stepped back a few paces as a third missile came whistling down and thumped into the ground, narrowly missing Sandy. 'Whatever they are, they aren't falling because they're ripe,' he yelled, 'something up there's having a go at us. Let's get back a little further, and then I'll move in again to see if it tries again.'

'If one of those nuts hits you, you'll have more than a head ache,' Ben commented wryly, 'so I wouldn't.'

Sandy just grinned and edged forward slowly, his eyes never off the green canopy above. A faint rustling indicated that something was moving its position, or another nut was on its way. Sandy sharply stepped a metre to one side, and a second later a nut hit the ground where he had been standing, and split open.

'Use your gun,' urged Ben, fearful his friend would receive a direct hit if he taunted the creature above any more.

'No need to,' Sandy replied calmly, 'anyway, it wouldn't be fair, it's only defending its territory.'

'It's a bloody good shot, so watch it.' Greg was unhappy at the situation, but did not have the courage to order his senior out of the area. There was an almost audible sigh of relief as Sandy slowly backed out from the area under bombardment.

'Got a feeling about those nuts,' Sandy said, picking a piece up and tasting it, 'I think it's edible, I almost recognize that taste, it's ...' Just then an ear splitting scream rent the air from up high, accompanied by the vigorous rustling of the greenery, and then silence. They looked at each other, wondering what had happened. 'I think something took a dislike, or maybe an extreme liking to our missile thrower, so it doesn't look as if we'll get any more nuts for a while. Let's collect these up.'

'You know, there's something odd about a wild creature throwing missiles at us,' mused Greg, a thought at the back of his mind refusing to fully form, 'it reminds me of something ...'

'It certainly smacks of a level of intelligence above what you'd expect from an animal, if that's what you mean,' Sandy replied, 'it had a bloody good eye too.'

They gathered up the unbroken nuts, looked around the grassy clearing to make sure nothing else posed a threat, and headed back the way they had come.

Apart from the continual buzz of very active insect life, and the gentle rustle of the giant trees, there was no other sound, except the occasional snap of a twig as someone trod on it.

Lulled into a sense of false security by the idyllic surroundings, the group went from glade to linking glade, blissfully unaware of several sets of eyes watching their every move.

'What's that smell?' asked Greg, who had stopped a few steps ahead of the others and was sniffing the air. 'If we could bottle that, we'd make a fortune.'

'I think it might be coming from those.' Ben replied, pointing to several large white trumpet shaped flowers adorning the strands of rope like vine hanging from one of the trees. 'I didn't notice it before.'

Greg went over to the plant, cradling one of the delicate blooms in his hands, and taking a deep draft of the heady perfume. Within seconds, his eyes glazed over, and he staggered about like a drunk, giggling childishly.

He would have fallen to the ground in a stupor if the others had not grabbed him and dragged him away from the flower's hypnotic influence. Sandy slapped his face hard, twice, but he just continued to giggle.

'There's nothing we can do except let that stuff work its way out of his system,' Sandy said, deeply concerned, 'I think we got him away just in time.'

Ben had gone over to the cluster of vines bearing the deadly flowers, taking a deep breath and holding it as he drew near.

'There are some little white sticks around the base of this tree,' he exclaimed, poking about in the grass with his foot, 'and some feathery things. Hey, these aren't sticks, they're bones! Good God, there's hundreds of 'em.'

Leaving Greg, Sandy went over to see what Ben had found.

'Now that's interesting,' he remarked, 'some of those bones have begun to break down, see how soft and crumbly they are. That means something in the ground or perhaps exuded from the tree, is doing that. Bones don't normally go soft, unless something attacks their structure.'

'That implies the vine is trapping creatures to use as food, but you said the ground here is very rich from volcanic ash, so why would the plant need to do that?' asked Ben.

'The ash is rich in minerals, but plants also need nitrogen, some more than others, and they can get it from breaking down flesh, or almost anything else which grows.'

Sandy walked around the huge tree trunk, keeping well away from the enticing white flowers as he did so.

'I think there's a symbiotic relationship between the vine and this tree,' he began, 'there's no sign of the vine roots reaching the ground, so it must have tapped into the tree somewhere. The vine catches nitrogen bearing creatures by stupefying them with its perfume, and they quickly die near the tree base. The tree releases some sort of enzyme which breaks the bodies down, the roots absorb it, and as it gets transported around the tree, the vine takes its share. Don't like it, but it's bloody neat.' he concluded.

'I think we'd better get away from that plant, me legs are getting a bit wobbly.' Sandy's words were slightly slurred, showing how powerful the perfume could be.

Greg was now sitting upright, and looking very foolish.

'That's one of the most weird experiences I've ever had,' he exclaimed, as the others gathered around. 'It was like dreaming, but only of pleasant things. I felt great but sleepy, and my body felt like lead, but I didn't seem to mind.'

They continued on towards the open plain, the eyes still watching them, fascinated by the strange little bipeds and wondering if they would make a good meal.

'Must say, I feel a bit safer out here,' Ben said, as they left the last of the trees behind, 'at least you can see what's around you.' The others nodded, but still kept a good lookout for anything which did not seem to fit in naturally with the landscape, but then, what was natural?

The ground changed from being a hard crust with shattered pieces of rock protruding from its surface, to one of sand, and this slowed them down considerably. The high cliffs of the volcano's base still towered above them on their left, while on their right, the endless plain of sand and gravel banks seemed to go on to the horizon, finally disappearing in the distant blue haze.

The sand eventually gave way to firmer ground again, and they stopped for a meal break, their legs aching from the struggle of tramping through the soft sand.

'We'll go on 'till evening, and then make camp. Tomorrow we'll have to head back home as our water will run out if we don't find any, and the others will get worried if we stay away too long.' Sandy announced.

They walked on, with less of a spring in their footsteps than they had earlier.

Six:
The Fires Speak

Rounding a spur of frozen lava which jutted out from the main mass of the cliffs, they stopped. Ahead, an enormous ledge of rock hung out from the cliffs above like a huge shelf, throwing a dark shadow beneath it.

'What the hell's that?' Ben eventually said.

'Looks like an ancient lava flow, and the ground beneath it has been cut away,' Sandy offered as an explanation of the impossible, 'but I don't see how so much rock can sustain itself without breaking off under its own weight.'

'It doesn't look safe to me.' Greg muttered, knowing full well they would have to get considerably closer, if only to satisfy Sandy's curiosity of such things.

As they drew nearer to the massive overhang, the true size of the rock shelf became apparent. One hundred metres above their heads, the underside of the old lava flow leaned out for a distance of some six hundred metres, casting an area of gloom beneath it.

'It looks as if the lava flowed out over a bed of sandstone, and the softer stone has been eroded away over the years.' Sandy stated, his memory of geology returning as he looked at the bizarre freak of nature. 'It's been like this for God knows how long, so it should be safe enough for us to go underneath it.' So saying, he strode forward, the others following reluctantly on behind and frequently glancing upwards, fearing the worst.

Having reached the centre of the overhang, they turned and looked out over the plain, the shadow they stood in making the rest of the world look much brighter.

Ben, who was in front of the others and still feeling nervous about the overhang, turned to face them, when his eyes locked straight ahead and his jaw dropped.

Slowly he raised his arm, pointing at the back of the ledge where it met the cliff and nodding his head up and down.

The others turned as one, and they too froze at what they saw. At the base of the cliff in the deepest shadows, a vast oval silver object lay on the ground, the back edge slightly raised as though it had skidded to a stop, the front end having dug itself into the soft ground and then met the hard rock of the cliff.

'What the hell is that,' gasped Greg, when he was able to draw breath, 'don't tell me that grew here!'

'It certainly didn't,' Sandy said quietly, 'that's been manufactured, and I think I know what it might be.'

'What?' the others chorused in unison.

'Can't be sure yet, so let's get a little closer.' Sandy replied, taking a few tentative steps towards the huge shape.

Their natural fear of the unknown made the others hold back, while Ben warned Sandy to be careful.

'I think it's been here a long time, look at the way the wind has blown the sand up around it in ripples, that doesn't happen overnight. Come on, it's quite safe as long as we don't fiddle with anything.' He now strode out confidently towards the silver object, waving his arm to bring the others forward.

As they drew nearer, the full size of the vehicle became apparent, towering over them by some fifteen metres.

'What's it doing here? Do you think someone put it here to keep it out of sight?' asked Ben.

'I don't think so.' Sandy replied, turning and looking back towards the open plain. 'There's a shallow furrow going out some way onto the plain which I didn't notice before. It's got partly filled with wind blown sand, so it only shows up from this angle, and then only faintly.'

Ben, having lost some of his fear, reached up and hit the side of the vehicle with his clenched fist. He had expected a hollow booming sound, but there was no more response than if he had hit a piece of solid rock.

'Not quite what you expected.' commented Sandy, who had stooped down to look underneath the curved body of the craft. 'See these marks under here, I'll bet they're access panels and if we could get them open, we could get inside.'

'You're joking!' Greg exploded, 'you're not seriously thinking of going into that thing. God knows what would happen.'

What do you think would happen?' asked Sandy calmly. 'It's been sitting here for years, so there'll be no sign of life in it. It's just a mechanical thing someone has made, and if we don't push any buttons or tweak any switches, it should just sit there.' The others were not convinced.

They walked around the huge shape, looking for an entry point, but found nothing which was an obvious doorway into the interior of the craft.

'I've found something!' the distant voice of Ben echoed around the huge cave-like overhang of rock, 'it's different to the other markings we've found.' The others hurried around to where Ben was looking intently at a slight recess in the outer skin of the vehicle.

'It's a sort of inviting shape,' he said, 'something I feel I should put my hand on.'

'Well, go on then,' Sandy said, 'I don't see what harm it'll do.' Ben placed his hand in the shallow recess. A faint only just discernible hum sounded, and a pulse of light flashed beneath Ben's hand. Greg, who had been standing behind Ben, now went flying as Ben accelerated backwards, a look of horror on his face.

'Hey, take it easy,' Sandy yelled, as he too was thrust to one side, 'we're going to injure each other more than that craft is likely to.'

Having got over their shock, they regrouped around the mystery panel. This time Sandy placed his hand in the recess. Again, the quiet hum, the panel flashed, but nothing else happened.

'What do you think it's supposed to do?' asked Ben contritely, 'it must have a purpose.'

'Of course it has,' replied Sandy sharply, 'it's just that we haven't figured it out yet.' He placed his hand in the recess again, with the same result, then stood back, deep in thought.

'I think this is a means of identifying those allowed to enter the craft, and it won't open for others, like us. So what's the difference between hands?'

'There're all different,' said Ben, 'some are large, some small, others have knobbly joints. Surely that thing can't tell differences like that.'

'It would seem to.' replied Sandy, pensively.

Each tried their hands in turn, but the door, if indeed there was one, remained stubbornly shut.

Frustration was beginning to get the better of them, and they were about to give up on the idea of trying to fool the door sensor, when Greg said he would like to give it a kick.

'And just how are you going to reach it?' asked Ben.

'Hey, wait a minute you two, that's the only thing we haven't tried.' said Sandy, hopefully.

'You've got to be bloody joking.' Ben said, wondering if his mentor had finally cracked under the strain.

'No, I don't mean kick it, I mean stick a foot on it.'

'Oh, come on. People don't go around opening doors by plonking their feet on them.' Ben retorted tartly.

Sandy untied the holding cords and kicked his home-made shoes off.

'Come on, someone help me up.' They all stood around in disbelief while Sandy tried in vain to fling his leg high enough to reach the recess.

'What are you lot waiting for?' he asked angrily. 'I need a hand up.'

'You need something, and it's not a hand.' mumbled Ben, and then wished he had kept his counsel.

Reluctant hands lifted Sandy up until he could place his foot firmly into the recess. The gentle hum was followed by the light flash, a faint 'ting' from somewhere within the craft, and a door hissed open beside the sensor panel, emitting a gush of stale and fetid air. Angrily Sandy heaved himself back to his feet and dusted himself down, after being dropped by his helpers when the door unexpectedly opened.

'What's the matter with you lot?' he growled. 'You're as jumpy as a bunch of bloody girls.'

'How the hell did that work?' asked Greg, the first to recover his composure.

'That thing recognizes hand shapes, and a foot has the same number of digits, only a different shape. From that we can deduce that those allowed to enter have long hands and stubby fingers, while we don't, and aren't allowed in.'

Apologies were offered, but were shrugged off by a still seething Sandy, and it was only when he suggested they try to climb into the now inviting hole in the side of the craft that things returned to near normal.

'OK, I'll go in first then.' he said, noticing the others had taken a step backwards immediately after the suggestion.

Sandy heaved himself up into the opening, and vanished, only to return a few seconds later, with a grin on his face.

'Come along girls, who's next?' Sandy was enjoying himself having made his point and gained entry to the alien transport vessel.

One by one, they climbed on board, wrinkling their noses at the tainted air, but driven forward by their curiosity.

They found themselves in a long passage, and although there was no direct light source as such, the walls themselves seemed to gently glow, giving adequate light to safely move about.

'Why are you lot whispering?' Sandy's voice boomed out in the confined space, 'there's no one alive on this thing!'

They tramped on, the passage ending in what they thought at first was a blank wall, but it was just that the door had been carefully designed to blend in with its surroundings.

'Right, shoes off,' someone called from the back, but Sandy had already found the release stud, and the door swung open.

Again, that whoosh of stale air, and they all held their breath for a moment, allowing fresh air from outside to swirl in.

'Looks like this could be the control room,' Sandy announced confidently, 'and those are the controller's chairs,' he said, pointing to three high backed seats in front of a huge viewing screen.

Sandy was the first to approach the seats, and he stopped dead in his tracks. The others, sensing something was amiss, hurried to his side and stopped also. Three mummified figures occupied the three seats, safety harnesses still holding the withered bodies in place, but all three had their heads bent forward at an unnatural angle.

'Good God, look at those hands,' exclaimed Ben, pointing at the first figure, whose arms lay stretched out before him. 'Sandy was right after all!'

The alien's hand was twice the length of theirs, and the fingers were considerably shorter, but apart from that it bore no resemblance to a foot.

'What do you think happened to them?' Ben said quietly. 'Can't be old age, as all three snuffed it at the same time.'

'What I think happened,' Sandy began, speaking slowly so that he could have time to think, 'is that this ship lost its way in the cloud or developed a fault, and tried to land here. Something went wrong, and the craft hit the sands outside and the whole thing skidded in under the lava overhang.

'It looks as if these three had their necks broken by the impact when the front edge of the craft hit the solid rock of the cliff.

'Even if a search craft was sent out, it would have difficulty in locating this one, tucked up under the overhang as it is. Only a ground search would find it, and they obviously didn't do one of those.' He felt pleased with his analysis of the situation, and he was getting better at it.

'Do you think it has anything to do with the Great Lights?' asked Greg, wondering if yet another mystery would now be cleared up.

'Could well be.' Sandy answered, looking around the control room, searching for anything which would help him determine what the vessel had been used for. 'Let's take a look at the rest of it.' he added.

On the opposite side to which they had entered, another doorway beckoned and Sandy soon had it open. A short passage led to a flight of steps, and they cautiously went down them to another small room, which looked out onto a large area below. Row upon row of coffin like boxes lay in neat lines, transparent covers allowing the visitors full view of the gruesome contents.

'Poor sods,' muttered Sandy, 'on their way to a new home, and never made it.'

'You mean, we came like this?' asked Ben, catching on quicker than Sandy thought he would.

'Almost certainly, I know I did, although I don't remember this part of the journey.'

'What do you remember?' Ben asked gently, aware he might be treading on dangerous ground.

'I remember a 'nothingness', which is quite different to being asleep, and then falling and hitting the sand with a thump. Nan was there to help me up, and took me in to meet you lot. Bits of memory from my former life come back to me sometimes, especially when I'm trying to work something out. I know I've lived somewhere else, but I don't know where at the moment.'

'Look down there,' Greg was peering out of the window of the despatch room, 'there's a clear space in the middle with a piece of machinery to one side of it. Do you think that's what they used to throw us out?'

'I don't think they throw us out exactly, we'd break our bloody necks falling that distance. It's probably some device which lowers us down, and then tips us out when we're nearer the ground. That's what it felt like to me.'

Ben found the door leading down to the storage room floor, but they were in two minds about going down to view the unfortunates who lay there.

'We may as well,' said Ben a last, 'they can't hurt us.'

As they walked up and down the rows of transport boxes, they noticed there were many different types of people entombed in their containers, some of which looked barely human. All their bodies had dehydrated to a mummified state, disguising their true likeness.

'Look, here's three like that bunch who tried to annihilate us,' Greg called out, 'just as well they didn't join the others, or we may not have been able to get 'em all in the tunnel at the same time.'

They returned to the main control room, glad to be out of the morbid atmosphere of the holding store, and looked around for anything else which would add to their fast growing reservoir of knowledge. It was Ben who found the clinching detail which proved Sandy's theory of what had happened to them all.

He had idly lent against the control console, and in doing so touched the activating button. A screen lit up showing a perfect outline of the crater, and around its edge were the various positions of the groups which inhabited it.

It was Greg who located their old home site in the crater, remembering the rocky promontory which jutted out into the sands, the only one he knew of in their area.

'This certainly gives you a good idea of how big the crater is,' said Sandy, 'and it's a damn sight bigger than I ever thought.'

They all stared at the illuminated crater map, and then Ben notice a series of small markings, one against each cave site.

'I'll bet if we compared those marks with the ones on the boxes down below, we'd know who was going where, if you see what I mean. There might have been some for us.'

'There probably were, but it's academic now, they all died long ago.' Sandy had lost interest in what had passed, and plans for the future were already beginning to form.

'I wonder if we could get this craft airborne again?' he mused out loud.

A look of horror crossed the other five faces, finding the ship was enough, flying it was certainly not on the menu.

Sandy was a little surprised when he saw their faces, and decided to back track a bit quickly.

'Just kidding men. I doubt this thing would ever fly again anyway, something must have failed to bring it down in the first place, and we certainly don't have the know-how to repair it.'

They went to the exit door of the craft, and found the light outside had dropped to a point where they could hardly make out details of the distant desert, the ground below them being in complete darkness.

'How do you feel about making camp in here for the night?' asked Sandy, 'it'll be a lot safer than going outside.'

They all agreed, and soon a meal was laid out from the various containers each had brought.

'Sure could do with one of Mop's stews right now,' Ben said, spitting out crumbs from one of Mop's somewhat hardened grain buns, 'damn good cook, that woman.' Sandy grinned, he knew Ben was trying to make a point about something, but was unsure exactly what it was.

None of them felt tired after their meal, so they continued to explore the alien craft, finding doors which led them ever deeper into the workings of the vessel, but finding little they could understand, except Sandy, and he was saying nothing for the time being.

The three mummified figures were unceremoniously removed from their seats, allowing three of the team a reasonably comfortable sleeping place. Fortunately two of the team were a little squeamish about occupying the dead men's last resting places, so they were quite happy to sleep on the floor of the control room. By next morning, they had changed their views, but a quick meal and the promise of going home cheered them up considerably.

The group left the alien ship under the lava ledge and headed out into the bright light of day. Sandy and Ben were a little reluctant to leave it behind before they could learn more about it, and Sandy fully intended to return as soon as possible.

They discussed what they had found as they walked along, Sandy being the only one to whom the implications of their discovery rang true to any great extent. Ben and Greg could see the logic of it all, but still found it difficult to accept.

Conversation dwindled somewhat as they struggled across the soft sand area, a wind adding to their difficulties as it whipped up the finer grains in a series of flurries, getting in their eyes and making breathing arduous. Ben suggested they make masks from some of the fine cloth they had acquired, if they ever came this way again.

Feeling greatly relieved when the sand gave way to the more compacted ground of the plain, they took a break. Greg removed his footwear to get rid of the sand, and found it had cut into his skin creating sores on his feet, and suggested that the others do likewise.

'I wouldn't have expected sand to have done this,' Greg announced, carefully wiping the last few grains from the angry red patches, 'the crater sand never cut into our feet.'

Sandy then had a close look at the raw places on his feet.

'You're right, it shouldn't have done this, must be something different about it.' He took a few grains from his crudely formed foot coverings, and examined them closely.

'Looks like this sand is a lot sharper, the edges of the grains are like little knife edges as though whatever it came from has shattered instead of being worn down like normal sand.

'We'll have to take extra care when we come back, this stuff could cripple us if we're not careful.'

The others exchanged glances, Ben being the only one who knew for certain Sandy's intention to return.

'Make sure you've got every little bit of this damn stuff out of your foot coverings,' Sandy instructed, 'we've a long way to go yet, and we can't afford any delays with the water running low.'

Once they were under way again, the sore feet were soon forgotten and they returned to their normal marching pace, the kilometres speeding by.

They stopped for another break when they reached the fringes of the forested area, retrieving the huge nuts they had left where the forest spilled out onto the plain.

'These should make a good addition to our diet.' Sandy said, sharing out one of the broken nuts. 'I didn't notice any adverse effects when I tried it earlier, so it should be all right for the rest of you.'

'You know, it reminds me of something,' Ben said, chewing on the firm but succulent flesh of the nut, 'but I'm damned if I can recall what.'

'Know what you mean,' one of the others replied, 'pity we can't get our memories back.'

I'm not so sure we can't,' Sandy said firmly, 'I have recovered quite a lot, and I intend trying the same method on you lot, when we have time.'

They were about half way back between the forested area and their home valley, when Greg drew their attention to something large and dark, flying high in the sky above them.

'I don't like the look of that.' he exclaimed.

'It looks like a bird of some sort,' Sandy said, and then had to explain to the others what a bird was, although Ben seemed to know after his furrowed brow relaxed a little.

The dark shape wheeled overhead, watching them.

'I think it's coming lower.' Greg sounded nervous, and moved a little closer to the rest of the group.

Six pairs of eyes were hypnotically locked onto the ominous shape as it spiralled around, gradually losing height and getting bigger by the minute.

'It's difficult to tell just how large it is as there's nothing to use as a reference point up there.' Sandy was getting a bit edgy now, as with a twitch of its huge wings, the flying creature corrected its flight path to home in on the watchers below. 'I think we'd better take cover, if we can find any,' Sandy added, 'it's coming down quite quickly now.'

They turned as one, and ran for the rock strewn border along the cliffs, hoping to find a small cave or a pile of rocks in which to hide.

A deep whistling sound was just audible above their panting lungs as they reached the cliff face and scrambled in among the rocks, looking for a cavity large enough to hold them all.

'This looks all right.' Ben gasped, pointing to a small opening in the otherwise solid rock face. As they dived in, a small four legged furry creature shot out between Greg's legs, bringing him down to his knees. Ben turned around, grabbed him by the arm, and pulled him into the cave just as the whack whack of huge wings announced the arrival of the flying creature.

Sandy wriggled himself to the front of the petrified group, the laser weapon in his hand, and gingerly peered out of the cave. There was nothing to be seen except the nearby scattered rocks and never ending desert beyond, so he leaned out a little further. A metre long black curved beak slashed down from above, missing his head by millimetres and buried itself in the ground with a thud.

'Bloody hell,' Sandy exclaimed loudly, wriggling back into the sanctuary of the cave, 'the bastard nearly got me.'

'Shoot it,' screamed Ben, who was next in line after Sandy should the beak reach into the cave.

Sandy took careful aim at the black scythe like mandible of the creature as it wriggled to free itself, and when the red dot showed clearly on the middle of the beak, pressed the firing stud a bit harder.

The faint hiss of the laser weapon was drowned out by a scream of pain and anger from the monster, accompanied by a loud crackling noise as the beak splintered into many fragments.

'Give it another one,' yelled Ben frantically, pushing Sandy forwards, 'that won't have killed it.'

'I know,' said Sandy calmly, 'just wait a minute, and get back in. If we go out now, it could still get us, but if we wait it may move away, and then we'll stand a better chance.'

They waited, huddled in the little cave, with barely enough room to move, not that they could move much as they were still paralysed with fear.

Sundry scratching and scraping noises drifted into the cave from time to time, but none dared stick their head out to see what was happening. Eventually the external noises died down, and Sandy drew his knife, using the polished blade as a mirror to see if the creature had moved far enough away for him to take another shot at it.

'Can't see anything,' he said, 'so I suppose it's all right. I'll crawl out a little way, and if things get hectic, grab my feet and pull me back in.' First he poked this head out, looked around, and then quietly wriggled forward a metre or so, 'Can't see anything yet, but it could be hiding behind any of these large rock,' he whispered huskily.

Sandy picked up a small stone and threw it at the nearest pile of rocks large enough to hide the creature. The stone rattled and clattered its way from rock to rock, but that was the only sound, and no ugly head reared up to see what was causing it.

'I think it must have moved away,' Sandy said cheerfully, hiding his inner fear, 'you can come out now.'

One by one, the group emerged from the cave, each taking a good look around before exposing his body to possible attack, and straining Sandy's patience almost to the limit in doing so, as he wanted to eliminate the possible threat to their survival and get back to the valley before nightfall.

When all six had assembled in a little clearing between the scattered rocks, Sandy suggested they climb the highest one for a good look around. As no one volunteered for the honour, Sandy took the hint and went himself. He called back from the top that there was no sign of the creature, as it had probably gone home to lick its wounds.

They regrouped and began working their way out of the rock field, and back to the open ground of the plain. A startled shout from Ben, who was bringing up the rear of the party, made them all turn to look.

Fifty metres away, the creature had crawled out from behind a rock hardly large enough to have hidden it, and was slowly humping itself along the ground towards them, its shattered stump of a beak making it look more comical than threatening.

Sandy stood his ground with legs splayed out to steady his balance, while the others quickly ran around behind him, uttering words of encouragement.

'I'll wait until it gets a little closer, as I don't know how many shots this thing has left, and I don't want to miss.'

'It might have already run out of shots,' Ben said nervously, 'there's no way of telling, is there?'

'No,' Sandy replied, taking careful aim, 'and if it doesn't fire, run like hell.'

The little tell tale spot of red light appeared on the creature's head for a split second, then there was the faint hiss as the laser discharged and the creature's head disintegrated in a mess of bone and flesh.

'God, that's horrible.' Greg said quietly.

When the creature had stopped twitching and quivering, they went over to see exactly what they had killed.

The main body was some three metres in length, with a tail section of another two metres. Flat scales, which they later found were composed of closely compacted hair, covered the entire body of the creature, right up to the top of the neck where it joined the shattered head.

They estimated the wings would stretch out to some eight metres on either side of the body when in flight, and seemed to be covered in some sort of tough leathery skin, Sandy's knife hardly marking the surface when he tried to cut it.

A latticework of fine bones formed the main wing frames supporting the skin, and one of these had broken and now protruded through the membrane, the cleanly broken end showing a hollow structure.

'I wonder how such a clumsy great thing could ever get airborne,' Sandy mused aloud, 'its legs don't look long enough to give the wings clearance to flap.'

'Perhaps it climbs onto something, and then jumps off.' suggested Ben, and then wondered how it could haul its huge bulk onto anything high enough in the first place.

'Well, that's something else we'll have to keep a look out for.' said Sandy, as they resumed their march homewards.

The light was just beginning to fail as they climbed the last step in the long series of escarpments which led up to their valley. Waiting at the top, three of those who had stayed behind raised their arms in welcome, one of them immediately turning to run back to the main settlement to spread the good news.

Mop, quite unabashed, welcomed Sandy home with open arms, totally oblivious of those who stood around, some of whom dared to make suggestive comments, thereby forfeiting any chance of second helpings when there was a surplus.

The meal that night was something they would remember for some time to come, Mop having excelled herself yet again. The new sweet nuts the team had brought back suited everyone's palate, and there was no shortage of volunteers to set forth and retrieve more, until the story of the bird creature was told.

By the time all the food had been consumed, and all tales told, it was quite late, and everyone was ready to retire.

Sandy surprised himself when he discovered just how pleased he was to be back safely in the ample arms of Mop.

He did his best to show that appreciation, much to Mop's delight. Unfortunately, this set a precedent for future performances, Sandy realizing this too late to tone down the whole procedure.

The climate in the valley suited the plants they had brought with them, and they grew quicker and more prolifically than up in the crater.

Bell could now expand her gardening efforts on a scale never before dreamed of, and several more areas of land were enclosed with stone walls to protect the crops from some creature which no one had seen, but nevertheless ate anything unprotected.

Although no one kept a record of the passing days, as there seemed little point in doing so, it was noticed that the planet was subject to climatic change, something they had not experienced when up in the crater.

They had been in the valley for some forty days when Ben remarked that he thought the evenings were getting quite chilly, but not as cold as the nights up in the crater had been.

As the days rolled on, it became more evident that the planet was going through a cool cycle, and some means of heating the caves had to be found.

As there was no shortage of firewood, a large fireplace was constructed just inside the main entrance to the cave complex, a convenient hole in the rocks above taking the smoke and fumes away, leaving the radiant heat of the fire to warm the air in the caves to a tolerable level.

They awoke one morning to another surprise, the ground had been dusted with a fine coating of snow, which quickly disappeared. It was when someone had gone to the end of the valley to gather fruit, and had a good view of the plains beyond, that they came back with the startling news that the snow on the plains had not melted, and they were still a glistening sheet of white.

Remembering the effect cold could have on plants, Bell and her helpers quickly took their seedlings from the nursery beds and transplanted them into the old growing boxes, taking them into the caves at night.

As the days were noticeably shorter, more time was spent in the caves at night, and Sandy got on with his memory recovery program. Only a few were interested in the project to begin with, but when it became evident that old skills could be recovered, nearly all joined in with a degree of enthusiasm which surprised him.

Very little had been said about the alien craft they had found under the lava overhang, although Ben suspected Sandy still intended to visit the site again. He brought it up one evening when they were having a general chat, and Sandy admitted he was going back, just as soon as the snow layer on the plains below had cleared.

The Valley remained clear of snow, except for a little sprinkling each morning, but the plains did not appear to thaw, the snow building up each night until even the few rocky outcrops on it had disappeared under the dazzling white blanket, leaving a smooth uninterrupted surface.

At what they thought was the peak of the shorter days, the remaining cloud layer disappeared, leaving clear blue skies during the day and a brilliant display of stars by night.

What they found difficult to understand was the fact that there was now more heat from the sun, yet the snow on the plains did not melt. Sandy thought during the cool period all the moisture in the air condensed out to form snow, so exposing the world to the naked rays of the sun, but as the snow failed to melt under this extra heat, he was unable to explain how the process would reverse itself, and the cloud cover return.

One day, someone noticed a few dark patches on the otherwise unblemished snows of the plain. The cool period was coming to an end and rocks were increasingly exposed.

The snow was being absorbed back into the atmosphere and thin wisps of cloud began to form high above.

The usual dusting of snow in their valley failed to appear one morning, so the plants which had been so carefully nurtured during the cool spell were brought out for replanting, and everyone looked forward to the warmer days to come.

A few days later, and the plains had lost all their snow, trees in the valley burst into bloom, and new grass shoots sprang up replacing the old discoloured blades of last season.

Greg remarked one day that he thought it strange they had seen no rain, when it was obvious that moisture could condense out as snow. No one could offer an explanation which made any sense, and then two mornings later they were greeted by a thick white mist when they tried to leave the sanctuary of the caves, and were unable to go more than a few metres from the entrance.

The mist lasted for three days, gradually thinning to be replaced by a warm gentle rain. They got wet, but were at least able to harvest fresh fruit again, although it was last seasons, and often overripe.

The rain turned into spasmodic bursts of drizzle over the next few days, and then it was dry again, the cloud layer having stabilized itself for another season.

Once everything was back to what they assumed to be normal, Sandy tactfully broached the subject of the alien craft one evening, and his intention of visiting it once more.

'What is to be gained from going there again?' a somewhat conservative member of the group asked.

'I have two things in mind.' Sandy replied. 'One, we could strip it for anything useful. It would be a good source of materials, and we could possibly learn something about the people who brought us here. The other is that we may be able to make it work again, it didn't look too damaged.'

'Do you then intend to go to other worlds?'

'No, the craft wasn't designed for interstellar travel, its smooth shape means it was for atmospheric work, probably journeying from the main orbiting ship to the planet's surface.' Sandy could feel resistance building to his plans.

'If it would only work on this planet, what would be the point?' Someone asked.

'We could visit the rest of the world, and see if there is somewhere better to live. We could go up to the crater and see if there are any more people who would like to join us, that's if there are any like us. There are many things we could do. A transport device like that could be very useful.'

After much discussion, it was decided to send an expedition composed of two parts. One party would stop off at the forested area where the nuts were found, look for anything useful to add to their food stocks, and collect more nuts if the nut throwers would co-operate. The other group going on to the ship, where Sandy would decide what to do it.

If Sandy's team failed to return to the forested area within three days, the other group would then go on to the lava overhang to see what had happened to them.

Mop was not overjoyed at the idea of her chosen one exposing himself to the unknown dangers of the alien craft, but reluctantly gave in, realizing the nature of her man demanded an adventurous and inquisitive life.

The two groups set off the following day as soon as it was light enough to navigate the steep escarpments leading down to the plain, and made good time reaching their first objective. Sandy warned them of the accuracy of the nut throwers, the possibility of a visit from the flying creature's relatives, and wished them good luck.

The alien craft was just as they had left it, and Greg wondered why no one had come looking for their lost comrades when they had failed to return to base.

'How the hell could they see 'em under the overhang?' was the short answer he got from Sandy, impatient to explore the inner working of the craft.

Ben was ordered to remove his footwear, and was then unceremoniously hoisted up to plant his bare foot on the sensor, the door obediently opened, and they were soon in the control room.

'First we'll have to get rid of these bodies,' said Sandy, 'or we'll be tripping over 'em.' The desiccated remains of the previous occupants were thrown out of the open hatchway, their bones making a strange rattling sound which echoed around under the vast overhang of the lava sheet.

Sandy tried pushing the many knobs and buttons on the control console, but nothing happened. It was Ben who found the main power switch, quite by accident.

'I wonder why this bit sticks up?' he said. A small square section of the control console was raised a few millimetres above the surrounding surface, and he put his hand on it.

There was a faint click, the square dropped level with the rest of the surface, and a deep humming sound came from below the floor. The huge viewing screen lit up, and they were looking out on the cliff face as though the front of the craft had suddenly gone transparent.

After they had got over the shock, no one was too keen to touch any of the controls they had so nonchalantly tinkered with before.

'How could they have shut off the power if they were killed in the crash?' asked Greg, who liked things to be logical.

'Probably an inertia switch,' Sandy replied, 'when the craft impacted, it automatically cut off the power, I guess.'

'Well, what do we do now?' asked Ben hesitantly, not so sure he wanted a ride in what might prove to be a coffin.

Sandy sat down in the main seat in front of the control console, a determined look on his face, and a few beads of perspiration just beginning to form on his forehead.

A small panel on the main control board had slid back, revealing two levers, and Sandy nervously rested a finger on the larger one. The others watched with bated breath.

'Well, here goes,' he said, and moved the lever the smallest amount possible towards him. The hum below them deepened, and with the screech of metal on rock, the craft edged slowly away from the cliff face and stopped as he released the lever.

'Well, that wasn't so bad,' Sandy said, trembling, as were the others, 'let's try the other lever.'

The craft lifted a metre or so from the crushed rock below, and using the larger control, Sandy eased it out from under the lava overhang, and out into the open air.

Once the shaking had stopped, and a degree of calm restored, Sandy lowered the craft gently down to the ground, while they worked out what they would do next.

'I'm surprised it's so easy to handle,' Ben remarked, 'so how did they manage to crash it under the overhang?'

'There might have been a thick mist at the time and they'd lost their way, who knows. What matters is, we have a viable means of transport for as long as the fuel lasts, and I suspect that might be some time.'

They took the craft up again, turning it this way and that, and then headed out across the plain until the cliffs of the volcano were only a smudge on the horizon, the rest of the huge mountain of rock being shrouded in cloud.

'Right, we'll head back to the cliffs, and pick up the others,' Sandy announced, feeling more confident now that he had got the feel of the controls.

The huge craft slipped through the air effortlessly, and when the forested area came into view, he slowed down and carefully lowered it to the ground just short of the trees.

'A couple of you go and see if you can find the others, tell 'em what we've done so they don't get too much of a fright when they see the craft.' he added with a chuckle.

Getting the food collecting team to enter the ship with their collection of nuts proved easier said than done. Eventually, after much coaxing and not a little swearing, everyone was safely on board, and Sandy raised the craft slowly upwards and headed for their valley.

'I reckon we could land in that grassy area,' he said, gently easing the vessel downwards, 'just hope it doesn't wreck the grain harvest.'

Seeing the huge silver shape approaching them, the rest of the group had fled to the safety of the caves, one brave soul peering out to see what would emerge from the craft.

Once they were recognized, all hell broke loose as extreme fear gave way to relief and joy at the safe return of the explorers.

Ben's main concern, once the initial greetings were over, was that the craft might be spotted by other craft visiting the crater, but Sandy put his mind at rest by explaining the others only came during the time of darkness, and then only into the confines of the crater.

Greg was the first to notice that several of the women had acquired rather large bulges in front, and this happened shortly after the last of the plants they had brought down from the crater had withered up and died.

It took very little time for Sandy to add two and two together, come up with five, subtract one and arrive at a reasonable explanation for the phenomenon.

'I think the plants we used up there must have been initially supplied by those who dumped us there, so that we couldn't reproduce, the rotten sods.'

There were mixed feelings about the forthcoming births, as no one knew what to do about it. 'Leave it to nature' was Sandy's advice, and as they had no other option, they did.

Over the next few days, Sandy took the craft out over the plains, looking for another home site, as their valley would be restrictive if their numbers grew to any extent, and he felt sure they would in time.

They returned one evening with the glad news that an ideal area had been located. It was some distance away, but the flat grassy plain fringed a large lake, with a ridge of hills backed by a mountain range cutting them off from the plains below their present valley. To either side, there were vast forests, some of the trees even bigger than the ones found in the valley of nuts, as it was now referred to.

Greg thought the lake might be a sea, as the water went right out to the horizon and probably beyond, but it was not salty, so they settled for a very large lake,

A meeting was held to decide whether or not to move their homestead to the new site. Sandy was all for it, but some of the more conservative members of the group were quite happy to stay where they were, it not being real that in time their valley would not be big enough to support them all.

With Ben's backing, and some forceful persuading from Greg, the last of the dissenters gave way, and agreement was reached that they would begin preparing the new site next day. As there were plenty of trees available, a team was flown out to begin the felling, large saws having been made from some of the more robust metal strips brought down from the crater. Wooden huts would be constructed along the lake shore, and when they were ready for habitation, the rest of their possessions would be sent, ready for the general exodus which was to follow.

The tree felling went ahead far better than Sandy had expected, the first hut being constructed within three days, and roofed over with turfs two days later.

The principle for the first huts was to cut down small trees, notch the ends so that they could be stacked one upon the other so forming a self locking system of construction. They would be crude square rooms, but would give protection from the weather and the cool cycle, which they felt sure would come around again in time.

Once they had made the necessary tools, and perfected the skills of converting the trees to planked wood, 'real' houses as Ben called them, could be constructed.

The local forests provided plenty of food for the hut builders, and no dangerous animals had been encountered so far, much to the relief of all.

The hut building was nearing completion when the next tumultuous event took place. It was late evening, the meal finished, and everyone was relaxing, when the ground trembled beneath them. A series of shudders ran through the cave system, rattling anything which was loose and adding to the fearful grinding noises coming from within the body of the volcano.

Ben shouted 'outside everyone' but most were already heading for the open ground as he said it. The deep rumbling noises died down after a while, but no one felt like going back into the caves. As the temperature dropped, they made their way back in, one by one, but none slept that night as ears strained for the next sign of the awakening volcano.

All was quiet for the next few days, and the horror of being buried alive faded as the building work on the huts neared completion. Next, Ben's store of raw materials brought down from the crater were shipped out to the new site.

After much trial, error, and nervous experimentation, they managed to coax the machine used for lowering bodies to the surface of the planet to work. Systematically, the dried out corpses of those intended for the crater were emptied out on the fringe of the forest in the 'nut valley', and the empty containers stacked in a pile on the new site for future use as raw materials.

Just in case the alien flying machine should fail in flight, the group was split into four sections, and ferried out to the new homestead on the shores of the lake.

It was with some sadness that Sandy oversaw the last group to leave the cave system. They had made a very comfortable home for themselves at the base of the volcano, and although there had been no rumbling for some time, it was thought that one day the sleeping fires below would come alive once more, and it would be a very unhealthy place to be in should that happen.

As the alien silver craft touched down gently on the lake shore to disgorge its last cargo of settlers, Ben came running up to Sandy in great excitement.

'You'd better hurry, Mop's making one hell of a noise, I think she's about to give birth, or blow up, or something.'

They hurried over to the hut where a small group had gathered at the entrance, mainly composed of men, the women being inside consoling the loudly protesting Mop.

Sandy pushed his way to the entrance to go inside, but a large red grim faced well muscled woman barred his way.

'You can stay outside, this is woman's work.' she said, and slammed the hut door in his face. This at least cut down the volume of Mop's screams as she struggled to expel the large lump she had been carrying around for so long. Ben and Greg took Sandy for a long walk along the lake shore.

Over the next few weeks, more births occurred, but by now a small group of midwives had generated itself and took over on such occasions, making the whole process more dignified and very much safer.

Mop took to motherhood as naturally as day follows night, her whole attitude to life changing to accommodate the new arrival into their lives. Two women bravely took over the cooking detail, but try as they might, it failed to come up to Mop's standard, and all were looking forward to the day when Mop could be heard banging her pots around again.

The lake produced an abundance of fish and everyone wanted to go fishing. That is, until the day when someone saw a very large bow wave caused by the mother of all fishes heading towards them, and they all raced for the shore, breaking two of their paddles in the panic driven process.

Greg was in two minds as to whether the story was true, or whether it had been put about by those who really enjoyed fishing and could see their fishing time curtailed by the over exuberance of the others.

He mentioned his thoughts to Sandy one day, who just grinned and said, 'They're getting more cunning by the day. Still, it's good survival tactics, and it does little harm, while it preserves their job. And they are the best at it.'

Crude tables and chairs were made by splitting logs into rough planks, and pinning them together with wooden studs. A scrape with a flat metal blade on the working surfaces gave a good smooth finish, and soon all huts were equipped with a set. Other pieces of furniture appeared as and when requested, the carpenter's skills being stretched to the limit when Greg asked for a wheeled wagon to be made. It was.

The question of whether they should invite some of the others still up in the crater to join them, came up again.

A meeting was held early that evening around a large camp fire on the sandy shore of the lake, the group being mainly in favour of inviting a selected number of the others to join them, although how the choice was to be made, and who would do it, was still open to debate.

The situation was taken completely out of their hands in one fell swoop some few minutes later, when the volcano became active again.

The concussion wave hit them first, a push pull effect which rattled the huts and knocked over anything which was not stable. This was followed by a loud booming roar as countless millions of tonnes of sand were sent hurtling into the upper atmosphere as the volcano cleared its throat ready for the real business of the day.

Within seconds, a dark cloud had formed in the sky to the north of them, lightning flashes ripped through the towering column as the fine rising particles generated a charge of electricity which from time to time they could no longer hold, discharging it in violent purple flashes of light.

Small wavelets formed on the lake, growing in size by the minute as the shock waves travelled through the planet's crust, bouncing back and forth from the harder ridges of rock strata below.

'I'm taking the craft up to see what's happening,' Sandy shouted, 'anyone want to come?' Only six sprinted for the ship, Ben and Greg in the forefront with Sandy.

They scrambled aboard, knocking shins and elbows as they raced for the main control room, the screen coming to life as Sandy hit the activating plate. Within seconds the huge craft was hurtling skywards, far faster than they had ever done before, and a couple were sick as a consequence of the violent surge upwards.

Stabilizing the craft at two thousand metres, they watched open mouthed as the volcano spewed forth a massive river of glistening molten rock, running down its sides like thick red and orange treacle, streaked with yellow where the magma was at full temperature.

A towering black thunder cloud had gathered over the erupting vent in the earth's crust, lightning sizzling between the rolling clouds of sand and ash, illuminating the landscape in harsh relief.

'What about those poor devils in the crater?' asked Greg.

'I doubt if they even knew what happened,' Sandy replied, 'it was all so quick, nothing could have survived the initial blast, let alone the heat released once the lava began flowing.

'I'm afraid there's only us left now, and with the crater all but gone, they won't be bringing any more people here.'

They stood in the alien craft, watching through the huge viewing screen the destruction of what was once their home, the high pinnacles of the rim melting under the onslaught from the fires beneath, adding to the cascade of liquid rock which spilled out onto the plain below.

It seemed as if the whole world was alight, the forested area where they got the nuts was blazing like a huge torch, sending writhing columns of black smoke high into the air along with showers of red hot sparks as the tree trunks exploded under the extreme heat.

They returned the craft to the lake shore where the waves had grown into huge rollers. These threatened to swamp the huts, despite having built them on the raised ground bordering the turbulent waters.

Although it was far from night, the light was fading steadily as increasing amounts of ash were hurled into the upper atmosphere, occluding the already weak sunlight.

For the next twenty days they lived in a twilight zone before the ash clouds were scrubbed from the skies by horrendous rain storms. The area around their huts became a sea of mud, not that anyone wanted to go out much, but life had to go on and food needed to be gathered from the battered forest.

The hours of daylight were only half what they used to be, and then it was more like dusk. The nights were correspondingly longer, and very dark.

Their next concern was the dwindling oil supplies for lighting. The extra time the lamps needed to be lit due to the elongated evenings had taken its toll, despite being extra careful in their use. So far, they had failed to locate any of the black tar-like substance they had found back in their valley, and no one could think of a substitute.

Strict rationing of the lamps was now called for, which meant going to bed a lot earlier than normal. This of course had the inevitable effect of increasing the birth rate, but this would not be apparent for some time to come.

Some sixty days after the volcano had destroyed itself and the surrounding countryside, things were almost back to normal. They flew out to see if there was anything left of the old valley and the tar cave, but the whole area had been reduced to a vast flat lava field, no sign of the towering cliffs remaining, just a huge caldera where the volcano had been, a vast open smoking sore on the surface of the planet.

The thirty strong members of the group had produced twelve children, three of the women remaining barren for some inexplicable reason, but some were pregnant again.

Ben and Greg also became pilots of the alien craft, but the dreaded feeling that the fuel supply might run out in mid flight was never far from their minds.

The oil problem solved itself one day. A team had marched through the forest to the east of the settlement, and out the other side. Here the countryside was totally different, being mainly composed of rough tumbled rocks and gravel banks, a little fine sand appearing in pockets between the rock clusters.

It was while one of the team was walking through one of these sand patches that he complained of some black sticky stuff adhering to his foot. Ben recognized it as 'tar sand', something which had been used on his home planet to produce oil.

Samples were taken back to the settlement, and upon examination, Sandy concluded that it would be far more efficient to make a distillation plant close to the other side of the forest near the lake, and then bring the resultant oil back, as such a large quantity of sand would have to be put through the plant to extract only a small quantity of oil.

The plant was constructed from Ben's supply of metallic bits and pieces, and hauled out to the site on the new wheeled wagons. The forest supplied the large amounts of wood needed to provide heat to drive the more volatile constituents of the oil out of the sand, and the lake provided the cooling water for the condensing tubes.

It took a few days to set up the plant, and it only produced a trickle of oil compared to that of the thick treacle like tar from the valley, but the tar sands seemed inexhaustible, and they had plenty of time.

Once more sophisticated tools were made, the carpenters went to work not only on plank constructed houses, as opposed to one room huts they had originally made, but equipped them with elaborate furniture, their skills and designs improving with time and experience.

Metallic ores were found one day while exploring the range of hills behind the grass plain of the settlement, and although no one knew how to smelt and refine them, the knowledge that it could be done spurred them on in their quest to be independent of Ben's dwindling supply of metallic bits and pieces.

A system of education was introduced for the young ones, passing on all the knowledge they could muster from their former lives, but it was some time before they were able to manufacture a reliable paper on which to write their history and the data for survival they were accumulating.

Sandy insisted that no dispute should go unresolved, no matter how small, and to this end a forum was inaugurated to handle any disagreements which would threaten the stability of the settlement. On the rare occasions when things did get out of hand, justice was swift, clean, and final, the whole membership of the settlement voting on the outcome.

The inevitable happened one day. Sandy, Ben, and a few others decided to check out the far mountain range for raw materials. Ben pressed the initiating plate to start the drive of their only powered transport, and nothing happened. They concluded the fuel had run out, and after two days of probing and searching, they were unable to locate any spare fuel, not even knowing what it looked like, or even if it existed.

The lake provided a plentiful supply of fish, and although there was a large predator out in the deeper part of the inland sea, it was rarely seen, and so far had not posed a threat to those who ventured out on the clear blue waters.

An organized method of farming soon established itself, the larger of the grass grains being sifted out from the harvest for planting the next season's crop, thus increasing the yield per plant and reducing the amount of labour involved.

The creatures of the forest were many and diverse, but none proved a serious threat to those who ventured into the wooded areas for food. Only one creature had to be treated with a fair amount of respect, and that was one of the smallest of the mammals. A half metre long furry four legged carnivore had no respect for the size of its intended meal, and as it seemed such an innocuous beast, several humans had been attacked, one being quite badly bitten.

A loud shout and a whack with a stick usually drove them off, and fortunately for the settlers, the creatures were slow to breed, so not too many of them were encountered.

Someone suggested they have an all out massacre of the creatures, but Sandy would not entertain the proposal, as he considered the creatures had as much right to the forest as they did, quietly hoping they would die out naturally in time.

When plank making became a little more accurate, a boat was built, as it was considered quicker to sail around the forested peninsula to the oil refining site than travel the tortuous paths through the forest.

When not in use collecting the oil, which was most of the time, the boat ventured further and further out onto the broad expanse of the lake, as the fishing was better there.

Ben and two others had taken the boat almost out of sight of land one day, when they wished they had been a little more cautious. They were pulling in the heavily laden nets, when the water around the boat erupted, and a thirty metre dark grey shape slowly rose to the surface. The enormous head, as wide as their boat was long, reared up a good ten metres, and two jet black eyes stared down at them, flicking from one to the other of the terrified fishers.

As the net was heavy and almost in, the boat would become unstable if they raised the sail.

The two baleful black eyes watched every move as Ben and one of the other men finished hauling the net onboard.

'Run the sail up slowly and quietly,' Ben whispered, 'don't make any sudden moves.'

As the sail slowly creaked its way up the mast on its wooden rings, the three fishers watched the shining grey head, hardly daring to breathe. Gradually the light wind filled the sail, and the boat turned slowly around to face the distant shore, and picked up speed.

Looking back over the stern, they saw the giant head with the glistening black eyes still watching them, and then a white crested bow wave gradually built up, the huge creature surging forward and closing the distance between them.

'If it hits the bloody boat we're all gone,' Ben yelled, 'keep zig-zagging if you can, we'll probably have to swim for it.'

The huge grey head loomed above them, and the smooth glistening snout of the creature touched the stern of the boat as gently as a falling leaf, and then it pushed. The bow of the boat lifted clear of the water and they were racing for the shore, too petrified to realise what was happening for the first few moments.

'I just don't believe this,' Ben exclaimed after he had got over the initial shock, and realized the creature meant no harm, 'get the sail down quickly, it's making the boat unstable and we'll tip over if it goes any faster.'

The coastline drew nearer at a phenomenal rate, with several watchers on the shore gazing open mouthed at the spectacle of the huge creature pushing the tiny boat along so fast the front half was out of the water.

As they neared the shallows, the creature slowed down and then stopped. It turned its massive body sideways, throwing up a huge wave which raced for the boat.

The stern of the boat lifted on the advancing wave, throwing all three fishers off balance and tumbling them into the bottom of the now speeding craft. Approaching the shore, the wave had spent most of its energy, and the boat coasted on gently to beach itself on the sand.

Sandy and several others had been watching the whole incident, apart from the initial meeting far out on the lake.

'I can hardly believe it, but it looks as if we have a friend out there,' he said, turning to Mop who was holding their youngest, 'I know the long snouted creature back in the valley was friendly, but this one is intelligent. I think we'll try to make some sort of contact, it could be most useful.'

Mop gave him one of those looks she always did when he mentioned something which could be dangerous, but knowing her man, she knew he would go ahead with it, come hell or high water.

The colony continued to grow and skills improve, but sadly time was catching up with some of the more elderly of its members, and deaths from sheer old age became more frequent. Strangely, there had been no trouble from the illnesses humans were normally prone to, and Ben put it down to clean living and good fresh food.

It was Ben's eldest son who found the fuel slugs for the alien transporter, and brought the craft back to life. The planet was explored from pole to pole, the elderly Sandy now having to take a back seat while the next generation did the actual physical work, which he found most frustrating.

Mop had slimmed down considerably after her third and final child, and was now a most desirable and handsome woman in all respects, the bond between them still growing.

The threesome of Sandy, Ben, and Greg, still went about their business together, but at a more sedate pace now.

The colony continued to grow and split many times over the coming years, spreading across the main land mass in all directions and occupying the choicest areas.

Unfortunately, as time went by, the skills which Sandy had been so adamant about passing down through the coming generations, were largely lost as the various groups expanded into new areas, and a return to a more simple and basic way of life resulted. Stories of the old skills were still talked about, but it was in the guise of magic and myth, and in time they too were forgotten.

Very many generations later, those who had started populating the crater so long ago, returned to deposit more groups of people on the planet. Their method of memory screening had been improved to the point where the depositee's were unable to recall anything at all from their past existence's, and so new groups of diverse humanoids were deposited between the already existing tribes who had escaped from the crater so long ago before it had erupted.

Although the new importee groups had different coloured skins and were different in stature from group to group, they were all basically humanoid, and shared the same genetic material despite coming from different worlds within the galaxy.

The Confederation continued to dump its unwanted outcasts on the planet for many millennia to come, until the teeming hordes threatened to overcome the planet's ability to support them. Eventually, the Confederation found another suitable world on the outer rim of the galaxy to send their least desirables to, but the population of Sandy's planet had taken off in an uncontrolled manner, and deforestation on a vast scale had altered the weather patterns, despoiling huge areas which then turned into deserts.

Sandy's world had been built with broken straws, and although he had realized the need for a just and civilized approach to life to ensure a comfortable survival for all, once the population had grown and expanded out into other groups, the old ways which had got them there in the first place, returned with a vengeance.

The fact that the Confederation had continued to add more people of the same ilk, only added to the decline in standards which he had fought so hard to establish, and it was fortunate that he had not lived long enough to see his dream crumble into the shambles it now was.

Left to 'nature', most things will work out all right given enough time. Famine, pestilence, disease, drought, and massive earthquakes, could be relied upon to limit the population to some extent, and reduce its avaricious appetite.

Once nature is interfered with to the extent it now was, with the new sciences being used in a cavalier and irresponsible way, it would only be a matter of time before the whole thing would end in tears, on a planet wide scale, unless another Sandy came along, with a very big stick ....

But that's another story …

The End

More from sci-fi-cafe.com
by David Reynolds-Moreton

Anthology of Futures
Anthology of Possibilities
Divergence
Enslavement
Exchange Rate
Extreme Difference
Flight of the Tristan
Fully Guaranteed
Greenways
Inheritance
Light Quest
The Martian Enigma
The Power Seeds
The Seed Garden
The Single Twin
The Sweepers
The Tribe
Transplant
Of Wood, Metal and Glass

www.ingramcontent.com/pod-product-compliance
Lightning Source LLC
Chambersburg PA
CBHW050533190726
48284CB00003B/1058